JO MAY

Flawed Liaisons

One ordinary man. One imperfect inheritance

Second edition

This book was professionally typeset on Reedsy.
Find out more at reedsy.com

To my siblings Nick and Sally

Also by Jo May

Biographical stories of Jo's boating adventures

A Barge at Large
A Barge at Large II
A Narrowboat at Large

Fiction

Operation Vegetable
Flawed Liaisons

Chapter 1

Thirty-Eight years ago

Four men sat on the sea wall at Llandudno, North Wales.

Below them was a bank of pebbles.

Below the pebbles was smooth, wet sand, then the Irish Sea.

Three men rose and walked away.

The fourth remained, head in hands, weeping.

The present

It was twenty past four in the morning – the moment he learned he was alone.

He opened the door to two uniformed police officers, one male, one female. They stood in the harsh glare of the outside light as rain dripped from the porch roof on to the steps behind them. They removed their caps simultaneously and held them with a sort of embarrassed reverence. He knew something was wrong – you do don't you, you can just tell.

'Mr Dunn?' asked the female. 'Mr Harry Dunn?'

His heart thumped. 'Yes.'

'I am PC Davidson and this,' indicating a tall black officer to he left, 'is my colleague, PC Brent. I'm sorry to have to tell you, but there has been an accident.'

'What do you mean, what kind of accident?'

'I think it best if we come inside. May we come in please?'

After a moment Harry ushered them down the hallway into the kitchen.

The woman retrieved a clear plastic bag from the pocket of her yellow jacket and passed it across. Inside was a watch. 'Do you recognize this?'

It was charred and the strap slightly misshapen but Harry turned it over and could make out the engraving on the back. 'To John. With my love always.' and below, '3rd September 1989'. A present from his mother to his father on his fortieth birthday. It was a gold Omega and the only material thing that his father treasured. His only possession of any real value.

'Yes, it's my fathers. What's happened?'

'Do your parents live at Knowle Farm, Pentryn?'

'Yes.'

She paused and looked down momentarily before meeting Harry's eye once again.

'There has been a fire Mr Dunn, at the farm. This watch was taken from the body of a male recovered from the premises.'

Harry stared at the polythene bag. Stared at his father's watch.

'He's dead?'

'I'm afraid it looks that way, yes.'

'Oh god, no. My mother?'

'We also discovered the body of a female. No formal identification has been made but we believe the victims to be your mother and father. I'm truly sorry.'

'They're gone?'

'I'm sorry, yes Mr Dunn.'

Harry slowly shook his head. 'What happened? Tell me what happened.'

'We don't know fully, but we are investigating. We can't be certain, but at this stage we believe it to have been a tragic accident.'

Harry turned away. It was dark outside as he faced the window above the sink. His reflection stared back, surrounded by the black night.

'Is there anyone you would like us to contact Mr Dunn? A relative or friend perhaps?' PC Brent spoke for the first time. A fit-looking man who appeared to genuinely share Harry's pain.

Harry slowly shook his head.

His wife, Susan, slept on upstairs. He'd no inclination to wake her.

'Would you mind if we asked you a couple of questions?' asked PC Brent.

'What? Oh, no. Go ahead.'

'Do you believe that anyone would have reason to harm either or both of your parents?'

Harry looked aghast. 'What are you saying? That it wasn't an accident?'

'Of course not, it is just something we have to ask.'

'To cover all eventualities, I suppose.'

'Yes, precisely.'

Harry answered tetchily. 'The answer is no.' He paused and continued quietly. 'No, they were quiet people who kept themselves to themselves. They didn't have a wide circle of friends but certainly no enemies – at least as far as I'm aware.' He paused again. 'No, I'm sure. There was nobody who would want to hurt them. They never did anybody any harm.' His eyes filled with tears.

The family dog came into the kitchen behind the police officers. The brown labradoodle called Benny looked at the strangers and wagged his tail half-heartedly. Sensing unease, he headed for his bowl for a noisy drink of water before disappearing back into the hall.

'Were your parents financially stable? Did they owe money to anyone?'

Harry wiped his eyes on his dressing gown sleeve. 'They weren't well off but they always had enough. My father believed that if you couldn't afford something you did without. He never borrowed money from anyone. As soon as a bill arrived he paid it. He hated the thought of being in debt.'

'They never mentioned anything suspicious around the farm? Strangers in the area for example?'

'No, not as far as I know. If there was anything serious my mother would have told me. My father was stubborn and proud - the life they led up there was one of self-sufficiency. If anything had been wrong he wouldn't have told me but he would have told my mother and I would have found out.'

'There had no issues with you or other members of the family?'

'No they did not. I loved and respected them both. In fact, I resent the implication.'

'I apologize. But we have to ask these questions. Look, we'll leave you alone now. Are you sure you don't want us to call anyone for you?'

'There is no one. I have no siblings.' He was silent for a moment, then added quietly, 'They were my only living relatives.'

'Once again Mr Dunn you have our sincere sympathy. Please call us if you think of anything.'

Harry nodded.

The officers let themselves out and Harry sat on a buffet at the kitchen counter. As the front door clicked closed his head slumped onto his forearms.

He wept for his Mum and Dad. Gentle, simple folk who worked hard, did their best. He looked up to a framed photograph on the wall above the small, pine dining table. Taken about six years ago they were standing in front of their barn. His father, wearing his ever-present blue overalls and a tweed flat cap had his hands in pockets. Mum had linked her arm through his and they were smiling. She sported her favourite summer dress, knee-length and simple pale yellow with light blue flowers. They were on their way to the local agricultural show, and they were happy. The adjacent photograph was one of his in-laws, John and Helen Wainwright. They were dressed for a summer ball, he in white tuxedo, she in an ivory, lace ball-gown. She had perfectly coiffured hair and a diamond choker with matching earrings. Unsmiling, they looked at the camera with a confident, haughty air. The look of the comfortable, the detached. But happy?

His Mum and Dad had scratched and cajoled a living from their small-holding. A routine geared to having enough because hard as they toiled, the reluctant land refused to yield excess. No comfort zone, but always just enough. Despite the austerity his childhood had been carefree when the responsibilities of adulthood were clouds as yet unformed. Home during Harry's younger days, four miles from town yet a world away from the fakery he now endured.

He sat for a time, numb, then went to dress. He had to go and see for himself.

'Where are you going?' demanded his wife from the top of the stairs as he opened the front door.

'Something's happened, go back to bed.'

'Harry!?' she called. But he was gone.

From the bedroom window Susan watched him drive away before going back to bed. She wondered briefly why her useless lump of a husband had dashed off in the middle of the night – but only briefly. She was asleep again within minutes.

The farm was across the far side of town. On the way he passed Wainwrights Timber Merchants where he worked. It was silent at this time of day but brightly lit by sodium security lights. The company was owned by his wife's father.

The previous day had passed like hundreds before, a dull slog, devoid of satisfaction or ambition. Harry was an accounts manager in his Father-in Law's company. He ticked boxes and filled in forms. He'd been ticking and filling for what felt like a lifetime, waiting in vain for a promotion so he could tick more important boxes in a larger office. He hated it. The company was successful, a supplier of timber to local construction companies. In addition, they specialised in hardwoods bought in and sold to high-end furniture manufacturers. Harry had worked there for eighteen years but had never bonded with his colleagues – yes, he hated the place.

Four miles through town Harry turned right onto the pitted lane that led up to the farm. The road was cordoned off by blue and white exclusion tape so he got out and began to walk the remaining half mile up the hillside.

As he crested a rise and passed through a copse of trees two hundred yards short of the farm he stopped. He gazed in near disbelief at the wreckage, hardly able to believe what his eyes were telling him - he was looking at a set from an apocalyptic movie. The outer walls stood firm but most of the roof timbers had gone. Three of the four blackened window frames had lost their glass and the front door hung drunkenly from one hinge. Firemen in hard hats and yellow waterproofs were busy, tidying equipment. The practised routine of professional fire-fighters, selectively immune to tragedy. Three policemen stood in a huddle talking and occasionally pointing. A few chickens scratched and pecked in the yard.

The only thing untouched by the fire was the small, slate-roofed barn across the courtyard. Within would be his father's old Massey-Ferguson tractor. Never again would it be called upon to bounce and buck his Dad over the rocky fields. Doubtless the remainder of the rudimentary machinery would slowly rot away. Up on the hill a small herd of sheep gnawed at tufty, straw-coloured grass. Lambing season was not too far away. Who would look after them now? The rain had stopped and as the dawn mist slowly cleared from the valley, a soggy blanket was lifted from the carnage. Tears once again filled his eyes.

In the yard blinking blue lights from three fire engines and two police cars flashed out a kaleidoscopic, neon code. Wisps of smoke carried away Harry's childhood memories.

He looked up to the right. Perhaps four hundred yards away, above the sheep, above the dry stone wall that marked the boundary of the farm, Harry saw the indistinct silhouette of a person. Whoever it was remained still for a moment before moving away west along the ridge – a dark grey ghost before the misty sky.

He had a last look at the ruined farm then turned and walked back down the hill.

Harry drove back to the house his father-in law paid for - indirectly at least. Harry depended on 'Pop' Wainwright for his salary. Most of what was left after paying the mortgage went on Susan, either down her throat or on clothes deemed suitably expensive for the daughter of a successful local businessman. He hadn't been in a good place before the tragedy because most of the ebullience he'd felt through school and university had long ago leached into the damp, misty landscape of North Wales. With this he was near desolate.

Any sympathy Harry had received following the death of his parents was distant and somehow practised. Neither his colleagues at work nor members of his peripheral social circle, largely comprising fellow members of the local golf club, seemed to offer any genuine solace. He'd only joined the club because it had been suggested by 'The Family'. He was tethered to his meal-ticket. Susan had unenthusiastically helped organise the funerals and dealt with some legalities but even she seemed to be merely acting a part. Harry felt she was morose not from mourning, more because she actually had to make some sort of effort. He felt utterly bereft and had never felt so alone.

Chapter 2

Three months later

'I'm so sorry Harry, truly. How devastating for you.'

He had just told Mary about his Mum and Dad. She was his best friend. His only friend in fact.

They were in a café next to the bus station in Shrewsbury. It is a lovely market town. Some high-end shops, cobbled streets and ancient, higgledy-piggledy buildings. Not the café though – the like of which can be found in every town and city in the world. Concrete outside, plastic within, it is a cheap haven for the underclass, the ranks of whom Harry had joined.

He'd been living in the town for three months, initially with an old school friend. He'd slept on an inflatable mattress in the attic room among old carpets and cardboard boxes until his mate had chucked him out after getting a dog. 'Really haven't got the space, what with the new mutt and all,' he'd said, 'awfully sorry. Been great having you to stay though, we must keep in touch.'

Sorry my foot, thought Harry, he'd probably bought the dog on purpose – or borrowed it!

After that he'd rented a horrid room in a horrid house.

Harry had two things that gave him at least some sense of purpose. One was the café in which he now shared a table with Mary. Here he felt relatively safe. The patrons were largely people either on the way down or who had already reached the bottom. At least nobody asked questions and he was anonymous. He was regularly enveloped in cigarette smoke and smeared with grease

7

from various sandwiches that would make a dietician baulk. Before Mary had arrived this morning he'd tackled a bacon sandwich. With a politesse summoned from a previous life he'd dabbed his lips on a paper tissue. The lout in the scruffy raincoat on the next table, noticed the gesture, arched a pair of unruly eyebrows and wiped his mouth on his sleeve. Then he smiled at Harry, who grinned back. Manners maketh man, the saying goes. Not in here it doesn't.

Grimy condensation clung to the single-plate glass window trapping them all in a vile sauna. As long as you didn't come into contact with the toxic film on the window you were safe enough and it helped preserve customers anonymity.

The second ray of light for Harry was Mary herself. Yes, she was scruffy but she was also kind and her bright, green eyes sparkled with mischief when she smiled. She was known locally as Ale Mary because she drank Guinness and over the previous months had become Harry's friend. She was an intelligent and thoughtful person and Harry wondered what her story was. She wore a light brown wig, often covered by a rose-patterned headscarf. They rarely spoke of the future, preferring to maintain a relative optimism. Harry had begun to share his recent past but Mary was unforthcoming. He didn't push her. She preferred to share her troubles with the figure on a cross above the altar in St Chads Church. Here she would go most afternoons to sit next to a radiator to warm up or dry out.

'It gets worse Mary. Much worse,' continued Harry. He sighed. 'I was stitched up. Really and properly stitched up. And the worst of it is that I've no idea why or by whom.'

'Goodness me. What happened?

'Remember I told you I worked for a timber merchants? Mary nodded. 'Well, the top man, John Wainwright, known as 'Pop', called me into his office about eight weeks after my parents died and told me that photographs of child pornography had been found on my works computer. Hundreds and hundreds of images – some of it apparently really revolting stuff. He showed me one or two which were bad enough, but he told me those were mild, some were very twisted indeed. He flat out accused me of being a pervert and a paedophile. I denied it of course but mud sticks.'

He sighed. 'They had been downloaded onto my PC not from the internet but from disc. There was no way to trace their origin.'

'They scratched around for two weeks - a 'thorough internal investigation' they called it, but as far as I could see it was sketchy at best. Pop called me in again and I was called to account for something about which I knew absolutely nothing. I pleaded, but nobody believed me. They said I was peculiar and aloof – they even held my childless sixteen-year marriage against me – as if having no children was my fault for goodness sake. The family closed ranks. That was 'Pop', Jane (his secretary - and niece) and Peter (senior manager, hardwoods – and nephew) - they knew nothing, had seen nothing, believed the worst. Susan sided with the family. They couldn't prove that I was responsible but more importantly I couldn't prove either my innocence or who was guilty. It all happened so fast.'

Mary stared and slowly shook her head. 'Why didn't you go to the police?'

'What could they do? The photos were in my office on my computer. Anyone they asked would swear that very few people apart from me go in that office, never mind use my computer.

'How did they find the photographs in the first place?'

'They were in a file. That was found by someone Pop had employed to improve the 'local network', whatever the hell that is. It was hidden in a sub-directory I didn't even know existed - and there they were. The file's password was the date of the fatal fire would you believe? Even I'm not stupid enough to choose such an obvious password. No, whoever did it was just reminding me of my predicament, really rubbing it in. I was really frightened at this stage I can tell you.'

Harry sat there with look of a terrified deer caught in the headlights the instant before impact.

'Blimey Harry, how terrible. What did you do?'

'What could I do? A few days later Pop called me in again and offered me the 'opportunity' to resign. I would disappear from his daughter's life and leave the area. The scandal would lose its fire in time and the company would prevail. The alternative was prosecution through the courts. 'Don't really want the police involved', Pop said.

'Whatever he actually believed he was reckoning to protect his livelihood and his daughter. A swift exorcism was the only way. 'If you think anything of Susan just leave' he told me. I burnt my bridges at this point when I finally snapped. I told him to 'fuck off' – then resigned.' He looked at Mary. 'Sorry about the language.'

'Don't worry. I don't blame you.' After a pause, 'So you came to Shrews-bury?'

'Yes. Packed a case and left. But not before I'd suffered the unspoken disgust of just about anyone I came in contact with. Whispers in the workplace leached into the town and a thousand silent knives ripped me up. It was horrible and I was powerless to respond. Not being in control is the worst thing. In everyday life when things beyond your control wind you up it's bad enough, but if you're accused of this sort of thing with no come-back whatsoever, it's..., well, it's literally soul destroying.'

'I got a doorstep visit from a mate from the golf club - the only farewell I got. He told me that a mutual 'friend' had been eyeing Susan up for 'some time'. I was being told because I deserved to know. Deserved? What the hell is that supposed to mean?'

'Susan had moved back to her parents at this stage, we hadn't spoken for a couple of weeks. I do miss the dog though. I left with twelve hundred pounds in cash, a suitcase of clothes and a burden like a lead weight.'

He looked up; Mary just stared back. 'I even sold the farm for next to nothing. A local bloke offered me cash and the state I was in I accepted. That went into the deposit account and the deposit account went straight in Susan's handbag.'

They were silent before Mary finally asked, 'so what now?'

Harry just raised his eyebrows and shook his head. 'Right now, I'm going to get some kip. I was taken out last night and ended up pickled in some nightclub down near the police station. Some chap I know vaguely took me out for my birthday because he'd won a few quid on the dogs. I can't even remember his name. I ended up with a bump on the head. No idea how it got there but I spent the night in hospital. Look.' He showed her a cut just above his hairline and a blood stain on his jumper. He got up to leave. 'I feel knackered. I'll see you later maybe.'

He felt ill and had walked back to his lodgings.

He didn't know, but things were about to change.

Closing the outer door quietly he entered the gloomy passage. He had one foot on a stair and one hand on the bannister when the first door on the right opened spilling a wedge of yellow light onto the filthy carpet. A pudgy face smirked at him from the gloom with mean, piggy eyes. His landlady. Her flowery, grubby dress stretched to bursting around her fat carcass. This creature's dominance of him was the embodiment of Harry's circumstance. She didn't say anything but watched Harry haul himself upstairs.

His rented room was dank and depressing. The bathroom down the hall, shared with the two other inmates he'd never spoken to, clunked and spluttered when water flowed. He'd paid a month in advance for two consecutive months and it was now four days before the next rent was due – four days till he would be chucked out. He'd finally run out of money, though he hadn't admitted that to Mary. He was just too embarrassed.

Alcohol didn't prevent him from doing his job because he didn't have one – he hadn't even the will to sign on the dole.

He no longer noticed the carpet, like wet soil set in chewing gum.

He squelched into his room and saw his few items of clothing thinly spread between the grubby bed, old ladder-back chair and chest of drawers. A bare, low-wattage bulb clung doggedly to a cracked ceiling rose and a muddy puddle of light dissolved in the gloom. The whole house smelled of damp dog. He'd never even seen a dog.

He stepped on a hand-written note that had been slipped under the door. It was similar to the notes he'd received on each of the previous three days. This one read: 'Four days'.

His landlady was evicting him by degrees.

She was the fixer, winding up the pressure, strangling the life out of his only sanctuary. Four days - no cash, nowhere to go - in fact, nothing at all.

There was no contract here, no security, no questions asked.

Accompanying the warning notice there was a letter. Official looking - 'Parker and Williams' printed in red letters, top left. It would doubtless be from her solicitor. 'Her' - his ex. Ex everything - wife, partner, lover, friend. Gone now – the relationship smashed apart by something he still didn't understand. Till death us do part – well, he was pretty close.

This was the second letter that Harry had received in three months. The first had contained his passport, decree absolute that ended his marriage and a few other bits including birth certificate. They were accompanied by a note 'requesting' that he complete the enclosed documents to sign the house over to Susan. He was told that funds in their deposit account would be retained to cover bills till the house was sold. He was warned in no uncertain terms that failure to agree would result in consequences most dire. The letter, written on behalf of his Father-in-Law by his secretary, said that the shame and embarrassment had driven his wife to seek succour with a man fifteen years her junior with a Mercedes and a four handicap. He was a financial consultant with a golden retriever and a flat in Marbella.

Fickle cow.

He was considered expunged from his former life. He'd lost everything including his few golf club friends. Mates as long as they were equals, but at the first sniff of trouble they'd disappeared like ghosts in the mist.

With a throbbing head he peeled the note and letter off the floor and threw them on the bed. Then he'd followed them and slept.

He woke and stumbled to the bathroom.

The mirror flung back a cruel image. A pasty face, bloated through months of alcohol, trying to remain anonymous behind scruffy brown / grey stubble. His image grimaced back. He was in the bathroom with an animal. The mirror told him that something had better change, and soon. Judging by the face in the mirror nothing could get much worse but he didn't want to push it.

Why? Why had he been stitched up, hounded out, discredited in the worst way imaginable? But there was time for all that – sometime.

She must have changed her solicitors because the red type stamped above his address spelt unfamiliar names. Marbella Mick's solicitors?

He opened the letter.

Mr E.M. Parker of Parker and Williams, Solicitors, regretted to inform him of the death of his uncle, William Davis. Mr Davis had died suddenly in a tragic accident while walking in the Lake District. As sole executor, Mr Parker was pleased to inform him of an inheritance subject to the provision of proof of identity and subsequent signing of papers, blah blah,

Who the hell was Uncle William Davis? Never mind that, how much? A sliver of moon in his darkest night. Dad never mentioned a brother, neither did Mum. Proof of identity – what was that? Passport or birth certificate presumably.

He staggered to the phone box round the corner and arranged a meeting with Mr Parker through his secretary, for the following morning. Liversthorpe near Chorley – where on earth was that?

He went to the café and made enquiries.

'Somewhere near Peterborough' said Sid, the owner.

'Rubbish!' laughed Mary, who appeared to know her geography. 'It's up Wigan way.'

'Wig-on?' laughed Sid.

'Get lost,' she hissed. Then to Harry, 'it's up in Lancashire love.'

'Know where that is?'

'Uh, yes. Thank you Sid.'

Harry walked over with two cups of tea.

'Sit down Harry. What's in Chorley anyway?'

'I'm seeing a solicitor. My uncle died and left me something.'

'My, my. Remember us when you're on your yacht won't you.'

'Sure, I'll take you for a spin but don't hold your breath.'

'In the meantime, that'll be 55p Mr Branston,' said Sid, 'one pound ten if you're treating Mary.'

Mary was genuinely pleased for Harry. She'd begun to fear for him having seen him arrive in a mess a few months ago and get gradually worse. And what he'd told her yesterday had really shocked her. Perhaps the guy had got a break at last.

Harry paid and smiled at Mary before he left.

'Best of luck love,' she called as he dragged some of the café's fug with him into the gloomy morning. As the door clanged shut behind him he heard Mary say, 'I think you'll find it's Branson, Sid.'

For the first time in six months Harry had a spring in his step as he'd walked to the bus station. Well, not a spring exactly, more less of a slouch, but there was at least a purpose about his movements. The return bus fare would use up all but fifteen pounds of his final reserves but staying put was not an option. He reserved a seat for early the following morning and went home to check his suitcase hadn't rotted away in the damp. He looked at his motley assortment of things and sighed. He set out for the pub to celebrate but stopped on the threshold. He'd need all his wits about him tomorrow, and he'd better preserve his remaining cash. He ignored the cafe too wishing to avoid inevitable inquisition, so went back to his room.

The following morning he dressed in the cleanest clothes he could find, left the rest to the mice and trudged down the stairs for the final time. He threw his keys on the floor near the door to his landlady's flat. A curtain twitched in a ground floor window as he closed the door - and he was gone.

Chapter 3

Harry stood in the recessed doorway of 47 Broad Street, Liversthorpe, Lancashire.

He'd arrived on the early bus and walked from the bus station to the solicitor's office where he now waited, dripping and gently steaming. He was forty-five minutes early for his appointment and he was nervous.

The office was yet to open so he just stood and fidgeted.

It was a Tuesday in late March, 8.15 AM. A former industrial mill town, Liversthorpe looked much as you would expect in the heavy drizzle of a grey, wet morning – grim and sour. The mill chimneys were gone and the giant buildings either demolished or re-developed into apartments or arty units selling hand-made soap and the like. The remaining mills were reborn but the soot-stained terraced houses stood dark and bleak, oozing broken dreams.

Harry was five feet seven inches tall and dishevelled. In fact, had a policeman happened by he may well have been asked to move along. A few cars hissed by on the wet road and anyone glancing over would have seen a forty-three-year-old man gone to seed. His blue eyes had once sparkled with mischief but they now looked bone weary – like those of a dying dog. Too much booze had turned his scleras yellow – his over-stretched liver issuing a visual warning. He was clean-shaven and had a full head of wavy brown hair, which needed a cut and tidy up.

Under a mottled waxed jacket his brown sweater and grey pants were damp and frayed. The only indication of better times were his brown brogues. From Barkers of London, they needed a polish but quality had assured their survival whilst everything else crumbled above.

He'd been waiting in the damp and drizzle for three-quarters of an hour and he was aching from head to toe.

'Push off, go on, away with you,' said a woman with a pink umbrella. Her attempt at an authoritative frown came from a friendly face wholly unsuited to the task.

Fearing a poke from the brolly, Harry moved aside muttering, 'sorry, I'm here to see Mr Parker. I arrived a little early.'

'Oh! Really? It's Mr ....?'

'Dunn. Harry Dunn.' And sensing a slight shift in the balance of power; 'MR Harry Dunn. I made the appointment yesterday afternoon with a lady called Ms. Daniels. Is she expected? I'm sure she will confirm the arrangements.'

'Oh yes, you called yesterday. And it's Miss. I am Miss Daniels.'

'Oh. Well. I was expecting someone older. Good morning Miss Daniels.'

Harry stood in the rain fully expecting a slash round the ear from a pink umbrella but after a tense few seconds was rewarded with a miniscule smirk. 'Please come in out of the rain.' she said, 'I would hate to see your clothes ruined.'

Harry smiled grimly at her retreating back.

Miss Daniels busied herself at the start of her working day and presented Harry with a coffee. Separates no less - cup, saucer, sugar, milk all on a small silver tray – not at all what he was used to.

'Would you like a slice of toast? I normally make myself some when I arrive early.'

He politely declined as the heavy, underbaked teacake consumed in the bus-station café an hour previously was only now approaching his stomach.

Quite apart from that, nervous anticipation had dulled his appetite.

Harry studied the guilt-framed prints dotted around the waiting room. Local scenes, including a couple of Pendle Hill, hung on Magnolia walls. He prodded, then smashed his teaspoon into his cup in an effort to make the brown rocks of sugar dissolve. Miss Daniels peered over half-moons at the racket so Harry busied himself with a 'Making a Will' leaflet taken from a neat fan on the glass-topped chrome table. Even opened to its full extent the leaflet failed to cover the coffee slick, the result of his battle with the sugar.

He smiled sheepishly at Miss Daniels who grinned back with a slow shake of the head.

Harry was daydreaming but was woken by a rattle. The outer door opened and a huge hooked nose arrived followed in by a tall, thin man wearing a black pinstriped suit under a long fawn raincoat. Upon the nose was a pair of gold-rimmed spectacles and above the shaggy eyebrows a most un-solicitor-like fishing hat – flies and all. 'Christ, what a bloody awful morning Irene,' said the newcomer.

Shaking itself like an uncoordinated jumble of letter 'K's, the apparition waggled it's brolly but dropped a newspaper and brief case on the wet tiles. He kicked the brief case and muttered 'bugger'.

'Ahem! Edward….uh Mr Parker, this is Mr Dunn, your nine o'clock.'

Mr Parker picked up his belongings, unravelled himself and stared at Miss Daniels. He then slowly rotated his head towards Harry who thought he was being leered at by a character from a Dickens novel. Harry had a rush of adrenaline and the teacake thudded into his belly. He suppressed a belch.

'You're rather early Mr Dunn.'

Mr Parker raised a hooded grey eyebrow dragging the right side of his face with it, raising a lip. The whole became an astonished sneer.

Harry felt he was being appraised by a tall thin eagle. An eagle that appeared less than impressed with his rumpled clothes and grubby brogues. Harry's unspoken reply to unasked question - 'despite your misgivings, I did make an effort to dress for the occasion.'

Harry raised his own eyebrows in a half-hearted silent challenge.

'Indeed. Yes. Good morning Mr Dunn. I do detest this time of year.'

'Indeed,' replied Harry.

'Well. Uh. Yes. Just allow me a few minutes to organise myself and we'll commence. Will you come in please Irene?'

A few minutes later Harry was sitting on a chair not dissimilar to the weathered carver in which his father used to sit at their farmhouse kitchen table. This one was highly polished and had a padded red cushion seat. Mr Parker (far better suited to sitting behind a desk than moving about) sat with hands resting on the polished desk-top, one palm resting on the back of his other hand. He peered out from behind a thatch of hooded eyebrows and asked Harry if he'd brought proof of identity. From his inside jacket pocket Harry produced his documents and handed them over. The solicitor flicked quickly through the passport but his eyes lingered for a moment on the birth certificate. Then, without comment, he handed them to his secretary who left the room.

And after a few moments silence he began to speak slowly and clearly without the use of notes.

'William Davis was your godfather. He was not a blood relative. Mr Davies, your father and I were friends at school together, indeed remained so for a while after we left. We agreed to be godparents to each other's first born. However, as neither William Davis nor I were blessed with issue, the only one able to honour our agreement was your godfather. He attended your Christening, as did I, but the day following your third birthday party he left. I don't believe your father spoke to him again.' He paused. 'Neither did I, except for the occasion, four years ago, when he came to see me to draw up his last will and testament.'

'It is very straightforward document, leaving you as sole beneficiary, excepting a modest donation to a private hospital in Wiltshire. It was completed within the morning – drawn up, typed and signed, all done. He left refusing my offer of lunch, and we did not speak again. The next I heard of him was a call from the police in Keswick in the Lake District informing me of his passing.'

My godfather's friend paused for a moment lost in memory as his head drooped during the telling of the story exaggerating his hawkish appearance. There was a sadness and a distance about him, possibly regret, and Harry felt a pang of sympathy for the man.

'He went into the army you see,' he continued 'married it in effect, and whatever life he had before then he gave up along with all his friends. Although I can't be sure, I believe he went abroad following your birthday and told no one outside the army where he was heading.

He was an only child and both his parents died before he was ten. His father was killed when a rock-wall collapsed at the stone quarry where he worked and his mother died twelve months later from cancer. He had no children and never married. The army became the only family he knew to the exclusion of anything else. I doubt you have any recollection of him?'

'No, none whatsoever.'

'Hardly surprising.' Pause. 'The police inspector told me that he fell from a steep ridge called Striding Edge to the east of a mountain called Helvellyn in The Lake District. His body lay undiscovered for forty-eight hours until it was spotted at the bottom of a rocky slope by a local sheep farmer. It appears to have been a tragic accident. He was buried a week last Thursday in a small graveyard close to where he lived in Shropshire and I'm sorry to say that attendance was sparse at best. In addition to me the only people there were the local vicar and three friends of your Godfather including Mrs Wilton who runs a local Bed and Breakfast. I had difficulty tracing you but did eventually through your father-in-law in Mold who provided me with your address in Shrewsbury.'

He paused and stared at Harry, unblinking, lost in a dream.

'What are you staring at me for?' asked Harry.

'I apologize, I was thinking about three young men and a little boy's third birthday party. It's hard to believe it's forty years ago. Mm, yes I do remember - I remember the exact date. I have thought about that day often, it was the end of a time of innocence for the three of us.'

Harry was getting nervous. Miss Daniels knocked gently and asked if they would like a drink. 'Scotch and water please' said Harry, attempting to lighten the mood.

'Tea or coffee?' asked Mr Parker.

'Coffee thanks.'

'Coffee for two please Irene.'

Mr Parker paused for a moment. 'I'm sorry. I got a little involved there but I thought you should have a little background on your godfather.'

'He obviously meant a lot to you despite your lack of contact.'

'He was a good childhood friend who became a good man all those years ago when we grew into adulthood. The man I saw four years ago was different, wiser but wary, but I don't believe the good had left him.'

Miss Daniels brought in a larger version of the coffee tray, this time including a bowl of granulated sugar and a supply of paper towels. She smiled at Harry and left.

Edward Parker poured coffee for the two of them and sat back cradling his saucer, lost in thought.

'Now to the will,' said Mr Parker suddenly, setting aside his cup.

Harry's teacake rumbled threateningly and his cup began to rattle on the saucer so he set it down on the desk with a clatter.

'There is a sum of money to the value seventy-four thousand four hundred and twenty-six pounds. Expenses, including funeral costs and our modest fee, have been deducted.' An eyebrow arched during a quick glance at Harry. 'In addition, you inherit his home, the keys for which you may collect from Mrs Wilton at her Bed and Breakfast. She lived near William and has been looking after Dave until the estate was finalised.'

Bloody Hell thought Harry. 'Who's Dave?' he asked.

'His dog.'

'Dog? Who on earth calls a dog Dave?'

'Your godfather. He didn't have many close friends.' Then he smiled. 'I spoke to Mrs Wilton and she told me that when William told people he was 'going out with Dave' it sounded like he was meeting a friend.' He smiled.

'Is that amusing or very sad?'

'Amusing I think. I hope.'

'Yes, me too.'

Mr Parker retrieved a buff folder from a drawer and placed it on the desk. He took out an envelope and two sheets of paper and began to read. Without lifting his head, he raised his eyes. Unblinking, he stared at Harry from beneath grey, bushy eyebrows. In that look Harry felt as if he was being handed a burden, his heart thumped and blood whooshed in his ears. An old clock ticked loudly on the marble mantelpiece. A drop of sweat trickled down his back and he wiped his clammy hands on his trousers. He felt tethered to the chair by an unseen restraint.

The solicitor appeared about to say something but looked away when Miss Daniels knocked and entered handing over Harry's documents. 'All in order

Irene?'

'Everything is in order Mr Parker.'

Everything should be fine, thought Harry. He felt sick. He needed fresh air and he needed a drink. How one was supposed to react when learning of considerable good fortune. Harry didn't know, but he felt there was something going on - so far his good fortune was proving a sizeable disappointment.

He shook hands with Mr Parker (who wiped his hand on his trousers) and was escorted to the door by Miss Daniels to the waiting area where Mr Parker's ten o'clock waited patiently. She was an elderly bespectacled lady muffled up in a tweed coat and wool hat. Harry needed to sit down for a moment. He picked up The Daily Telegraph but was denied the opportunity to read because the old lady insisted on telling him that she was experiencing difficulty with her neighbour's over-height fence. Harry muttered sympathetically before the lady eventually ran out of steam and Harry left her waiting for her audience.

The rain had stopped as he left Parker and Williams. He clutched an envelope containing a cheque and Mrs Wilton's address. He had fifty pounds from Mr Parker who had adjusted his cheque accordingly. 'Not really the done thing.' Mr Parker had muttered.

He left with the good wishes of Miss Daniels.

Eighteen minutes later he was back in the bus station, on his bus, awaiting departure. He didn't hear the gunshot that ended the life of Mr Edward Parker of Parker and Williams, Solicitors.

Unaware of the tragedy, Harry sat on his bus and contemplated. He racked his brain to find a childhood memory of his uncle but nothing came. With fifty extra pounds in his pocket and the promise of more to come his financial problems had eased, but as he wiped condensation from the window with his coat sleeve and looked out at the drizzle, another bead of sweat trickled down his back and he shivered. Sure, there was a ray of light ahead but the storm through which he had lived loomed behind him. He saw himself staggering out of the surf against the rip of returning water, a great grey wave at his back, white topped and thunderous, ready to break and swamp him.

Chapter 4

Harry rapped on the door having failed to spot the bell – situated most inconveniently right beside the door jamb above a 'please ring for attention' sign. While waiting he turned and looked at the garden separating the house from the road. Snowdrops and the green shoots of what he presumed to be daffodils the only hint of approaching spring. A huge green tractor rumbled by pulling a large steaming trailer. The revolting vapour trail reminded him of his childhood and he shivered. 'Chicken poo' he thought to himself and wrinkled his nose. He turned to knock again at the precise moment the door opened.

'Ah. Sorry, thought you hadn't heard,' said Harry, hiding his offending knuckles in his trouser pocket. 'Er, good morning. Mrs Wilton?'

'Yes, that's right.'

'Harry Dunn.'

'Oh dear...I mean, oh yes of course. I didn't know you were coming. It's a bit of a surprise that's all.'

'Yes, I'm sorry I didn't phone but I was, well, rather nervous and thought I'd just come along and see if you were about.'

'As you can see I am about. And I'm about to have a cup of tea. May I offer you one? Please, come in. Mr Parker told me to expect you in due course. Such a tragedy. How could he do that to himself?'

'Do what to himself? What do you mean?'

'Kill himself.'

Harry frowned. 'It was an accident surely.'

Mrs Wilton stared at Harry. 'He shot himself, how can that be an accident?'

'I was told he fell down a mountain.'

'No, no. Oh my. You haven't heard. Mr Parker committed suicide.'

Harry felt weak. The rush of adrenaline nearly floored him and left him sick to the stomach. 'Suicide? When?'

'Not long after you left his office I believe. He must have just come off the phone to me by all accounts. Has no-one spoken to you?'

Not yet, thought Harry. 'No,' he muttered.

She led the way through a short hallway past a flight of stairs and into the large kitchen, the beating heart of many a country home. An Aga in a huge, stone inglenook dominated the outer wall of the room. Country pine proliferated - kitchen cupboards and low-level units topped with a gravel-grey. granite worktops. An enormous pine table, weathered and well used, in the centre of the room held biscuits and a chocolate cake on wire racks cooling from the Aga. The fabulous smell made Harry's mouth water. A picture window looked onto a pebbled courtyard where he presumed guests would lounge around in the summer months. The whole scene could have been straight from Country Life if it hadn't been such a tip, thought Harry uncharitably. As if reading his thoughts, she said, 'I've no guests at the moment so am taking the chance to catch up with a few things. Please, take a seat. Milk and sugar?'

'Both please Mrs Wilton' he said shifting his eyes sideways towards the biscuits.

'Call me Jan. And help yourself.'

'Sorry?'

'I'm not daft, go, help yourself to a biscuit.'

'Oh those,' said Harry in his best innocent voice. Their eyes met and they smiled at one another.

A little older than Harry, she wore no make-up but didn't need any, she was just one of those fortunate people who is naturally attractive. She was short and trim and her ash blond hair was flecked with grey and styled in a neat bob. Wearing a blue and white striped apron she placed Harry's tea before him and sat across the table with her back to the Aga.

Harry's attempt to ingest a warm crunchy biscuit was curtailed by a low growl. 'Christ!' he spluttered.

Jan laughed.

'That's Dave,' she said, 'that's her "would you mind awfully if I had a taste" growl or "who invited you in" snarl. I'm still learning her language but if you give her some biscuit she won't mind who you are or whether you're invited or not.'

The dog sat and stared at Harry who thought it prudent to share his snack. He snapped off a little of the biscuit and dropped it in front of the dog who didn't move a muscle and continued to stare.

'You have to hand it to her gently and don't short-change her. She seems to know when she's not getting at least half.'

Harry went to retrieve the morsel on the floor but the dog put a paw on it and gave the faintest of growls.

'You've lost that bit for good – that's just her bonus because you don't understand the rules. It's half what's in your hand she wants.'

Harry carefully broke the remaining biscuit in half and offered it to the dog who leaned forward and gently took it. With tail wagging to and fro along the tiled floor fifty percent of the 'crunchy farmhouse' was dispatched in seconds and the mutt padded round the table to sit with Jan.

'So why doesn't she want half yours?'

'I gave her some earlier – she's not greedy and knows how far to push it.'

'What breed is she?'

'Black,' replied Jan grinning 'she's a rescue dog that the vet reckons is a collie / retriever cross. A she dog called Dave. Will always wanted a dog called Dave for some reason but fell in love with this one at the rescue centre. He thought that shouting 'Davina' to bring her to heel would have been bad for his image. So, it's Dave.'

It gets worse, thought Harry. Inheriting a dog is responsibility enough but it's a female called Dave of indeterminate parentage with a taste for home-made biscuits.

'She's a lovely girl and she was a good friend to Will,' said Jan, 'I always looked after her when he went away so she feels at home here.' She untied her apron and hung it over the back of her chair and continued, 'when you get a dog from a rescue centre whoever takes them on is not allowed to own them outright. First you are questioned to see if you are deemed to be suitable 'parents'. Then you foster for a probationary period and if all goes well you adopt them. You never actually own the dog as such and you're not allowed to sell them. If you want to get rid of it for any reason you must inform the rescue centre and they will take it back. They keep a close eye on their animals so they don't end up back at square one – on the street - which is fine, I'm sure you agree.' Harry raised his eyebrows and nodded. 'I have spoken to them and explained our situation. If you want her she's yours by right, subject to the necessary suitability tests.' She glanced at Harry who looked down into his tea. 'You must however contact the centre to tell them if you are taking on the responsibility.'

Harry bent down and looked at Dave under the table and was rewarded with a soulful stare and the briefest flicker of the tail. He'd have to think about this.

'Let's just see if we get on,' he said, 'the dog will decide. If I do take her you can be nanny, great aunt or whatever.'

Jan smiled.

The grandfather clock ticked as Jan retrieved a set of keys from a hook above the phone. 'These are yours.' She said.

Harry took the bunch of keys and his heart thumped.

'The silver one's the door key and the black one is for the engine. I'm not sure about the other two.'

'Engine?'

'Yes. How else are you going to move it?'

Harry stared and couldn't correlate this information.

'It's a boat – a narrowboat. Moored in the marina just down the road - that's where Will lived.'

Bloody hell, though Harry. What else? 'My Uncle lived on a boat? I thought it was a hou...' but he ran out of steam.

'You didn't know then?'

Dave crept up, leaned on Harry's leg and looked up at his new dad as if to say, 'Yes, and what's wrong with that then?'

He patted the dog's head who returned to sit by Jan.

'Oh, I forget to tell you. A policeman phoned at lunchtime and asked if I could get you to give him a call when you turned up. I have the number here. Why don't you call him and then go and have a look at your boat? Here use my phone.'

As Harry dialled his hand trembled and he spoke briefly to a Detective Inspector Warren who said he wished to come and ask Harry a few questions – tomorrow morning would be convenient. They agreed to meet at the B & B at 10.30 am if Mrs Wilton was agreeable - which she was.

Chapter 5

Harry walked through the gate - Leebank Marina said the sign, in letters that needed a touch-up. He was amazed by the size of the place – unbelievable. A huge lake, full of boats, in the middle of the countryside. A man pushed a wheelbarrow full of logs down a gravel path and smoke curled from the chimneys of two or three boats. He walked down the drive and obeyed the sign, 'all visitors must report to the shop'. The automatic door alarm sounded like it needed new batteries, or a more drastic measure. Harry thought it sounded like a mouse being trodden on but didn't mention this to the grey-haired man sitting behind a counter working on a computer because when he dragged himself away from the screen, he wore a threatening scowl.

He muttered, 'bloody technology,' then, 'can I help you?'

'Hello, I'm Harry Dunn. My uncle lived here.'

'Oh yes, I've been expecting you. Sorry about Will, nice chap. Always paid up front, never any bother, kept himself very much to himself. Didn't even know he'd gone till Jan told me he wouldn't be coming back. I'm Tom Knight.'

'Nice to meet you Mr Knight.'

'Yes, you too. Intend staying? Rent's paid till the end of June but if you want to go somewhere else there will be a refund. Less one month's rent in lieu of notice of course. I've got a waiting list as long as my arm so it's no matter to me either way. Call me Tom.'

The phone rang. 'Excuse me a mo'.'

Harry looked around as Tom dealt with his call. The shop was not large, maybe twelve or fourteen paces square, but it was crammed full of stuff, some of which was a mystery to him. A few paintings hung on the walls, canal scenes, presumably by local artists, mediocre but colourful. On the shelves were plastic tubs containing what looked like plumbing spares, both copper and plastic, also tins of paints and a shelf of edibles, confectionery, tins of fruit and the like. Coils of rope, an assortment of odd-shaped lumps of brass and a few books – many items meant little to Harry – apart from the food.

Through the plate glass window he watched a man walk past and if he had had any worries about not being suitably attired these were now dispelled. The resident (at least Harry presumed he was) wore old jogging pants tucked into calf-length work boots, steel toe-capped and light brown, like they wear on the building sites. Above, an old waterproof jacket over a green knitted sweater - and a flat cap. He was pushing a bag of coal in a rusty wheelbarrow.

'Will's boat's down there towards the bridge, first right, second boat on the left. I hope you've got a key because I haven't.'

'Yes, Mrs Wilton gave me one. I'll go over and have a look then.'

Tom went back to his lap-top with a growl as Harry made his way to his uncle's boat – his boat. It was parked second along a long line of boats pointing nose-in to a rusty metal pontoon. It was dark green with a yellow coach lines – reminding Harry of a packet of Golden Virginia that he smoked in his youth. It had a grey roof and written in big scarlet letters towards the back, the words 'Box Car Willy'.

Harry smiled to himself thinking the name sounded like a complaint with which you would visit an STD clinic.

He unzipped a canvas cover, clambered down onto a small deck and unlocked the wooden double door with his silver key. He was bending down stepping down into the boat when a loud voice rang out behind him, 'Hello there.' Startled and unbalanced Harry straightened and crunched the back of his head on the top of the door frame. 'Bugger,' he muttered and staggered out rubbing his head.

'Sorry, didn't mean to startle you.' A chap dressed in jeans and blue sweatshirt stood on the pontoon. 'I'm Ralph. I live over there.' Pointing vaguely towards the shop.

'Hi. I'm Harry. That's the first time I have ever cracked my head on the top of a door. Thank you for instigating a whole new experience.' He smiled.

'Are you a relative of Will's then?'

'Not exactly, I'm his godson.'

'Oh, right. I was really sorry to hear about the accident. He was OK Will - kept himself to himself but friendly enough.'

'Did you know him well then?'

'No, as I say, he was a bit of a loner, kept his own council. He was also away quite a bit, enjoyed travelling, but he never said much about his trips. Bit of a mystery really. He kept some of the residents here guessing, drove them mad actually.'

Harry looked up as a pair of swans whooshed overhead and landed with elongated splashes at the far end of the marina. Wow, what a sight, thought Harry.

'They're amazing aren't they? Look Ralph, you obviously know your way around. Would you mind showing me what's what on here? I've never even been on a barge before. I don't want to sink the damn thing.'

'Don't let the purists hear you call it a barge - these are narrowboats. But yes, sure I'll help. On you go, I'll follow. Watch your nut.' Ralph glanced quickly around before following Harry.

As they stepped down into what was obviously the lounge, Harry noticed a slightly musty smell with a hint of dog, it was cold, but it looked homely. There was a wooden floor (oak Harry recognised from his timber days), green painted walls up to the gunwale with the remainder of the walls and roof covered in aged pine tongue and groove. To his immediate left was a wood-burning stove (unlit) and to his right, low-level cupboards on which stood a television. A single leather lazy-boy chair with matching foot stool, fold-down table and a rumpled dog's bed were the main furnishings. Beyond the lounge, a kitchen and on the draining board a single cup. A lone piece of crockery and a single teaspoon that made Harry feel like a trespasser and rather miserable.

There were two photographs in frames screwed to the wall. One man was common to both photos. It was the first time Harry had actually seen Will, or who he presumed to be Will. He was a tall, dark-haired man. He had a tanned face and in the left-hand photo he wore army fatigues under an open quilted coat and had a pair of sunglasses perched on the top of his head. In that photo Will was with a group of men all dressed in cold-weather gear, the backdrop a range of snow-covered mountains. The other was of Will with three men, two of whom Harry recognised as his father and Edward Parker. The fourth was a good-looking chap with fair hair. They were all sitting around a table outside what looked like a café, the mystery man had his back to the photographer but was looking towards the camera over his shoulder. All four were smiling and from the detritus on the table, they looked to be having a celebration. Harry looked at his father for a moment and shivered before moving on down the boat into the kitchen.

The cupboards were oak and with sink, double oven and microwave all in stainless steel it all came as a pleasant surprise. On the right down a short corridor was a sliding door into the small bathroom with shower cubicle, washbasin and toilet and beyond here, the bedroom. The 'nearly double' bed was covered in a red / white quilted bedspread and a small cupboard above the pillows housed a car stereo unit, a pair of inset speakers and a reading light. At the foot of the bed was a double wardrobe in the bottom of one half of which was some kind of boiler.

'That's a diesel-fuelled central heating boiler,' said Ralph, following Harry's gaze, 'probably only lit that when we have a prolonged spell of really cold weather.'

'This is fabulous,' said Harry 'not at all what I imagined.'

Two steps ran up beside the wardrobe into a small rear cabin. 'What on earth are all that lot?' asked Harry indicating a multitude of tiny red and yellow lights set in a large black panel.

'Those are the LED lights for all the electrical equipment. It's not as complicated as it looks, each light represents a different circuit and they're all labelled. Look, this top one is the cabin lighting circuit, this one is the water pump, this one the fridge etc. etc. If a light goes out the switch has tripped and there may be a problem somewhere.'

'Really.'

'Don't worry you'll soon get the hang of it all. Below us is the engine and those double doors there open up onto the rear deck. You have to lift the hatch here above your head and slide it back then the doors will open.'

Harry stood on the small deck and felt a bit queasy. The deck was roughly semi-circular and it was only three feet from the rear doors to the back edge at the furthest point. 'At least I've got this stick to hang onto.'

'Tiller,' Said Ralph. 'Besides, you won't fall in more than once! It's bloody cold in there, especially at this time of year. That thick blue wire is your mains hook-up – connected to an electricity supply on the pontoon near the bow. Most of the boat will run off 12-volt electricity powered by big batteries under our feet but there is a mains circuit so you can use a kettle, toaster or whatever while moored here on the marina. Come on why don't we get the fire going.'

Fifteen minutes later Harry was sprawled in his lazy-boy and Ralph was perched on a leather footstool, the coal fire belting out a very satisfactory warmth. They were drinking coffee found in the cupboards with coffee-mate. Harry went to see if he could figure out the television when he spotted the telephone tucked in behind it. The answer machine message light was winking and after a moment's hesitation he pressed 'play'. The first call was timed at 8.52 am eight days previously but whoever it was hung up without leaving a message. The second was 7.34 pm a day later and was from a dead man.

Chapter 6

'**H**arry, it's uncle Will.' A pump of adrenaline took his breath away as he heard an unfamiliar voice. 'I hope you don't have to hear this message but if you do, you will require an explanation. It's all in a file on my lap-top which is with Dave. He has one of the passwords – you will know the other.'

He sat down as the machine clicked off. Bloody Hell, he thought.

'That's extraordinary', said Ralph, 'explanation of what?'

'I've no idea.'

'Who's Dave?'

'Will's dog. She's living with Jan at the B & B round the corner till I can get myself sorted out. IF I can get myself sorted out.'

Ralph looked doubtful particularly with the 'she' reference but kept quiet.

'Look, I'll get off and leave you to it. Let you have a good poke around. Look me up if there's anything I can help you with.'

'OK, thanks for your help, I'll be fine.'

Harry sat and puzzled. He didn't blame his uncle for keeping himself to himself, nor for the lack of contact. In fact, until a week ago he had never even heard of William Davies.

He replayed the message then erased it along with its silent accomplice - then realised that a 1471 could have told him where the call originated. Not that he necessarily needed to know but it might have helped. Or would it? Truth be told he was rather flummoxed.

He went to see if Uncle Will had any booze in - which he didn't. Probably a good job - three days dry now and he was getting a bit agitated. Sweaty palms and a bit shaky but he didn't want to break this spell of good fortune and disappear down the toilet again.

He made his way to the bedroom making a mental note to get hold of a toothbrush tomorrow. As he lay on the bed, unfamiliar noises assaulted from all angles. He skimmed a book on boats electrics, understanding little, and made himself another coffee before finally dropping to sleep in the early evening accompanied by the gently slapping of the water on the hull and creaking of the mooring ropes. The words of Edward Parker echoed round his mind.

He awoke to the sound of tapping.

Someone knocking on the side of the boat. It was 8.30am and he'd slept like a log for over twelve hours. He made himself look semi-respectable and clambered out of the front to investigate. 'Morning, sorry to bother you, hope I didn't wake you. I'm just off into the village and wondered if you needed anything. Paper, milk, bread or whatever.'

'Er, no thanks, I'll be going in myself later on. But thanks anyway. I'm Harry.'

'Welcome. Gandalf said we had a new inmate. How's the boat?'

'Well, I've only had a quick look, but it looks fantastic. I slept like the dead. I'm glad you came and knocked; I would have been there till lunchtime. I can't believe how quiet it is. Who on earth is Gandalf?'

'Old Tom in the office, mane of grey hair etc. I wouldn't let him hear you call him that though. Have you boated before?'

'No, yesterday was the first time I'd stepped on one. It's not what I expected at all. I think it's fantastic.'

'Good, I'm glad you like it. Will was proud of his boat, he did quite a lot of the work himself. Anyway, I must be off – got a dental check-up. I'll see you later if you're about. Cheerio. I'm Ralph by the way.'

'Another Ralph? That's a coincidence.'

'What do you mean?'

'Well, the chap who showed me round the boat yesterday afternoon was called Ralph. Lives over there.' Pointing up the jetty.

'My boat's up there. I didn't get home till after midnight. Quiz night at the local. As far as I know I'm the only Ralph here.'

'Who was that bloke other then?' A fear gripped him. 'Oh no!'

Chapter 7

Harry called the B & B, the number on the card that Jan had given him. No reply. Fifteen minutes later he was rapping on the door. 'Jan.' he called. No reply. 'Jan!' This was making him feel very uneasy. He rang the bell and knocked again before making his way round to the patio. He peered through the French windows into the kitchen. Nothing, not even a dog bark. He tried the door which slid open. 'Jan. Are you there?' Silence.

He'd dressed in a hurry and run the short distance to the B & B. Something was very wrong. He was breathing heavily and blood hissed in his ears when he spotted that the door in the far corner of the room beyond the Aga was ajar. Jan was lying on the bed, hands, knees and feet bound with parcel tape. Her head lolled to one side and blood had dripped from her nose onto the bed sheet. Her chest rose and fell but in a shallow staccato motion. There was a bluish tinge to her lips and her eyes were closed.

Harry called an ambulance from the phone by the bed. 'Bed & Breakfast down the road from Leebank Marina' was all he could tell the controller. 'Run by a lady called Jan.' That was good enough. Most local people knew of Sycamores B & B. Harry cut Jan's bonds with a sharp kitchen knife and sat on the edge of the bed holding her hand. He gently stroked her forehead and spoke to her in a manner he hoped was reassuring.

Then she stopped breathing.

Harry knew he had to act fast. He knew a bit about this – come on son. On the edge of panic. The ambulance was on its way but he knew that every second was critical.

The chain of survival.

He opened her mouth and saw what some sort of cloth in the back of Jan's throat. Why the hell hadn't he checked earlier? He pulled out a bloodied handkerchief. He rolled her onto her back, placed one hand on the forehead and lifted Jan's chin using his first two fingers of his other hand to open her airway. He was shaking. Look, listen and feel. He bent so his ear was close to Jan's nose, placed the flat of his hand on her upper chest and looked along the length of her body for any sign of breathing. Christ, nothing!

He dragged her off the bed onto the floor. Come on now, just calm down. He pinched her nose, opened her mouth with his other hand sealed his lips over Jan's and breathed in. Too fast. Slow down.

Come on think!. Breathe slowly – long breath, two seconds. He tried again, this time properly. He raised his head slightly and released the nose, the air was expelled, the chest fell. Then again. Good. Now, chest compressions. It's coming back – relax. Arms straight, fingers interlocked, centre of the chest. OK. Press down about 2 / 3 inches. Rocking motion. One, two .... fourteen fifteen. Come on, come on..... Back to the breaths - two more. Fifteen compressions.

How long he carried on he couldn't say but he was out of breath and his muscles trembled. He looked up to see the blue flashing lights of an ambulance distorted through the frosted window. He picked up an onyx ornament from the bedside table and hurled it through the window. 'In here!' He yelled. 'Quick! Help!'

He watched the paramedics apply a defibrillator and give her some sort of injection. They asked him questions he couldn't remember and praised him for his efforts. The metallic voice prompts of the automatic machine filled the room. 'Do not touch the patient.' Harry began to shake.

There was a momentary calm.

'You've probably saved her life' he said looking Harry squarely in the eye for a second. 'Do you know her name and if she's on any medication?'

'She's called Jan but I've no idea about the medication. I only met her for the first time yesterday.'

'Ok.' But well done, you did a good job.'

Harry didn't feel superb. He shook from head to foot; his hands were sweating and his head buzzed.

'Are you going to be alright?'

'Yes, I'll be OK, sure,' replied Harry 'what about Jan?'

'Looks like she'll be alright. We'll get her off to hospital, but she has a pulse and is breathing. Hopefully she'll be OK.'

Harry stood bent at the hips, hands on knees trying to get his breath back. He suddenly wanted to be far away. What the hell was going on?

The ambulance pulled away, lights flashing but surely the police must be on the way. Gradually he began to think straight. There was only one place he would find any answers. He'd have to find Will's computer, unless bogus Ralph had found it.

He ran through the kitchen into the hall and nearly fell over the dog lying at the foot of the stairs, tongue hanging out, snoring. Fat lot of bloody good you are, he thought. He shook the dog but nothing. Drugged? How easy for someone to pose as a guest, befriend and drug the dog? There was a disc on the dog's collar, 'Dave' on one side, on the other a number. A password? Maybe, but no damn good without somewhere to put it He removed the dog's collar and put it in his pocket.

'It's with Dave', Uncle Will had said. What the hell did that mean? The dog wasn't much good to anybody in its present condition but at least it was alive.

He went back into the kitchen and spotted the dog's bed. Nothing in there, or under it. In the pantry however he got lucky. There was a nearly-full 24-pack of dog food in tins on a shelf in a shallow cardboard tray. Lying flat beneath the tins, a black Dell lap-top computer.

Still no police.

Why he ran he didn't know. Or perhaps he did – fear. He'd done nothing wrong but for some reason he ran back to the boat and called a taxi. He collected his passport, birth certificate and cash (twenty-seven quid). He had found the case for the laptop the previous evening which contained various leads so he slipped the computer into it, locked his boat and went out the gate to wait for his cab. The taxi took him to the local town of Wem passing a police patrol car en route. From there he caught a bus to Shrewsbury.

There was only one person whom he could really trust and she would be found either in a grubby café, in church or in the boozer. He found her huddled next to a radiator in church.

Chapter 8

'**N**ever thought I'd see you again love,' said Mary. 'Come here to say thank you have you?'

'I think he's handed me a poisoned chalice Mary. To be honest, I could use your help.'

'You need my help. Bloody hell.... oops,' looking at the altar, 'sorry Lord,' then back to Harry, 'my my, you must be in a pickle if you need my help.'

'I don't have anywhere else to go Mary.'

'Let's go and have a beer and talk about it.'

'Actually, I'm trying to stay off the ale. Four days now and I'm beginning to think straight. Let me buy you one though.'

'No, we'll stay here. Providing what you're going to tell me is suitable for sensitive ears.' Looking up again.

He told her what had happened over the previous couple of days, ending by saying that he needed somewhere to look at the lap-top, away from prying eyes. Well out of the way of the police.

'Good grief. Not delusional are you through lack of alcohol?' She asked with a nervous smile.

'I've got a set of boat keys and a computer as physical evidence.'

'And a trail of devastation behind you - a dead man, a mystery psychopath, a hospitalised landlady and a poorly dog. You'd have been better off missing your bus.'

'I'm beginning to think it's more than one dead man. Yes, we've got the solicitor, but there's also my uncle who left me a mysterious phone message the day before he died - and my mother and father whose deaths were never properly explained, at least to me.'

'Hell fire Harry. Oh damn, sorry Lord.' She looked up at the east wall then at Harry, 'can't do with upsetting him, it's the only time I get warm.'

Mary stared down at her lap, then looked Harry in the eye for a moment.

She was suddenly quiet. She smiled briefly, then looked very serious. Then she knelt and prayed.

She was motionless for a full five minutes. Harry began to calm down and apart from a gentle ticking from the radiator next to Mary, it was silent. Mary heaved herself back onto the pew and looked Harry in the eye. Her face was serious and she somehow looked distant. 'Of course I'll help.' She fumbled in the folds of her worn clothing and came up with a plain key ring upon which were two keys, one for a yale lock and one mortice.

'Flat 5, 11 Belmont Gardens. Go down to the river, turn left and follow it until you see the Tesco supermarket. Belmont Gardens is across the car park down Hind Road. Go down the alley beside number 15, the entrance is round the back. The big key is for the outer door, the small one is flat 5 on the third floor. Please don't ask questions just now and please be careful, I'll join you later.' He stared at her but she gave him a gentle shove and said, 'Go on, off you go.'

Harry's mind reeled as he left the Church. He was at the address in fifteen minutes having walked quickly, head down, expecting a tap on the shoulder at any moment. Harry barely noticed the River Severn that flowed by to his right and tried to ignore the throng milling around the Tesco superstore.

But now he was climbing the stairs which exclusively served flat 5. What he saw when he opened the door left him stunned.

Chapter 9

He entered a square hallway off which were four doors, one in the facing wall, two to the left and one to the right - all closed. There was a skylight in the ceiling that illuminated the hall and the salmon pink carpet was thick and looked to be of high quality. On an oak table in the far right corner stood a telephone alongside two glass ornaments, identical birds on plinths arranged to face each other. Beside the table, an oak carver. A large painting, a hunting scene, in substantial guilt frame hung on the wall to the right under a picture light.

He thought back to first school art class when he had presented his painting to the teacher, Mrs Hoyle. She examined the offering for a moment or two then proclaimed 'astonishing'. He only knew what this meant when he was presented with a lump of clay at the following class. His ability to judge the quality of a painting was in some doubt but he knew an expensive 'looking' item when he came across one – and this was one.

He nervously explored. The door immediately to the left led into a cloakroom with toilet and small basin, the other into a large bedroom with king-size bed and fitted, oak wardrobes and a further door to an en suite bathroom.

The right-hand door opened into a large kitchen. Above a central island unit hung pots, pans and utensils suspended from a stainless steel frame. A run of white, steel-handled kitchen units was broken only by a huge cooker with overhead extractor, also in stainless steel. An archway led to a dining area where a highly polished table was surrounded by six ladder-back chairs.

To the left of the archway another door led to the large rectangular lounge. A three-seat black leather sofa faced a magnificent slate grey fireplace flanked by two matching armchairs. Above the fire a large guilt mirror. A glass-topped, oak frame table sat within reach of the sofa and chairs. Behind the sofa, against the wall opposite the fireplace, sat a large mahogany writing desk upon which stood a brass reading light and a further telephone. Three Georgian sash windows looked out over a park and a Wedgwood blue carpet covered the entire room. The flat occupied the entire top floor of the Georgian terraced house. This was not the residence of a down-and-out.

He was dumbfounded. In the centre of the lounge he slowly turned a complete circle wondering what on earth was going on. Don't ask questions.

Harry set his computer on the writing desk, plugged in the power lead and fired it up. He took Dave's tag from his pocket and entered the six-figure number at the password prompt. He was in. In the 'my documents' folder were twelve files. Most appeared to relate to either the boat or day to day living but one was called Harry. He double-clicked the icon and was prompted for the second password. "You will know this." Did he?

He tried Davis and Dunn. No go. Box Car Willy. No. Dates, dates. Harry's birthday – no. Damn it. He thought about Uncle Will. No idea of his birthday and it couldn't be the day he died – surely. It wasn't - stupid attempt.

He walked round the flat racking his brains then stood looking out over the park. A mother was pushing with her young child on the swings. Think! Child – that's it! Harry as a child, the last time he saw Uncle Will – his third birthday.

121163. He was in.

The file opened. A word document. A lengthy document that began: Dear Harry....

Chapter 10

Thirty-Eight years ago

The fourth man stood and began to walk. Spent, cried out, numb. He walked along the sea-front and up the hill called the Great Orme, Llandudno. He stood on the edge of the cliff staring, unseeing – way below crashed waves from the grey, soulless sea. The wind buffeted and thrashed his tortured mind. The rain came - failed to wash away his guilt. He fell forward......

The Present

Dear Harry

I'm so sorry my boy. My regret at failing to contact you has grown year on year like an untreated sore. The longer it went, the more impossible it became. This is my heartfelt yet cowardly attempt to put things right - to say what I should have said many years ago.

It's dramatic I know, but the fact is, if you are reading this, I am dead.

I could not look you in the eye so this is my poor attempt at atonement. My past has caught up with me. It is a past I could not face. I joined the army and ran away but I could never forget.

I remember your third birthday as if it were yesterday. It was the last time I saw you and it was the occasion that my friendship with three of my childhood friends came to an end.

The four of us were at school together in Cardigan, West Wales. Your father, Edward Parker, Derek Crabtree and myself. Derek took his own life many years ago. I look back and believe perhaps that he was the only one with any guts.

We were inseparable at school, played rugby together, met each evening after lessons, shared our lives. Our favourite pastime was orienteering and we joined the school cadets which gave us the chance to learn the basic skills that would later stand me in some stead when I joined the army. We would spend days and nights in the Welsh mountains, 'living off the land' we called it (except when we cheated and ate our emergency beans cooked on a primus). We loved the camping, the walking and the freedom, taking the worst weather and danger in our stride with naive confidence. We would pull together, we were indestructible.

Looking back on my life, those were the days the sun shone.

We had no leader as such, we all had our strengths. Your father, John, was the talker, the one to approach a local farmer in an effort to persuade him the give up a chicken for four lost, hungry boys. He would boast that his success rate was 70%. On the occasions he failed, Derek would take over and go and steal one anyway. We called him the fox. Twice he ended up with lead shot in the seat of his pants. Edward was the thinker, the schemer. When a plan was called for (generally because we were either lost or hungry) he would step forward with a battle plan. I was the navigator and trapper. I snared us the odd rabbit and usually got us up the correct mountain but when I bungled, someone else would jump in.

Before we left school we decided to have an adventure. We chose the hills surrounding a small town north east of Toulouse called Caylus. Edward had previously visited the area with his parents and as planner in chief we trusted his judgement. The plan was that after we left school we would work for three months saving all we could, then spend a month camping and trekking in France.

The journey was part of our adventure, a mixture of trains, buses, boats and for the final leg, we hitch-hiked. The man who gave us a lift on the last leg of our journey did so in the back of his clapped-out van. He lived on the edge of the village of Felines and unbeknown to us then he was the root to our troubles.

He dropped us off so we could buy provisions in Caylus. While looking for somewhere to camp, we unwittingly arrived at our benefactors farm gate so asked where we could safely pitch our tents. He appeared a little nervous as he pointed us towards a wooded ridge behind which was a stream – a couple of kilometres away. As he gave us our instructions a girl, about our age, came out of the house and stood nearby. She was a lovely young thing wearing a light blue summer dress with open sandals. She had long dark brown hair, dark eyes and a deep tan. A small wiry dog had followed her and sat by her side. She stared at us strangers but did not return our smiles. The exchange did not go unnoticed by the man who swiftly herded us away.

I took the lead and found us a suitable campsite in a clearing next to the small stream. It was a magical spot, shaded from the heat of the summer by silver birch trees that whispered and swayed in the breeze, the chatter of the stream our constant companion. We spent the next two days exhausting ourselves walking the surrounding hills, chatting and laughing till late in the night drinking cheap, tasteless lager and wine from plastic bottles bought from the little supermarket on the outskirts of Caylus.

We never encountered another soul. My mind however kept returning to the girl. I was intrigued and on the third day returned early from the hike feigning a stomach upset. I returned to the farm to catch a glimpse of her.

I sat in the bushes opposite the farm gate and watched. She played with her dog then lay reading on a rug in the garden under a parasol. She spotted me when I fell into a dry ditch. Desperate to relieve myself, I'd stood up to sneak back into the scrub but caught my foot on a root and fell, cracking dead twigs on the way down. I clambered out to see the girl waving me away frantically and pointing at the house. I had expected a sympathetic smile but saw a young girl who appeared nervous and frightened. She sat down again, blanking me completely as the man who had given us a lift a few days before, came out of the house. He didn't see me as I ducked down behind a bush.

He walked over and knelt down beside her and to my horror began to stroke her leg. She froze and screwed her eyes shut as his hand moved up beneath her dress. I was paralysed as he forced himself onto her - she lay motionless, arms outstretched - it was as if she was being crucified.

I have never forgotten that terrible, twisted scene. I can hear to this day the grunting and wheezing of that wicked bastard. When he had done he stood, fastened his clothes and walked back into the house, the girl covered her eyes with her hands. She curled up holding her little dog and sobbed.

I could hardly believe what I had witnessed. I felt nauseous. Finally, the girl stood. I came out from my hiding place and began to walk across the road towards her. She looked directly at me, held her hand up as would a traffic policeman at a junction and unhurriedly shook her head. Then she turned and walked slowly into the house.

I walked back to our camp in a trance to be greeted by my companions who immediately realized that something was badly wrong. I told them what had happened barely able to believe what I was saying. The guys listened then we sat in stunned silence in a ragged circle. We talked it through, all except Derek who remained strangely silent.

The next morning it was Derek who was adamant we move on. He was acting strangely, fidgeting and constantly walking to and fro. We thought we should go to the police but Derek insisted that it was none of our business and we should just clear off and forget it. We were in the middle of nowhere in a strange country and who's to say that we would be believed. He talked us round and we packed up and left. None of us was thinking straight but I should have figured that there was something more.

Three days later we found out what.

The farmers photograph was on the front page of the regional paper – he had been shot. Through our pidgin French we figured out that he had been shot twice, once in the back and once in the head, with a shotgun. Police had no clue as to why the man, named as Guillaume Leport, had been killed nor who was responsible. Monsieur Leport's niece was reported to be in deep shock but had told the police that she had been in the woods early in the morning collecting mushrooms and had heard what sounded like two shots. This was not unusual as local farmers regularly shot vermin, shooting was part of the way of life in rural France. Police were baffled by the murder.

Monsieur Leport was a former notaire (mayor) in Caylus and his niece, Celine, was now being cared for by a friend in the town.

Derek stared motionless at the photograph, his face blank, his eyes dead. Suddenly he was someone we no longer knew. A spirit had possessed him and we were terrified. Not that we felt in physical danger but something dark had come upon us.

Edward was the one who pulled us round. We had to get clear, make our way north. No-one associated us with the shooting - we had camped in the forest, and as far as we knew there were only two people who knew we had been in the area - and one of them was dead. There was nothing we could do about the girl; we couldn't go back. What would we do if we did? What would we say? Remorse was ripping me apart and I was desperate to return but I knew Edward was right.

We arrived back in England a week later and took the train back to Wales. We had spoken barely a word to each other. Your father was the one who insisted that we talk; we couldn't leave it like this. We rode to the end of the line, got off the train and made our way to Barmouth where we walked to the beach. We sat in silence for a few minutes, no-one knew where to start but we all knew from where the explanation would come.

Finally, Derek broke the spell. He told us what we already suspected. He had gone at first light to the farm and had seen the girl leave the house. He spoke quite matter-of-factly, with a detached calm.

He had gone into the house, found the gun by the kitchen door and shot the bastard as he slept. He spoke with no remorse. He told us that as he was leaving the house he saw the girl standing silently watching from the edge of the tree line. Frozen, he stood holding the weapon. The girl approached him with her arm outstretched, palm up. She said nothing as she took the gun from him and walked back into the woods. Derek told us it was as if they were acting in a macabre silent film, yet there was no set script. Scene followed scene as the players instinctively fulfilled their roles. Their audience, the trees, rustled in the breeze - beyond that, silence.

He'd arrived back at our camp to find us asleep. He'd been away less than an hour but the shock waves from that quiet corner of France would buffet us for the rest of our lives.

We met one final time three months later in Llandudno. It was in the autumn of 1960.

It was strained, a gathering of strangers, but once again Derek spoke.

He told us that he had been abused by his stepfather as a child. Threatened and terrified he had never said a word to his mother. She had never suspected a thing, or pretended not to. The stepfather had died when Derek was eight and he and his mother moved to Wales to be near her family.

He told us that our friendship had helped him bury his past although he knew that he had never resolved it. There was no-one to believe him - vile memories were no proof.

When I had told him about the girl at our campsite he returned to a place in his mind where the filth and horror lay in wait like a malignant pupa. He had walked to the farm in a trance, in a parallel world where an act of violence or revenge seemed so logical. He remembered the gun, the shooting, the girl, but it was like walking through a fog, he said, as if something had taken him, calmly possessed him and acted through him.

He was desperate to talk and we let him. Not one of us blamed him and he told us he had thought of little else since our return from France; he explained it to us in his own way. He said that we all have emotions. I remember his words so clearly - they were so logical. When someone tells a funny joke, you laugh because it's the natural thing to do. Laughter is a way to rid yourself of that particular emotion, then you start again with a clean slate. If something happens and you need to cry then you do. But you can suppress it – big boys don't cry. The problem if you hold on to tears or fear is that the emotion is stuck in your head unreleased. If it happens again and again the emotion inside is trapped like a clenched fist getting tighter and tighter. He said that he had a head full of all sorts of crap and at some stage he had to let go. He let go that day in France. He told us that he could see why people do violent unpredictable things. He knew exactly what he was doing but there was no rationale to stop himself.

Then he wept. He sobbed and to be honest we were all a bit self-conscious of our mate blubbering on that wall. Your dad put his arm round him but he went on and on. He shrugged your dad off, looked at us with swollen eyes and waved us away. And we left him.

He died that day. Jumped from the cliff. Took his demons with him and smashed them with his body on the rocks. Christ I regret leaving him. What a foul, shitty way to go. Yes, he had entered a tunnel from which he felt he would never emerge but, looking back, I truly believe that he thought he was helping us. Shouldering our burden and setting us free.

It didn't of course and things were never the same again. The bomb had exploded and blown our friendship apart.

I joined the army believing it as good a way as any to run away. Edward went to Liverpool University to study Law. He never married and moved to Chorley where he set up a practice, and there he remains. Within a few months your father met the girl he was to marry within the year. I am sure you know but as an interim step they lived with your mother in law in her small hill farm. She died suddenly a short time later and your mother and father lived in the house, content to live in near isolation. Until the fire.

You were born soon after they were married and I honoured the agreement to be your godfather.

I only saw you four times. At your Christening, then at each of your three birthdays. When you were three your father and I agreed that it was best that I no longer played a part in your life.

That was a long time ago.

I saw neither you nor your father again. I saw Edward recently; he helped me with my will, but there was nothing between us. He had changed, as had we all. He was thin and gaunt living quietly somewhere in his mind. But not at peace. I went to him in the hope that, should you two meet, he may offer some insight of me. You will probably have met him now; in some way it may close a chapter for him. Unfortunately, it has probably opened one for you.

Then in late August this year I received a threat. It wasn't the first because I have served in some sensitive areas throughout the world and dealt with some dangerous people. This one though was different because as far as I was aware no-one from that area of my life knew where I lived. I had been very careful who I told of my whereabouts and much of my mail came through an anonymous mail-drop address.

That is why I have chosen to live on a boat. What does concern me however was that the threat was addressed to the marina. What worries me more is the cryptic nature of the message which set alarm bells ringing:

BE VERY AFRAID. JUMP TO IT SOLDIER YOU'RE UNDER FIRE.

The inference was obvious. I don't like this. I have called some contacts but so far nothing has come up. I am away for a few days but when I get back I will get to the bottom of it.

BUT, something is wrong; I have a bad feeling about this.

I hope to finish this tale, rewrite some of it and explain my feelings more fully but if something

goes wrong, at least you have something.

And there it ended. He hadn't even signed it. Harry sat and stared at the screen. What the bloody hell was all this about? He began to read the story again and was part way through when he heard a key rattle in the front door. A few moments later the door to the lounge opened.

Chapter 11

'You found it then?' Mary stood in the doorway - shabby clothes, wig, dirty shoes and the ever-present grimy shopping basket.

Harry turned and stared, unable to think of a single thing to say.

'I've brought coffee and milk. Put the kettle on and I'll join you in a few minutes.' She took the shopping into the kitchen and a short while later he heard the shower running. Harry turned to look at the computer screen for a moment then went to do as he was told.

'I dropped out,' said Mary, sipping her coffee fifteen minutes later. They were sitting opposite one another at the kitchen table. 'It's a bit of a convoluted tale, but the time has come to get back on track - start again.'

Harry's mouth opened and closed like a floundering fish. Mary laughed. Gone was the woman he had known for the last months, the vagrant huddled by a radiator or swapping insults with Sid in the café.

The person before him was dressed in grey jogging pants, dark blue FCUK sweatshirt and pink trimmed running shoes. Her brown shoulder-length hair was tied back, held by a blue bow. She wore no make-up but didn't really need any as Harry's gaze was drawn to her sparkling eyes. Eyes that came alive as she laughed.

'Christ,' spluttered Harry. 'Where's Mary?'

'I'm here,' she smiled. 'Always have been. I've been in hiding for a while that's all. I had to take time out.' A shadow moved across her face for an instant and she bent her head to her coffee.

She looked up. 'I need to thank you Harry. You became my friend at my lowest point. I knew you were not at your best but nevertheless you took me for what I was. I'm not saying you saved me because I have discovered a strength I never knew I had and I know I would have come through. What you did do was make me believe that it's who, not what, you are that is important. You'll probably never understand what that means to me. I knew that the time would come for me to re-surface but never in my wildest dreams did I believe the chance would come in such circumstances.' She sighed and a tear was quickly wiped away. 'Enough, what about you?'

Harry re-engaged his brain and said, 'you look stun.....you're......it's brown' pointing at her hair. He swallowed and shook his head in amazement. Desperate for a diversion said, 'you'd better come read this.' He stood beckoning her into the lounge. Before he could move Mary put her hand on Harry's arm, drew him in and hugged him. 'Thank you,' she whispered.

While she read Harry stood and gazed over the park. The child in the buggy had gone and it had begun to rain. The trees whined and whipped in the wind. He glanced over his shoulder at Mary hunched over the screen still unable to take in the transformation.

He thought about Will's tale and his mind was drawn to his mother and father. Had they tried to escape or had they been overcome by smoke? Had they suffered? Was there more to it than an accident? Bloody right there was. Will had died in a fall but he had been in the army for God's sake, he wouldn't just fall off a mountain. He had known something was wrong. That's why he left the phone message and letter. With Edward Parker's suicide all four friends were gone. Why did he kill himself? Did the police think Harry was responsible? They must be looking for him. He had been scheduled to meet the Detective from Chorley. Running away seemed less and less smart.

They would know he ordered a taxi; know he caught a bus. Could they know anything else? They would know he had been at the B & B but couldn't blame him for the assault on Jan because he'd saved her — or at least she had been alive when the ambulance left. He hoped the dog was OK. He was raised from his musings by Mary.

'Blimey'. She said, turning to face him. 'This is almost beyond belief.'

'You're telling me,' replied Harry.

'What are you going to do?'

'I've no idea. But I think I should go to the police. I've done nothing wrong.'

'Well, presumably you can prove that you left Parker's office BEFORE the shooting by confirming what time the bus left.

'Presumably Irene Daniels will vouch that she shepherded me off the premises.'

'You left the B & B in a rush which looks rather suspicious. Did anyone else see the man that came onto your boat the previous afternoon?

'I've no idea. It's unlikely, not close up anyway – he wouldn't have wanted to be seen. He did know a bit about boats though.'

'You have to admit that there's been rather a lot going on and playing devil's advocate, you are in the thick of it.'

'Very re-assuring.'

Mary smiled. 'Look, I'm on your side, you know that. But if they can tie you in to something they will - especially if there's no-one else to go at?'

'I could offer up the computer. That could help.'

She thought for a moment. 'Would it? It might just open up another can of worms. If they start connecting Will to your dad and the others it would make it very complicated, especially when you don't know half the story yourself. I'm not sure where I'm going with this but the more you can keep to yourself without doing any damage the better in my opinion.'

'I liked you better in your wrinkled stockings,' said Harry smiling, 'it was nice and simple when we were a pair of tramps.' Mary smiled and Harry continued, 'Look, I feel I owe it to Will to try and find out what's going on and the only way I can do that is if I can get about without fear of being locked up. The only way to do that is for me to take the initiative and come clean. I won't mention any history. The longer I leave it, the worse it is going to get. This way I can march straight in and tell the truth. The more I think about it the more I'll confuse myself and the more likely I am to make a cock-up. I'm not a good liar.'

She thought for a few moments. 'Perhaps you're right but tread carefully.'

'Yes, I agree,' replied Harry, 'but a couple of things worry me. First the bloke who came on the boat. He heard Will's phone message then presumably went round to the B & B and nearly did for Jan. What was he after? The computer presumably. There's got to be something that Will knew that was serious enough to make him act like that. It must be the computer and the story Will left for me, so by extension he's still looking. That could make him dangerous. He can't know about you and it's got to stay that way.' He paused and looked meaningfully at Mary. 'I'll have to tell the police about him but I've no idea if anyone else saw him. I did tell another guy on the marina but I've only met him once and he's no idea about me. I might be a nutter, making it all up.' He sighed and shook his head slowly.

Mary said nothing but went into to the kitchen returning a couple of minutes later with two beakers of coffee. 'Here,' she said, 'have a breather, you're in a tizz.'

'I'm in the mire.'

She smiled. 'Just tell them the truth'

Harry looked at Mary for a long moment. 'How old are you?'

'What kind of question is that? That's not something to ask a lady.'

'You'd have told me in the café. Back then, this morning in fact, you were a lady of the street. You'd have given me an earful first, but you would have told me. There was no reason to hide anything then was there? Neither of us had anything to lose.' He continued; 'I told you why I was hounded out of Mold, why did you believe me?' Pause. 'Did you believe me?'

'Yes, I believed you. You wouldn't have told me if what they'd said about you was true. You had no reason to lie then, you don't now.'

He gave her a sheepish smile. 'Thanks.'

'You're welcome.' She walked and squatted in front of Harry and took his hand. 'I think you should go before you lose your bottle. Do you mind if I look over the computer, see if there's anything else?

'No, have a snoop by all means.'

'OK then, off you go and tell them your story. No lies and no boozing.' she smiled. 'Go on, off you go.'

So he did.

Chapter 12

They'd tied him in knots with endless questions.

He'd gone to Shrewsbury Police Station and asked to speak to D.I. Warren. They took him to a room with a Formica table, two chairs and not much else, including paint. He was given a cup of tea and asked to wait. The policeman arrived two hours later with a red nose and furrowed brow. The first enquiry, off the record presumably. 'Where the bloody hell have you been?' No softly softly approach then.

D.I. Warren was an overweight, bull-necked individual who'd come all the way from Chorley to Shropshire to speak to Jan and Harry about Edward Parker. Having spoken to Irene Daniels it appeared like suicide but why does a respected solicitor blow the top of his head off straight after a visit from a stranger.

The Detective Inspector was expecting things to be relatively straightforward but what he found when he arrived in Shropshire was a badly assaulted woman and a short scruffy individual who'd done a runner. He wasn't best pleased. The squally local weather had not been merciful to his straggly grey hair and his dark grey suit looked like it had been slept in. More Frank Cannon than Monsieur Poirot, thought Harry, trying to take the sting out of his fear.

'What the hell are you smiling at?'

Harry tried to shrivel up inside his clothes.

Warren and his female colleague, a fierce-looking blond lady, Detective Sergeant Groves, had prodded and probed. She had powerful hands that had lifted weights or hit something. No make-up, no bedside manner.

He had told his tale and answered questions. 'A load of bollocks' (Warren's summation) sounded apposite even to Harry - but he swore he was telling the truth. They'd fired questions at him, taking turns to try and tie him in knots.

No, he had never met William Davis, at least not since he was three....

Yes, he was my Godfather....

No, he hadn't tampered with the dog's food....

Yes, he had helped Jan....

I trained as a First Responder with the Welsh Ambulance Service....

I don't know why I ran away....

No, I didn't take anything from the house....

The bus left Chorley at eleven fifteen....

No, I threw the ticket away. You don't keep bus tickets.... The driver should remember.

There was a man on the boat. He was about fifty with grey hair, red sweatshirt and jogging pants – he heard Will's phone message....

I know 50 and grey hair doesn't narrow it down much....I wasn't paying too much attention.

Dark eyes and called Ralph, or said he was....

No, I hadn't seen him before....

Yes, I believe that Jan was a friend of Will....

I've been wandering around town since this morning wetting myself....

Because I was frightened and - well I suppose I just panicked....

My parents died a few months ago....

Yes, Mr Davies and my father were friends, but not for many years....

I don't know why they didn't see each other....

No, I had not met Edward Parker previously....

Yes, Mrs Wilton told me he had died.....

Certainly not, my Godfather's will is my business.....

OK, OK! He left me some money and his boat. A barge, er, narrowboat.....

Yes, I would love a cup of tea....

Well why did you ask me then?...

I AM telling you the truth....

No, I never visited Will's boat....

No, I have never been on a boat before....

Yes, I went to the Lake District about fifteen years ago....

A holiday....

Two weeks....

The Woolpack Hotel in Keswick....

Yes, I knew that he had been in the army....

Edward Parker told me....

Yes, I am married, or was.....

We grew apart....

About seven months ago....

With her father in Mold....

Wainwright....

The marriage just came to a full stop and I walked away....

Yes, I worked for Mr Wainwright....

Timber. I was a junior manager....

No, I wasn't sacked. I resigned, walked away from it....

It might sound suspicious but there was nothing left for me there....

I stayed with a friend for a while....

Jimmy Gale....

On the Battlefield Estate....

17 Grove Gardens....

I rented a room in town....

Yes, here in Shrewsbury....

Near the bus station, Flat 3, 17, Garden Street....

I told you he called himself Ralph and no I had never seen him before....

No, or since....

Yes, I would recognise him again....

No, I have not been to Chorley before or since....

Since I went the first time – only time....

I got on the bus at about eleven fifteen....

I'm sorry, I realise you're not deaf....

No, I have never owned a gun....

No, I have never fired a gun....

So on it went. Throughout the grilling he'd been at times indignant, stroppy, pathetic and rude. But always honest, well nearly. Economical perhaps, but generally honest – just about.

They kept him in overnight and released him at nine the following morning, after another salvo, 'pending further enquiries'.

He'd left the two police officers perplexed and untrusting but temporarily mollified. He was stiff and tired but at least they hadn't beaten him up – not physically. They had told him that Jan was holding her own. Stable but poorly was the official line - as of nine o'clock the previous evening. The dog was OK and had been taken away by the RSPCA.

No, he'd told them, he was not going to run away - nothing could be worse than the last twelve hours and yes, he understood that they may wish to speak to him again. He would call D.S. Groves on her mobile with the phone number on the boat. No, he did not know whether Will had owned a computer. Now he had actually lied outright, and shivered. Yes, if he thought of anything else he'd call straight away.

He phoned the flat from a public call box outside a nightclub. Christ, he thought, it's THE nightclub, the night of the bump on the head. Mary answered after barely one ring, urgent, concerned. Yes, he was fine and no he was not under arrest.

'I have to go to the boat. I have to give them the phone number there and I don't want to draw any attention to you. Thanks for being there. Look, I'll give you a call when I get back to the marina. You too....... and thank you. Bye.'

He set off for the station breathing a huge sigh of relief. From an upstairs window in the Police Station D.I. Warren watched him walk away.

Chapter 13

'W hat have you been up to?' It was Tom, the marina owner. He'd come hobbling out of the shop attached to a knobbly walking stick, accompanied by a huge German Shepherd. Man and dog met Harry halfway down the drive. 'We had the police crawling around half the day yesterday. Don't bring trouble here.'

'I'm sorry, truly, but none of it was anything to do with me.'

The dog alarmingly snuffled Harry's nether regions.

'You must be joking,' Tom continued, 'I suppose it's just coincidence that all hell lets loose as soon as you arrive. I've been beating off jackals from the newspapers all day, interfering buggers. You made the front page of the Shropshire Star and it's not the kind of publicity I need.'

'Look, I really am sorry,' said Harry trying to put distance between the dog's muzzle and his vitals. Then a thought struck him. 'Is Will's boat roadworthy – or whatever you call it?'

'I imagine so,' said Tom giving Harry a mean glare.

'Well, I presume I could get out of your way for a while then. Not to run away, but it might just suit us both if I make myself a little less conspicuous for a while. I'm only talking a few days till things get sorted out.'

'Good idea.' Snarled Tom. And marched back into his office.

Moron, thought Harry, and set off towards his boat.

There were more people about than yesterday. That is to say one more – total two, plus Harry. One was his neighbour Ralph, he presumed the real Ralph, and the other an elderly chap in jeans and blue windcheater - and a moth-eaten bobble cap with unreadable motif. A pencil behind his ear poked out of the bottom of his hat. They'd been watching the exchange on the drive.

'Meet whiplash,' said Ralph. And to Harry's unspoken, raised eyebrows, 'so called for his over-enthusiastic use of the throttle, otherwise known as Ron.'

Harry smiled. 'Pleased to meet you Ron. I'm Harry.'

'Oh, I know who you are,' said Ron, 'we haven't had as much fun round here for ages. Take no notice of that old duffer.' Looking over at the shop, 'Things must be serious, I haven't seen Tom move that fast for years. He's normally glued to his computer. And the walking stick is only seen on special occasions. We call it the 'goods inward' stick as it normally only comes out when there's a delivery and he wants to avoid doing any work.' He chuckled. 'Can I do anything to help, is everything OK?'

'Not great but not terminal, thankfully,' replied Harry. There was a moment's silence before he continued, 'but perhaps one of you guys could give me a hand. I've decided to tickle off for a few days and could do with a crash course in driving one of these things,' looking over his shoulder.

'If it's a crash course you want, Whiplash is just the man,' said Ralph, chuckling. He coughed and flipped the remains of his miniscule roll-up into the water.

'I don't want to go far, just out of the way a bit.'

'Tell you what,' said Ron, 'when you're ready I'll come with you a-ways then walk back. After you've gone through a couple of lift bridges just up there,' he said pointing vaguely, 'it's a clear run whichever way you go. Left towards Ellesmere, right towards Whitchurch. You can stop and tie up wherever you feel like it. On the tow-path side that is.'

Harry looked puzzled.

'That's the side with the path on it,' said Ralph helpfully. 'There's almost no wind today so it's a great time to learn the ropes. Wind is probably the boaters worst enemy – especially for beginners. You'll soon get the hang of it though. It takes some longer than others,' smirking at Ron, 'but you'll be fine.'

Ron glared at Ralph then turned to Harry, 'it's half-ten now; how about I come round about twelve? Give me chance to sort myself out and feed the dog, that'll give us plenty of time to make some progress.'

'That would be great, see you later. Thanks guys, I owe you.'

He left Ron and Ralph muttering about alternators and went aboard Box Car Willy to phone Mary. The message light was flashing – seven messages. Three were from D.I. Warren with progressively unhinged rants. Two ring-offs and two from Marcia Freeman, a journalist from the Shropshire Star, who left her number. Harry wiped them all and rang Mary's flat. If it was indeed Mary's flat.

He explained his plan about leaving the marina and merging, ghost-like into the Shropshire countryside. Mary laughed and told him she was glad he had perked up.

'Look, I've pushed my luck with the police but I really need to stay in contact with them so is it possible you could organise me a mobile phone? One of the guys here on the marina is going to give me a hand and I'll ask him a good place for me to stop. You can come and meet me there if you don't mind.'

'Sure, that's fine. Give me a ring before you set off.'

'Perhaps it's better ringing you when I get there – I don't know how long it will take to wherever I'm going.'

'How long is the extension lead on the boat phone then?'

He realized his mistake and chuckled. 'I'm an idiot.' he said as she giggled down the line.

'I'm aiming to find somewhere on the way to Ellesmere I think. Ron says there's a road bridge on the Shrewsbury to Ellesmere road. I'll try and stop somewhere near there.'

'Don't worry, I'll find you. See you in a while.'

He rang off and called D.S. Groves informing her of his plan.

'No monkey business,' she threatened, 'you're far from out of the woods on this Mr Dunn.'

He assured her that he would call with his new number as soon as possible and in any case, all she needed to do was find a narrow watery thing and he'd be somewhere not too far from Leebank.

He ended the call and went for a shower. The water was hot but space was restricted in the six-foot by four bathroom and he bashed various body parts.

While he dried his bruises he roughly worked it out - twenty-four square feet that included a shower over a four-foot bath, wash basin, a small cupboard, toilet, radiator and a window; amazing. There aren't many places you can live where you can have a poo, stir your soup and watch telly all at the same time. He emerged and dressed, supplementing jeans and t-shirt with one of Will's jumpers found in the wardrobe.

He opened the back hatch and doors and tried to fathom the mysteries of the boat's propulsion system – gave up, put the kettle on, made a brew and fell asleep. Dreamt he was strapped into a rocket on the launch pad. The engines had fired, he was terrified, claustrophobic, struggling to free himself of his harness, a tapping noise, there's something wrong, the tap becomes a rap, the spacecraft shook, there was shouting, the rap became a mind-numbing knock, have to get out, the knocks are now cracks, like gunshots, ripping the craft apart, going to die, have to get out ....

Ron woke him furiously rapping on the window. 'Come on. Wakey, wakey!'

Harry looked up to see a vaguely familiar face. He got out of his chair and poked his head out of the front door. With a ferocious look on his face he said, 'Do you mind, I'm trying to get this bloody spaceship launched?'

Ron stared.

'I was having a dream,' explained Harry, 'I was strapped in and I was trying to ......oh, never mind, come in.'

Ron's eyes widened and he took a pace back.

'Come on in, I'm not angry. I can always re-schedule the mission.'

'What the bloody hell are you on about?'

'Nothing, ignore me. Come on.'

'He's a lunatic,' mumbled Ron as he climbed inside.

Harry's instructor was as laid back as they come, completely unfazed by the prospect of a journey with a complete novice. In fact, he inspired confidence. He had boated for fifteen years and had lived aboard since his wife died four years ago. Harry phoned Mary and told her that he would be stopping near bridge 51 where the B3574 crossed the canal. He would expect her when he saw her; after dark he suggested.

'This is the morse control,' said Ron after they had made their way to the rear deck. They were peering into the rear cabin and Ron was pointing to a black handle about 9 inches long. 'You push it forward to go forward, and the opposite for reverse. Before you start the engine there are few things you need to do. First, check you've got fuel, which is Diesel. Unscrew the filler cap and dip it with this.' Handing Harry a three-foot cane with blue horizontal lines on it. 'That's fine,' said Ron wiping it his jeans. 'Over half a tank, that'll go for ages. Secondly, turn this brass handle through about 180 degrees. This forces grease onto the propeller shaft and stops it seizing up. You need to do this every six-hours cruising or so but I always do it after I've finished cruising for the day. If you do it before the grease thins with the heat and seeps out. It becomes a habit and it's important. Finally, push this red button in the centre of the morse and push the lever about a third of the way forward, like this. Pushing the button puts the gearbox in neutral. Right, turn the ignition key back a quarter turn until you hear this noise.' A rapid, shrill beeping came from inside the cupboard. 'In cold weather, like today, I count slowly to eight or nine. This warms the glow plugs. 'In warm weather or if the engine has run recently you don't need to turn the key backwards as the plugs will be warm enough,'

Harry looked puzzled. 'I'll explain later,' said Ron. 'Now, turn the key fully forwards until the engine starts then release the key which naturally settles in the 'run' position – like this.'

The engine fired up and a cloud of black smoke belched out to one side from below their feet. 'After a few moments you can return the morse to the upright position, which is tick-over speed, and the red button pops out. If you move the morse forwards of backwards now the propeller will engage.' Ron turned the engine off and said, 'right, now you have a go. You won't need to warm the plugs.'

Harry nervously talked Ron through the pre-flight checks and started the engine which settled down into a quiet throb.

'Well done. Right, now, leave it ticking over and let's untie and get off. Don't forget to unplug the phone line and mains electric, that's this blue lead here.' Harry followed instructions and coiled the leads on the boat roof. 'You untie the front and chuck the rope on top of the gas locker then come back down here. I'll get the back rope.'

'Come on, you're taking her out,' instructed Ron, 'pull the morse lever back till the prop engages.' Harry did as instructed, there was a muffled clunk and the boat slowly began to reverse away from the pontoon. Harry couldn't believe how nervous and excited he felt.

'Now, in reverse you have virtually no steering so the only way to do it is to engage forward gear. If you want to move the nose to the left, push the tiller to the right with a short burst of power.' The boat slowed but the nose did indeed do as it was told. 'Now, reverse again to keep moving and when you're ready repeat the forward thrust to move it further round. Once you start the boat swinging it will carry on for a while under its own momentum. To stop it swinging....'

'Forward thrust with the tiller the other way,' said Harry.

'You're getting it,' smiled Ron, 'using this technique you can virtually turn the boat on its own axis – providing there's not a gale blowing!'

In open water they spun the boat through ninety degrees and slowly set off.

'This is amazing,' shouted Harry.

'Great isn't it? replied Ron with a big grin.

'Nose to the right, tiller to the left,' Harry muttered to himself as they exited the marina under filthy glare of Tom. The two boaters looked at each other and smiled.

Within half-an-hour they had negotiated two lift bridges. One bridge wound up and down with a windlass (a right angled aluminium weapon with a square hole in one end that fitted onto the end of a ratchet on the bridge's winding gear) and the other was pulled up manually by a chain. Ron had jumped off to raise both bridges. Harry brought the boat to a standstill after each bridge and Ron hopped back on the back as it passed through the narrow openings.

They approached a bridge that crossed the canal. The waterway narrowed to the extent where was room for one boat with about a foot to spare on either side. Harry was concentrating on keeping on line so was taken by surprise by the woman standing on the bridge. 'Mr Dunn? Harry Dunn? Marcia Freeman, Shropshire Star. Can I have a word?' and without a pause, 'is it true that you left the scene of a crime ignoring a seriously injured woman?'

'Oh, for goodness sake,' muttered Harry.

The journalist took a series of photographs and continued; 'Do you have any comment on your arrest?'

'I was not arrested. I went to the police voluntarily. I did not do anything to Mrs Wilton, I helped her,' yelled Harry above the engine noise.

'By running away? Were you and Mrs Wilton having a relationship?'

'Just go away and leave me alone.'

'Mrs Freedom,' shouted Ron as they passed beneath the bridge, 'I am Mr Dunn's' solicitor and I'm afraid he has nothing to say at this moment. I believe you may find something interesting if you speak to Tom at the marina, he knows as much about this as anyone.'

Unsurprisingly, Marcia Freeman was not sated and ran from the bridge to join the towpath. The first two paces were accomplished in shoes and the ensuing ones in stocking feet as her shoes stuck fast in the cloying mud. Harry and Ron left her walking like someone with haemorrhoids back onto the bridge in mucky stockings carrying a pair of mucky shoes. Both men tittered. 'Serves her bloody right,' chortled Harry and looked at Ron, 'Solicitor eh?'

An hour later, after much huffing and puffing, Harry had tied up to the steel pilings near bridge 51. His multiple knots wouldn't win any awards but he felt safe enough. Ron had left him soon after the encounter with the journalist leaving Harry his phone number – emergencies only after seven pm.

Later that evening he was eating another tin of beans when there was a knock on the cabin side. It was Mary, dressed in her rags. Out of breath, she scrambled on board. She stood for a moment, 'Blimey this is posh isn't it?'

'It's great. I haven't got the hang of everything yet but there's a guy from the marina acting as the fourth emergency service so I'm not totally isolated.'

'You can show me later, right now we've got a problem.'

Chapter 14

'I got into Will's email programme using the numbers on the dog tag as a password,' said Mary. 'There was one new message addressed to Will. I hope you don't mind but I replied to it and explained what had happened to him. Anyhow, read this,' passing over a sheet of paper, 'Then I'll tell you what happened. I wrote down the emails word for word, here.'

While Harry read, Mary closed the curtains and changed in the bathroom. She still wore her FCUK sweatshirt under her scruffy coat and exchanged for her old skirt for jogging pants bought in her shopping basket and off came the wig.

12/3/01 09.44

We need to talk. Trouble. Call me. Quinn.

12/3/01 10.35

Dear Mr Quinn. I am a friend of Will's godson, Harry. I'm sorry to tell you that Will died a fortnight ago in the Lake District. Can we please talk? I promise you that I am a friend. Please email me your contact number. Mags.

12/3/01 12.14

07891 556772. Call from public phone. Delete all mails.

Harry looked at Mary. 'Mags?'

'I didn't want to give my real name. Quinn is obviously a friend of Will's, or a colleague. Anyhow, I called the number. As you can see it was some time before he emailed me back so I suppose he was checking up. He was very abrupt but wants to meet. There's a canal-side pub called The Lock Tavern. It's off the A49 heading north out of Whitchurch. We're to arrive there at 12.15 tomorrow. You wait inside, me out.'

'Didn't he say anything else? Who is he?'

'I don't know. I suppose there's only one way to find out.'

'Don't like it much, but it doesn't sound like it's the imposter who came on the boat does it?'

'No, he wouldn't have had Will's email address. Oh, and here, I've got a mobile phone for you. It's one I had in the flat, I just bought a new sim card. I charged it for a couple of hours so it should last a while. There's a charger here too. The number's on the back of the emails.'

Harry filled the kettle and lit the hob. 'Have you eaten?'

She looked at the half-finished beans. 'I'm fine thanks, but I'll have a cup of tea.'

Apart from the odd car crossing the nearby bridge, the quiet was tangible. Mary opened the side hatch opposite the kitchen and breathed in the evening air. The night was still and the moon reflected off the water through wisps of mist. She thought of Sid's café and smiled to herself. Close by in a copse an owl hooted, closer by Harry snored.

He'd had fallen asleep in the chair so Mary took the bed.

Harry was awoken by the passing of another boat sometime before eight the following morning. Box Car Willy strained at her moorings and rocked. Harry leapt up from the floor where he'd gravitated during the night wrapped in a rug. He looked around him with a look of terror in his eyes, as if someone were shooting at him and he couldn't work out where the shots were coming from.

'Don't panic,' said Mary, who was buttering some toast. She laughed.

'Christ, I'm a nervous wreck,' he said. He went to the bathroom.

Harry decided to ride Will's bicycle (which was lying on the boat's roof), Mary would leave ninety minutes earlier at 10.30 on foot. A vagrant riding a bike would not only look 'bloody ridiculous' (Mary's phrase) but the feeling was that they should appear unconnected. Whether they would fool anybody was anyone's guess.

By the time Harry arrived at The Lock Inn (great name he thought) Mary had walked some 200 meters beyond the pub and was sitting on a wooden bench looking suitably disinterested. Harry had passed a few dog walkers and the lightweight waterproof-suit he'd donned, found hanging by the rear doors, was splattered with mud from the tyres. He'd only used one of the eighteen gears. The only other person he'd seen was a British Waterways workman chopping canal-side saplings and tending a fire.

He could see why Quinn had chosen the pub. The only way to approach it was via a single-track gravel road, down each side of which ran a wooden rail fence. The road bisected a field and anyone approaching from the A49, 200 meters away, by whichever means, could be readily spotted. The only way to get from the car park to the pub was by walking up a path over the canal lock by means of an iron footbridge and down again to the pub's entrance.

Harry realized that there was 'private / service' access from the rear, a single track that crossed another field. Anyone approaching from this side would be also easily spotted. The track disappeared into a copse some distance away and there was nobody about.

The only other access was via the canal towpath. It was here, outside the pub, that Harry now dismounted like an arthritic octogenarian. He took off his splattered outer gear and went in ordering a large orange juice. He didn't have to pretend to be parched and worn out after a long cycle-ride. His legs wobbled and his backside throbbed. No food at the moment thanks.

To avoid speaking to anyone he sat in the snug. From here he had a view of the bar, and he buried himself in the previous day's Shropshire Star. He'd made the front page but not the lead. The main headline concerned a local labour councillor who had 're-directed' a consignment of computers destined for Ellesmere Secondary School and flogged them to his sister in law. He was photographed at his Florida retreat with his limbs wrapped round somebody else's wife.

The 'B & B Horror' story was only a hundred words or so, the journalists not having got their teeth into it, but there was a grainy photograph of Harry and Ron on the narrowboat. Different today perhaps.

Now 1.05pm, the place was filling up with lunchtime diners. The man he recognised as the tree feller came in, ordered a coke and sat down across the room from Harry and read the Daily Mirror. There he stayed for another quarter of an hour. Finally, with a 'mind if I join you', he came and sat at

Harry's table with his back to the wall.

'Sure,' replied Harry. He had little choice.

'The lady with you?'

'I'm sorry.' Said Harry.

'The scruffy one on the bench - Mags.' He paused and looked at Harry. 'Never, ever take me for an idiot.'

On the back foot, chastened and nervous, Harry offered the man a drink, declined with a shake of the head. Tall with grey/ginger hair and moustache, he was powerfully built. He had huge hands and a face that had spent much of its time open to the elements.

'I hope for your sake there's no-one else here you know.'

His husky voice sounded clipped ex-military and although his lips smiled, his grey eyes did anything but. Eyes that constantly flicked from side to side checking, checking.

'Tell me what you know.'

'What should I call you?' asked Harry

'Don't call me anything, just look at me and talk. I'll know if you're lying - so don't.'

'Look,' said Harry with a bravado he didn't feel, 'why should I say anything to you?'

'That is your last question,' said the man known only, and probably falsely, as Quinn. He paused. 'Let's just say that at this moment I think we are on the same side. You have one opportunity to confirm that. If I thought you were a threat I would not be here giving you this single chance. I knew Will - in our line friends are hard won, few in number and sometimes killed. I trust very few people – that's the way I keep breathing. Now face me and talk.'

Harry swallowed and talked. He talked because the alternative wasn't appealing. The first sound was a dry squeak so he had a gulp of orange, then told the guy everything starting from receipt of the letter in his fleapit. Everything except Mary's alter ego - and the flat.

Throughout, the man's eyes left Harry's only to scan the room every few seconds. He didn't say a word and when the tale was told Quinn stared, unblinking straight into Harry's soul. Harry's soul wasn't up to it.

'You're holding back. This is your last warning.'

'What do you mean?'

'Who's the woman on the bench and why is she dressed like that? What is her name and where does she fit in? Don't bullshit me. Her hands and face are not the hands and face of a dosser.'

So, Harry told him. 'She is a friend;' he said, 'we shared a gutter for a while. I honestly don't know why she is living the life she does, she hasn't told me. I think we are trying to climb out of our hole together but it's not proving straightforward. When I needed help, she was there and I trust her – I had to start somewhere. It turns out that she owns, or has access to, a flat in Shrewsbury. And you're right, being a tramp is not what she was designed for. To be honest I know very little about her.'

'That's not the kind of person I like. I want to meet her – alone.'

'I don't like that.'

'Tough shit. Stay here for at least at least fifteen minutes. She'll probably meet you back at your boat.' He looked at Harry. 'Yes, I know you're on the boat. If I feel we should speak again I will contact you.'

So Harry stayed. He'd ridden five miles to be psychologically roughed up by a substantial individual who could have physically crushed him like a beetle underfoot. He was someone in the same line of business as his Godfather, a business that appeared to involve regular dying. Harry had gushed while Quinn told him virtually nothing – an unequal distribution of knowledge, but at least he still had all his teeth intact.

He sat staring at someone else's newspaper imagining Mary's demise. Then he cycled back to the boat. This time it felt like fifteen miles.

As Harry lumbered onto the boat, the man standing on the bridge smiled, donned his helmet and rode away on his motorcycle.

Chapter 15

I t was two days before they heard from Quinn.

Mary had returned to the boat at 4.15pm. She didn't appear shaken but was unforthcoming except to say that she had told him all she knew, believed that Quinn was sound and that they were to wait. He would contact via email which meant that Mary had left again almost immediately and returned to the flat to wait.

Harry used his mobile and called the police station, giving them his new number. He asked how Jan was. 'She wants to see you. Probably wants to tell you to get out of her life.' said D.S. Groves. 'We're still looking for your mystery man. If he's a figment of your imagination I'll make life so bloody miserable for you, you'll wish you'd never been born. Don't suppose by any slim chance he's paid you another visit?'

'No, I'm sorry, he hasn't. Where is Jan?'

'Shrewsbury Hospital, ward 4. Were you having a relationship with her?'

'No, I was not. I'd only met her once before she was attacked. I presume you've got that story out of the paper have you? There was a journalist waiting for me yesterday. Totally irrelevant that I denied her allegation.'

'Who was the other man? If he's a solicitor I'm a Dutchman.'

'A guy teaching me to drive the boat with an aversion to nosy women,' said Harry wincing. There followed a threatening silence.

'I want you to come back and make a full statement. As soon as possible.'

'Does that mean that you actually believe me?'

'No, it means I'm worried someone will kill you before you get the chance. Possibly me.'

'Charming.'

'Today would be convenient.'

'Will I be there long?'

'If I've got anything to do with it – years.'

'I'll be there by midday.' And he rang off before she could shrivel him further.

He called the hospital (visiting two till four) then Mary and told her that Jan was improving, and that he was seeing her later that afternoon. He said he would call her later.

His statement was dictated, typed and signed by 1.45pm and he set off for the hospital. He had walked two miles, under protest from newly discovered cycling muscles, to Ellesmere and caught a bus to Shrewsbury. He now took another from the bus-station to the hospital, nearly a mile the opposite side of town. As his bus pulled out he looked over at Sid's café and grimaced as a man who'd just come out hacked and hawked and headed for the betting shop. He'd shared a table with him in another life.

Jan was in a side ward, propped up in bed attached to various tubes and wires. She opened her eyes as Harry entered to room and a tear rolled down her cheek. 'Thank you.' She said in a whisper. Harry pulled up a chair, smiled and held her hand. 'A policewoman told me what you did.'

'If it weren't for me you wouldn't be here in the first place.'

'It wasn't your fault. I know Will would never have hurt me intentionally but it must have been something to do with him.' She smiled weakly. 'Look, before I fall asleep again, I've not told the police this but the guy who attacked me asked what I knew about Lady.'

'Lady?' repeated Harry.

'That's what it sounded like although it was sort of elongated like lay dee.'

'It means nothing to me,' said Harry with a puzzled frown. 'Why didn't you tell the police?'

'I don't know – a feeling. I thought it might mean something to you.'

'Nothing.' Frowning again. 'What else happened?'

'He'd tied me up, asked his questions then stuffed the rag in my mouth. I heard him rooting around, looking for something I suppose. When the phone rang I reckon he must have run. I don't remember anything more.' Harry froze.

'You didn't tell the police about the computer did you?'

'No, I forgot all about it.' Harry visibly relaxed. He was somewhat reassured that the police hadn't mentioned it either on his second visit.

'Don't say anything please, I took it. When I knew you were in good hands I scarpered. There was some really personal stuff on the computer that Will had left for me in a file about his past and how he regretted not being in contact with me. I get the impression he was a good man but had been carrying a burden around for a long time. I'll tell you all about it when you're better. Soon, I hope.'

'He was a good man. At least to me. Poor guy.' Tears moistened Jan's eyes. She was, Harry could see, on the verge of letting go. They were quiet for a while.

'Dave was picked up by the RSPCA so he's OK,' said Harry in an attempt at something positive.

'You mean she's OK. Good. I hate to say it but I've not given her a thought. Will you collect her?'

'Can't get my head round that fact she's female. Anyhow, things need to settle down first but I will give them a ring.' Non-committal.

They said goodbyes. Harry would come again, he said, as soon as he could.

He left the hospital, desperate to see Mary, but resisted. Enough people had been hurt, he didn't want to lead anyone to her.

Outside the hospital, as he waited for the bus to take him into town he saw a man kneeling by a motorcycle fiddling with the engine. He saw the same motorcycle parked near the bus station and was very worried as he boarded his bus to Ellesmere.

Chapter 16

He phoned Mary and summarised his meeting with Jan telling her he thought he was being followed. They assured each other that they would be careful. She would only venture out in disguise and then when she had to, he would act like a sardine in his tin box.

Harry spent a nervous night alone on the boat and flinched when his phone rang at 8.45 the following morning. It was Mary. She'd had an email; Harry was to meet Quinn. He knows you are being followed but you're not to worry. If whoever it was had wanted to harm you he would already have done so. He says to walk east down the towpath, the direction of the pub. Leave the boat at 11.30 and keep walking. You alone Harry, she stressed. Oh, and I have given him your phone number, hope that's OK.'

'Yes, no problem.'

'Please be careful' she said.

'I will.'

Ron had given him some notes unkindly entitled 'Boating for idiots'. 'Something he'd put together for someone else and had proved useful,' Ron had said. It told Harry that he needed to run the engine for a couple of hours to re-charge the batteries and heat the water in the calorifier. Water in the main water supply tank should last up to a week, if you're careful – if it was full to begin with. He started the engine. Now wondering what a calorifier was in addition to glow-plugs.

He showered quickly and had a black coffee because there wasn't any milk and didn't have any toast because there wasn't any bread - he'd have to do some shopping. At least his stomach would soon begin to resume manageable proportions. He was still off the booze too and even though thinking straight had never been a strong point, at least he was giving himself the chance.

He set off on schedule. Will's boots were a couple of sizes too big but fine with thick socks - a minor difficulty against the considerable mess he was in generally. It was cool but dry.

He looked but didn't see a man or a motorbike and walked for thirty-five minutes until he saw Quinn beckoning him from a bridge. Harry scrambled up the slope and joined him – he was standing next to a motorcycle. 'Get on,' he said, mounting up.

Harry clambered up behind and they rode for five minutes at a steady pace. The single-track lanes that all looked the same. Neatly trimmed hedges sat atop three-foot high grassy banks - the maze of rural England. They pulled off onto a dirt track through an open gate and after a further 200 meters came to a stop in a muddy lay-by. 'Come with me,' said Quinn, hopping over a wooden gate.

They were hidden from the road and walked through the trees for a couple of minutes before coming on a gagged man suspended from a tree, upside down, bound hand and foot. It was only by his eyes and unintelligible mutterings that you could ascertain that he was a bit pissed off. 'Recognise him?' asked Quinn.

'The man from the boat, calls himself Ralph,' replied Harry. 'The bugger who nearly killed Jan. You scared the shit out of us you bloody tosser.' Tough as nails now the guy was strung up. He thought he saw Quinn smile. Quinn knew what was going on. Harry shut up before he made a complete arse of himself.

Quinn cut the gag away. 'One shout will be your last, not that there's anyone to hear you. Now start talking.'

'Cut me down and I will.'

A fist like a sack of coal hit the captive in the stomach. He retched and gasped for air. Trying to double up is tough upside down - further pain, no relief.

'The next two blows are in your face and your bollocks - now talk.'

So he did.

'I swear I didn't mean to hurt her.' He gasped and his eyes watered. 'I was only trying to get information that William Davies may, and only may, have known.' The man appeared younger upside down. He'd greyed his hair with some sort of white powder which now fell to the ground in a mini blizzard each time he looked from Quinn to Harry and back. Pleading to be believed. Pleading rather more with Quinn.

What's your name?

'Bernie Mason, I'm a private detective. I was employed to trace Mr Davies and find information about something that happened in France forty years ago. Anything connected with the death of a man named Leport in a village somewhere not far from Toulouse. I don't know why. I don't care why as long as I'm paid. All I know is that I was given the names Davies and Leport. I watched his boat on and off for three days, learned a bit about him. Then you turned up.' Looking at Harry. 'It was a woman who hired me. Said I'd come recommended, which is rubbish, it's what they all say - it's generally straight out of the Yellow Pages. She sent me a hundred quid cash and said the rest would follow. Another five hundred. She would call me back in a week. The only lead of any sort I got was the phone message on your boat so I went to find your computer. I'm afraid Jan was unforthcoming so I tied her up but I promise I never meant to do her any damage. That's not my way. I told the woman who hired me all this and, well, here I am.'

'Good start,' said Quinn.

'I don't know any more.'

'How did you know so much about my boat?' asked Harry.

'I've been on them a few times, holidays. I guess yours is not much different to any other.'

'What do you know about 'Lady,' asked Harry.

Quinn's jaw tightened; he knew nothing of this.

Shit, thought Harry. He inhaled, then coughed nervously.

'She told me to ask about Lady,' said Mason, 'that's the only thing I had to work with apart from the names. I was told nothing else. The only thing I can tell you is that the cash came in an envelope, hand-delivered, no post mark.'

Quinn whipped a knife from behind his back and cut the rope supporting the detective. He did it with such speed that neither the sleuth nor Harry had time to draw breath before the former was in a heap on the ground among the damp leaves. Quinn placed a substantial boot on the man's windpipe and said, 'If either me, or my friend ever see you again, you will never see anything else again. Is that clear?' He nodded, eyes wide. Quinn cut his bonds. 'On your bike.'

The dishevelled detective scrambled upright and ran through the trees. He wobbled a bit having been upside down for a while but Harry and Quinn soon heard the roar of a motorcycle starting.

Bernie Mason rode off, a smile spreading over his face.

Richard Burton, eat your heart out. You'll have to do better than that to catch out old Bernie. Bloody idiots. Bone-headed, hillbilly tossers, he said to himself.

He was laughing out loud as the bike touched fifty-five miles an hour, a tiny contact was made and the front wheel exploded.

'Why did you let him go?'

'He didn't know any more. More importantly, you know more than you've told me.' Pause. 'Don't you?'

A dull 'whump' in the distance made Harry turn.

Quinn was impassive.

Harry said that Bernie Mason had asked Jan about 'Lady', pronounced laydee, something to do with France a long time ago.

'My bullshit alarm's just gone off' said Quinn.

'Honestly, I went to see Jan in hospital. She told me that Mason had asked her if she knew anything about Lady – or lay dee, as she emphasised. That's it. That's all I know.'

The big man stared at Harry for a full minute, then growled.

Then they parted.

One very nervous, who disappeared back to his boat, one suspicious, who just disappeared.

Chapter 17

Mary and Harry had boarded a plane at East Midlands Airport and were heading for Toulouse. Quinn had told Harry not to worry about Ralph. Scared off he had said – Harry wondered if it was something a bit more radical than that but kept quiet.

BMI Baby had just fleeced them for a revolting cup of coffee and they were trying to figure out what was going on. Besides, just a change of scene for a while would be a bonus. Get to France and play it by ear was the best they could come up with so they sat back and dozed. Harry thought about the lady beside him. The riddle of her and their fledgling relationship posed questions beyond him.

It was the first time they'd spent together without worrying or feeling threatened. The maelstrom of the previous days had concentrated his mind on staying in one piece. After months of simmering his life had suddenly erupted.

Thinking back, it was only days ago that his existence revolved around searching out the next drink and clutching a glass.

This drink wouldn't save him but the next one might – there was always a next one.

Now he'd sobered up he was embarrassed by what he had become – he cringed at the memory and hated himself. His palms began to sweat and his heart raced. An unseen hand leant on his chest and began to push. His chest ached and his throat constricted. Suddenly his lungs were unable to take in sufficient air and his vision blurred. He ripped off his seat belt and stood leaning over the seat in front heaving, gasping. The more he fought the worse it became. His arms and hands tingled, Jesus, what was happening?

Then the pain started in his chest, his eyes widened in terror, the dizziness in his head became a buzz. Someone had planted electrodes in his brain and turned on the current. The old lady whose seat he had grabbed squawked - the current increased - all three occupants of the seats in front scrabbled into the aisle, backing away from the mad man.

'He's having a fit,' someone said.

He was dimly aware through the mist that people were staring at him, most as frightened for their own safety as he was for his.

He couldn't get his breath, his shoulders heaved as he tried to take in air, he shook his head which continued to buzz. He felt an arm round his shoulder restraining, constraining, he tried to shrug it off and in the distance, through the cacophony in his head, 'It's OK, it's OK, you're fine, relax,' his head lolled, trembling legs collapsed under him, then it went dark.

He came to with a sick bag clamped to his face.

Mary was next to him leaning over, one knee on her seat and a foot on the floor. She stroked his hair, 'breath slowly Harry - in, out slowly, that's it, try and relax.....slowly.' Her gentle soothing gradually penetrated the fuzz in his head and he flapped at the bag on his face as his heaving slowly eased. 'It's OK Harry, breath into the bag, nice and slow. You're OK.'

He looked at her wide-eyed, she was close to him, soothing, smiling.

Gradually his head cleared and his breathing steadied.

He trembled with shock and his eyes were wide as if he had seen a ghost - his own.

'Christ,' he mumbled through the bag, 'I thought I was a gonner.'

'You panicked. You've had a panic attack, that's all. You're OK now.'

'That's all? He said, 'I've never been as bloody scared.'

She lowered the bag and he leaned back and sighed. A stewardess sat to his right was holding his hand.

'Sorry.' He muttered shaking his head slowly. She patted his hand and passed him a glass of water. 'Here, drink this. You're OK now.'

Other passengers were looking at him. He lowered his eyes, covered his face with his hands. Mary gently hugged him and stroked his hair. 'I'm really sorry,' he said, 'what an idiot.'

'No, you're not,' she whispered. She placed her hands on his cheeks and turned his face towards her; she grinned, he grimaced.

By the time the plane landed the fear had gone replaced by an embarrassment so acute that he wanted to shrivel up inside his sick bag. He apologised to the lady in front whose hairdo had suffered as he had grabbed her seat. 'It's alright love.' She said. 'It gives me something to talk about anyway. Stuck on one of these things,' indicating the interior of the plane with a sweep of her eyes, 'is not the place to have a turn. I hope you'll be OK.'

Harry nodded and grinned sheepishly at her. 'Thank you. And sorry again.' he said.

His hands began to sweat again.

The Renault Meganne (with everything back to front according to Harry) headed north-east out of the city.

They were heading for Caylus about an hour away. Mary drove because Harry was still shaken up after his episode. He was quiet, still self-conscious. It was OK to be vulnerable on your own with another drink available, but in the confines of a small airliner he'd been claustrophobic and genuinely frightened. After it was over he'd just wanted to shrivel up. He mumbled another thank you to Mary and stared out of the window. It was half an hour before he was brought back to the present.

'How did you leave it with Quinn?' asked Mary.

'With a degree of suspicion on his part,' replied Harry, 'not that we ever had an open relationship.' He told her about questioning the man known as Ralph. 'Quinn's a dark character but I'm bloody glad he's on our side. At least I think he is.'

'What about the woman who hired the detective?'

'I've no idea and Quinn never said anything. I have a suspicion that her contract with the private eye has been broken.' He'd nearly said terminated and shivered at the thought.

'Quinn did agree that everything had started in Felines and suggested we go and have a poke around. I had told him most of Will's full story of course but there was no big speech about being careful or watchful, just go and have a poke around he said. We know that Will and the others went there and the chap Leport was killed but as to the link with recent events, I'm at a loss. Maybe the girl holds a clue, but the chances of finding her are almost nil I would think.'

'Something sure happened, but why the forty-year gap?'

'Perhaps we'll find out. I just hope we don't disturb a wasp's nest,' said Harry.

'Perhaps we should turn round and go home.'

'I'll leave it to you to tell Quinn we bottled out eh?'

Mary was quiet for a moment. 'Mm, yes, fair point.'

'Let's just go and have a look. We might even enjoy it.'

Arriving in the town of Caylus Mary pulled into a road-side cafe.

'Hotel de Ville', said Harry. 'That'll do.'

Mary said nothing but walked across the road to the Hotel du Bois and booked two single rooms.

Caylus was surrounded by wooded hills and the main road was on a steep slope heading away to the west through a valley. It looked a pleasant place with a couple of restaurants, a bakery, a deli and a general store. Granite buildings clung doggedly to the hillside above the main road and the only person moving was an elderly chap, pushing an old bike up the hill, doing a lot of puffing and panting.

'What's wrong with that one?' asked Harry indicating his choice of hotel.

'This one looks a little cosier, that's all,' replied Mary looking over her shoulder, 'come on, this one's fine.'

Mary took a shower so Harry went off to learn some local geography. The receptionist was a pretty young girl who spoke little English but he eventually ascertained that Felines was three kilometres away down the hill and over there, indicated with a waggle of the girl's arm and fingers. 'Mercy' tried Harry, to which the reply was lost.

It was six o'clock in the evening and dark so they had decided to wait till the following morning to explore.

Harry ordered a brandy in the cosy bar and sat down to look at some pictures in a magazine. It dawned on him that it was his first drink he'd had in over a week, he'd ordered it without thinking. The sweats had eased off but he was conscious of his aeroplane episode and he knew he wouldn't get into the same state again. He was thinking straight and was happy to appreciate Mary's company. The liquor burned his mouth and throat but tasted good. This was a 'positive' drink he thought to himself, one taken to enjoy and relax, not to hide in or obliterate problems.

He was lost in thought about his previous existence when Mary joined him, she looked at his near-empty glass and smiled. She knew he wouldn't go back, neither would she. He thought back again to the plane, left the remainder of the drink and they walked out of the hotel.

They dined in a small restaurant called Chez Claude and chatted over a wonderful meal, ordered by Mary, of Langoustines, fillet mignon and Le Desert Special. A desert that had no name, but Claude's concoction was both legendary and delicious - some sort of fruity suet pudding with cream.

'They sat back in the glow of wonderful grub and smiled at one another. Then Harry wrecked the mood when he said, 'Why did you drop out?' Then hurriedly, 'Don't say anything if you're not up to it.' He was suddenly fearful of alienating his only ally and wished he'd kept his trap shut. 'Oh, sorry, I shouldn't have mentioned it.'

Mary sighed, then turned and smiled. Then the smile dropped away. 'It was a dark time for me,' she said, 'I got ill.' She leant back and looked up with unseeing eyes, peering back at something in her past. 'For now, let's just say that my illness, it's breast cancer, was part of something far bigger.' She paused. Harry shuddered.

Mary went on, 'sometimes you need to back off to get a broader view of things and although burying myself under a mucky coat was an impulse, it was there I saw a fuller picture. I was also content to play my part, be anonymous and ignore any real decisions I suppose. I do have strength, more than I ever realized I guess, but bouncing back when you've exploded is not easy. There are other issues other than the illness that I'm not going to press on you now, just to say that they are things I can't see a way out of. It's all very personal and very frightening.'

They were quiet for a minute or two, absorbed in their own worlds. Mary knew more about Harry's history than vice versa but he knew she'd tell him if she wanted to. He was very keen not to lose the first friend he'd made for many a year. They were both learning lessons from dismal times and trying to clamber out the best they could. Harry was particularly aware of the huge risk Mary had taken by revealing herself to him. Placing that much trust in someone else when you're so vulnerable is faith indeed.

'You're the first person I've told about any of it.' she said, 'I know from our times in the ditch that you're a straight, honest guy, but you don't need this right now. I have finished my treatment and go to the hospital for check-ups every three months, privately. That's the only time my disguise comes off. The doctors are not forthcoming about what happens next.' She smiled again. 'You've begun to convince me I'm worth saving.'

Harry felt his throat clog up and couldn't speak. He patted her hand and gave her a gormless grin. The smile reached her eyes this time and she held his hand. She'd let go a little.

'Did you find out where Felines is?' changing the subject over coffee.

'Yes, it's down the hill over there,' he replied with a flourish and a wave.

'Oh, really?' said Mary smirking.

'Yes, it's not far at all.' He said with some authority. And closed the matter by disappearing to Les Hommes.

Back in their hotel, Harry had retired to bed, 'traumatised by his episode on the plane, he'd said, and Mary had lingered in the bar and started chatting in her basic French to the barman. Maurice, she soon discovered, was the hotel owner. It also transpired that Maurice spoke English fluently which enhanced their conversation. His wife, Sophie prepared the breakfasts so they would meet her in the morning and the young lady on reception was their daughter, Claudette.

Mary obtained a more reliable route to Felines than Harry's but when she mentioned the name Leport to Maurice there was an uncomfortable pause. Maurice was a small man with lively brown eyes set in a tanned face. His neat grey moustache twitched slightly as he stared at Mary. He wiped his hands on his white apron.

'That is a name I have not heard for many years,' he said, 'It is ancient history; best forgotten from our point of view in Caylus.' He paused and his moustache twitched again.

'What is your interest in Leport if you permit me to ask?'

Mary fibbed that they were on holiday but had been asked by a friend in England to enquire if any of Monsieur Leport's relatives still lived in the area. Our friend met him many years ago while on holiday and was just curious. He believed that he had a daughter.

Maurice busied himself polishing some glasses then poured Mary a second Drambuie which he placed on the bar 'with the compliments of Hotel du Bois'.

'Thank you,' said Mary. She could see she had touched a nerve and the barman was stalling, thinking. Finally, he said, 'I was much younger, I remember the name Leport but do not remember ever seeing him. People spoke of him after his death. I heard whispers over the years but never really understood what it was about him that put people on edge. I believe there were few who knew the full story. I have always felt that it is something the town wishes to forget. Perhaps it is better that you do not ask too many questions.' He paused. 'You are however nearly correct but the young girl was his niece, I believe and not his daughter.'

'Is she still here?' asked Mary.

'No. Soon after he died she came to live with Leport's sister, Madame Lauran, here in Caylus, but they left the area shortly afterwards. As I said, there were whispers. She may be the only one who knows the full story - maybe she took it with her. I get the feeling that the townspeople thought it for the best. Her leaving was not mourned.'

'Do you know where they went?'

'No.' He polished a glass, the same glass he had polished a few minutes earlier. Mary remained silent; knew he was debating whether to say anything further.

'I realise that you have come a long way and that are anxious for information.' He looked her in the eye. 'The only person who may know is Madame Chambrée. She lives in the run-down cottage on the left immediately after the river bridge at the bottom of the town. It is on the way to Felines; you'll pass it on your way. Whether she will tell you, I do not know. She was Madame

Lauran's neighbour on Rue Charmont at the time she left.'

With that he placed the highly polished glass on a shelf below a 'Paul Ricard' clock that read 11.15pm and disappeared through a door at the rear of the bar.

Both of them thought that 11.15pm was late enough – Mary also left the bar and headed upstairs to bed.

Chapter 18

The following morning over coffee and croissants Mary related her exchange with Maurice. She felt rather guilty about the conversation, her economy with the truth didn't sit well with her – and the barman's nervousness added to the puzzle. The name Leport had been the key. After she'd mentioned it he'd danced and feinted, closed up a little. Memories are long in these small places and there is obviously a raw nerve very close to the surface. It's virtually impossible to hide secrets in a town this size as whispers seep down through the years, but she had the feeling that there may be more. Maurice's reaction was too immediate for an isolated event forty years ago.

They drove down the hill passing villagers going about their business. Normally she would envy their belonging, life-long friendships and simple, uncluttered lives. Every person and every town had their secrets but age-old bonds sustained villages like this, the beating heart of the community passed from generation to generation. It felt like the place in her mind she had visited more and more recently - a comfortable, safe place where she could go to replenish herself when things were tough. A time before....

'People are looking at us,' said Harry as they drove down the hill. 'seems you've stirred something up.'

'Not nice is it?'

They crossed the bridge over the fast-flowing river Aude and pulled into a muddy lay-by in front of a cottage. Harry got out and looked over the house. 'Looks a bit run down.' he said.

'Yes, it's in a bit of a state for sure'

The cottage was symmetrical, a central front door with four windows either side, two on the ground floor and two on the first. Through the single chimney, to the right of the red-tiled roof, curled a wisp of smoke. There was an open sided lean-to at the right-hand end of the cottage with a part-used stack of logs. The small garden was about 10 feet deep from edge of the lay-by to the front of the property and extended the full width of the small house. The uncut lawn and neglected shrubs were enclosed on three sides by a picket fence in need of attention reminding Harry of a set of rotting teeth. A mossy path ran from a gate in the centre of the fence to the flaking door.

Harry knocked and looked at Mary.

He was about to knock again when the door was opened by a lady who was nearer ninety than eighty, dressed in a grubby floral dress, black cardigan and thick woollen stockings. One of her slippers had a hole in the toe and the other looked like she had been standing in the coal bucket. Her white hair was tied in a severe bun but she peered at her visitors with sharp blue eyes. She leaned on the door jamb while her other hand clung to an old cane walking stick.

'Oui? She said brusquely.

Mary asked in hesitant French whether they might speak with her.

They were here, she explained, at the suggestion of Maurice from Hotel du Bois, who though she may be able to help them search for an old friend who used to live nearby.

The old lady looked at each of them in turn with her piercing eyes before inviting them to follow her inside with a brief wave of her hand.

Harry gathered that Mary had declined the offer of coffee and the only word he recognised during her introduction was Leport. Madame Chambrée remained motionless – just stared at Mary who became increasingly uncomfortable and began to fiddle with the hem of her coat.

The meagre fire at one end of the room barely took the chill from the room and Harry could feel the cold and damp creeping through his layers of clothes. Their hostess sat in a single thread-bare armchair to the right of the fire. On a small table to her left sat an old reading lamp, a book and a chipped mug. Harry and Mary squeezed onto a small, matching settee. A tatty old rug lay between them; the remainder of the stone-flagged floor was uncovered. One door leading off the lounge was closed, the other led to the kitchen where a small pine table was visible in front of a stone sink. Harry scratched his leg, then the back of his scalp.

He asked Mary to explain to Madame Chambrée that he needed to return to the hotel as he had forgotten something and would wait for Mary outside in the car. She frowned at him and spoke to the old lady who silently watched him leave. Her expression didn't change as he mumbled a goodbye and regained his freedom.

Glad to be out of the cottage, he walked the half-mile back up to the village and bought a tourist map, a phrase book and a bottle of water from the épicerie before going to the café. He ordered himself 'un coffee' and sat at a table next to a radiator.

He knew his language skills weren't up to the job.

'Voila,' said the smiling proprietor, 'Un coffee.'

'Mercy,' replied Harry with a sheepish grin.

'Mind if I join you?' He asked with a West Country accent.

'Please. Be my guest.'

The man introduced himself as Robert Jackman and asked if Harry was staying long. Not 'where', thought Harry, 'how long'.

'Just a couple of nights I think. It's nice to be able to talk to someone without using sign-language. You must live here then?'

'Since last April, moved here from Woodbury, near Exeter, with my wife - chasing the quiet life.'

'Do you like it?' enquired Harry.

'We're just starting to be accepted nearly a year on. Not that people are unfriendly, just cautious. Can't say I blame them, I suppose we look like the big knobs wanting to wreck their way of life, but it's not like that. We come from a small place and we understand that we have to earn their respect. That doesn't happen through cash. What brings you here?'

Robert was a large man who looked to have rather over-indulged his own pastries, samples of which were displayed in the glass-fronted cabinet that doubled as a counter. In his fifties, nearly bald and with a ready smile, Harry thought he had the face of a man you could trust. Still, something told him to be wary.

'We're having a couple of days holiday,' said Harry.

'The locals might need some convincing,' replied his host with a knowing look, 'I've heard one or two mutterings in the village this morning.'

Harry swallowed.

'I stay out of the politics unless invited,' continued Robert, 'but there's been an unnatural amount of side-of-the-mouth stuff in dark corners, if you get my drift. They'll welcome you with open arms but don't try and mislead them or upset their equilibrium.'

'Oh.' said Harry looking down at the table.

'I'm neither warning nor threatening, merely stating. They're good people, please go carefully.'

'Thanks for the advice. I'm just trying to sort out one or two of my own demons, I've no intention of hurting anyone else.'

'I'm sure you've not. Another coffee?'

Harry looked at his watch. 'No thanks, I'll go back and meet my friend, she may be wondering where I've got to. She's seeing Madame Chambrée down the road there.'

Robert humphed. 'Now there's a strange one; rarely ventures out by all accounts. Lives down there all alone, has done for years I gather.'

Two customers came in. They babbled incessantly and Robert left to serve them. Though the odd phrase was directed at Robert, presumably to order something, the dialogue was unbroken and they continued as they took a table against the far wall. Harry smiled as he imagined the exchange:

'Well what about Mrs So and so at number twelve, have you ever heard such a thing?'

'Yes, and with her hips too.'

'Her daughter's no better, mixing it with that mechanic who lives two down, spanners everywhere that lad.'

'Never thought I'd see the day when one of hers got embroiled with one of his.'

'Two coffees please love, and two of our regular pastries, them with the jam in.'

'Nice man that Mr Robert. Now if the mechanic took after him it would be a different thing all together, we'd never have had this hoo-ha.'

'You need the rough 'uns to make the good 'uns shine through.'

'Aye, but there's rough and then there's really rough.....

Harry finished his daydream.

'Nice to chat, and thanks for the advice Robert, bye,' called Harry as he left. Robert nodded and smiled. The café's bell bing-bonged as he closed the door behind him.

He needn't have worried about leaving Mary on her own as it was another thirty-minutes before she re-appeared. When she did, her knocking on the window woke him up with a start.

Getting his retaliation in first he said, 'Thought you might get on better with me out of the way,' then regaining his composure added, 'Risque-t-il d'y avoir des avalanches?'

Stunned, she replied, 'I beg your pardon?'

Harry grinned and admitted he had bought a phrase book, 'What I said was, is there a danger of avalanches?'

'Oh, very useful I'm sure.' She laughed, then mock frowned. 'But you still ran out on me. I realize you couldn't understand a word in there - but you set me off scratching when you bolted.'

'Sorry.' He mumbled. 'What did she have to say anyway?'

'Not a great deal, but she knows far more than she's prepared to say about Madame Lauran. I got snippets from her while trying to gain some kind of confidence but she was mighty wary. Come on let's drive on and I'll tell you. It's not polite just sitting here. And we're being watched.' A curtain twitched as they pulled away.

They drove up the hill through woodland for a kilometre before forking left as the gradient increased and they entered the village of Felines three minutes later. A hamlet really, consisting of a dozen or so houses lining the single-track road. They drove slowly through passing a modern bungalow and an assortment of two-storey stone-built houses in varying states of disrepair, one of which was a B & B.

Two hundred metres after the houses petered out the road swung to the right and disappeared over a crest. On the bend was a rusty metal gate with a barely legible sign: Entrée Interdit.

'Entry prohibited,' said Mary.

They parked the Renault in a lay-by and approached the gate. The track beyond was barely discernible, almost totally overgrown. Thirty metres beyond the gate was a ruined house just visible through the straggly trees. They could see a sagging roof where a few tiles clung to charred rafters. The lower floor was obscured by shorter saplings, brambles and weeds.

Mary and Harry were thinking their own thoughts when they were startled by an old man who stood leaning on their car behind them.

'Dangereux,' he said, 'Très dangereux.'

Mary walked to the man who ignored her outstretched hand. He was dressed in ancient grey trousers and brown jacket, the outfit held together by string tied round his middle. Barely five feet tall and stooped, he wore old, but sturdy boots. Prominent tiny blood vessels on his nose and cheeks testament to a life outdoors. Large purple / red ears flapped below a cloth cap. His keen eyes moved between the two strangers then lingered on the house before settling on Mary. 'It's a bad place,' he told her in a husky drawl, flicking his eyes back to the ruin. As if on cue a wind sprung up, whistling and moaning through the skeleton of the house. Both Mary and Harry turned to look.

'It's a bad place,' the man repeated, 'no-one goes in there. No-one has been in there for many years. It is not advised.'

Mary translated for Harry looking a bit flustered.

Recovering her composure, she said, 'We've come a long way to find someone on behalf of a friend. A girl who lived here in the past. We believe her name was Leport and that she moved to Caylus after her uncle died.'

'It is not wise to resurrect the past. Leave it where it belongs.' And with that the man turned and walked slowly back down the track.

Mary returned to the gate and linked her arm through Harry's. He enjoyed the contact and was content to stand and stare at the house. When he looked back the old man was gone - back to his own time.

'I'm going to have a look,' he said finally, 'we've come this far, if I don't

I'll always be wondering.'

'I'll come with you,' replied Mary, 'but the place spooks me. In fact, the old guy spooked me, this whole place spooks me. I'll be glad to get out of here.'

They clambered over the gate individually, one holding it for the other as it rocked and creaked under their weight and battled their way between trees through the matted undergrowth. As they neared the house it was increasingly evident that it had been gutted by fire, but long ago. Moss clung to the remains of blackened window frames and the rotting front door hung was lying on the ground within the property. He couldn't help thinking about his parents' farm. Battling his way through the saplings and foliage Harry peered in through the doorway. There was no floor to the upper storey except for a few intermittent charred floor joists and the whole was open to the sky through the sparse remains of the roof.

The breeze whined a warning as he gingerly stepped inside on to the carpet of weeds. Whatever had occurred here and whoever had lived here had been exorcised by fire before nature had begun to conceal the carnage. A pigeon made a frantic escape through the roof and pieces of dried straw floated to the ground. Harry stepped back in surprise and bumped into Mary who had followed closely behind.

The remains of a stone fireplace built into the angle of the front and left-hand wall, was piled high with twigs and detritus, the result of birds nesting in the chimney. Running up and away from the fire against the left wall, a stone staircase rose to the upper floor, the charred stump of thick, wooden newel post was all that remained. To their right a door opening led to the kitchen, a stone sink all that was left save for some twisted, blackened lumps of wood. A passage ran away from them leading to two further rooms at the rear of the house, the way blocked by the remains of more fallen timbers and rubble.

It was Mary who noticed it. Scratched roughly into the seared stone chimneybreast were the words: Les Dix and below, Pourrir en enfer.

She beckoned Harry over and they were quiet for a moment before Mary said quietly; 'Les Dix, that's it. That's what Jan said, you know, not 'Lady' but Les Dix!'

'You're right.' said Harry, 'dix is ten isn't it?'

'Yes, pronounced 'dee', it translates as Ten or more accurately, The Ten.' She frowned then translated quietly, 'The Ten – Rot in hell.'

They stared at the words.

'What on earth does it mean?'

'I've no idea,' replied Harry, 'but there's not much left here to shed any light on it is there?'

'No, just the shell of a burned-out building that no one goes near. There's something manic about that carving, real hatred. Come on, let's get out of here, I've had enough.'

Harry stared at the stone stairs leading down from the void above to the defiled fireplace below - the stairway to hell.

With a last look at the burned-out wreckage they went outside and struggled to the rear of the building where they stood by the shell of a derelict barn. Inside sat the rusted corpse of an ancient tractor suffocated by the weeds.

Thirty yards beyond the barn they could see the start of a coniferous forest. The treeline stretched from the valley below to their left, up and over the crest of the hill to the right - endless and regimented by comparison to the self-seeded melee surrounding the wrecked house. Imposing and inert, the fir trees were dark sentinels of this miserable place.

According to Will's letter, this must be the spot where, over forty years ago, a young girl had stood.

It was silent now just as it had been silent all those years ago as she had accepted the instrument of death from her uncle's murderer. She had walked quietly from her hell into the dark.

They walked towards the forest. A short way in it was pitch black, light and life sucked from the trees, a young girl's torment trapped forever within.

They walked on, footfall cushioned to near silence by a billion pine needles, the whisper of the wind in the tree-tops above their only companion. They looked back towards the ruin. Apart from the lone pigeon, the area was dead. No rustle of small mammals, no birdsong - the beasts were waiting for the trees to reclaim their territory - waiting till it was safe.

Back in the car, Harry sighed deeply. Mary, silent, sat and stared.

'You OK?' he asked.

'I'm picturing the girl. How do you get over something like that? Did she ever get over it? Its things that happen to us over which we have no control that are the hardest to take. I know we have both had a rough patch but nothing like this.' She looked at the house for the last time. 'Come on let's go.'

They drove away. No sign of the old farmer, no sign of anyone.

Chapter 19

Back at the hotel, much subdued, they'd ordered sandwiches and a pot of tea which they ate in silence sitting in the lounge that overlooked the main street. A log fire danced in the hearth and Vivaldi played quietly through concealed speakers.

Eventually Harry asked Mary to tell her more about her exchange with Madame Chambrée.

'As I said, she didn't say a great deal. She may look doddery but she was sizing me up. She did say that Madame Lauran moved away within a week of the girl coming to live with her. I was open with her and told her what we know of forty years ago and the trouble it has caused since, especially recently. I thought the only way to get anything out of her was to be straight but I did ask her to keep it to herself.

'She appeared genuinely upset that people had been hurt, or worse, but still didn't give much away. She'd sworn an oath to Mme Lauran promising she would tell no-one what she knew. She has kept that promise for forty years. She said it is for Mme Lauran, and her alone, to tell her story - if she chooses. She wants us to go back and see her this evening - both of us this time. Her words not mine. I feel that us being here is intruding on something this town would rather forget.'

'There must be answers here though, maybe we'll get something. I spoke to the guy who runs the cafe over there, an English guy who warned me not to rock the boat. Not threateningly, but it was a warning nevertheless.'

Harry went to his room and phoned the Hospital in Shrewsbury to try and speak to Jan. He called back a quarter of an hour later by which time they had made a phone available for her. She sounded much more with it and said she was making good progress and should be home within a few days. Her daughter was coming to stay for a while till she was back on her feet.

'You do sound much brighter,' said Harry, 'thank goodness.'

He told her that he was in France trying to work things out but told her little. The less she knew the safer she was.

'Our story has moved off the front page,' she said, 'although I did get another visit from the two police officers and the nurse tells me that a particular female reporter has been sniffing around. Oh, and yes, the police were investigating a motorcycle accident and wondered if the injured man was the one who attacked me. They showed me a photo. He looked similar, but younger, and I told them I was pretty certain it wasn't him. Apparently he's in a pretty bad way.' There was a pause. 'Was it him?' she asked, a note of suspicion in her voice.

'I've no idea,' lied Harry; then shuddered involuntarily. 'I wouldn't be surprised if he's not long gone, especially with the press on to it and the police looking.'

'Mm' she said. 'When are you back?'

'A few days at the most. I'll come and see you.'

'I'd like that.'

'Get well Jan. See you soon.'

Motorbike accident my foot, though Harry. Should he phone D.S. Groves? No, bollocks to her. He fell asleep.

He was awoken by a knock at the door; he roused himself and opened up. Mary stood in her dressing gown, hair tousled with tears in her eyes.

'What on earth's the matter?' asked Harry.

She looked him in the eye then moved towards him and her face crumpled. She began to sob uncontrollably. She leaned close as Harry hugged her tight. Never had he experienced such despair, such desperation. Each breath a series of short gasps as she clung to him. Now and then a cry so awful it was as if her heart was being ripped from her body. He held her and gently rubbed her back.

On and on it went.

Wherever she had tumbled, this place in her mind, was a place of utter desolation. He had never seen anyone truly consumed by grief - it was awful.

Gradually she quietened, her cries diminished and her breathing steadied. 'They've taken so much Harry, all I ever had, all I ever was.' She leaned back and looked up at him - the little girl within was here, and she looked so sad.

He led her to the bed where she lay on her side. He covered her with the duvet. Gradually her breathing steadied and she slept. Harry sat in the chair by the window and looked at the husk of his friend now breathing softly and peacefully.

She'd put a great deal of trust in him and he felt an overpowering responsibility. He was determined not to let her down. There is something humbling when someone shares so much with you, especially a relative stranger. He felt compassion sure, but although her tears were instinctive, he felt she had placed a dependence on him, something he was determined to honour. If he needed a purpose, he now had one.

He remembered a silly quote on a friend's fridge magnet, 'If you want to help yourself; help somebody else'. His chance had come.

He slept and when he woke it was light outside. He looked out of the window and watched the people of the small town beginning their day, going about their business. Low, grey clouds hugged the forested hill tops, smothering secrets. Outsiders knew nothing of the town's hidden past - dormant yes, but never truly buried. The soul of the town would not let them forget. Ghosts looked on.

They tapped on the door of the nameless cottage and were ushered inside. The old lady looked more alert, more alive as her eyes flicked between Mary and Harry. They resumed their positions of the previous day. The fire had died and though the old lady seemed oblivious to the chill and damp, her two guests huddled within their coats. She was silent for many minutes and stared predominantly at Harry. When she spoke, to their astonishment, it was in near perfect English.

'I understand that you want answers. I also understand that what happened many years ago caused great suffering. However, it is because it has caused more torment in recent times that I am prepared to try and help you.'

She looked at Harry and continued, 'your friend told me that your family has suffered, and if possible I want to help you to put an end to it. I suspect that you will go on probing and the only way to ensure that innocent people are not hurt is for you to understand properly. It has gone on long enough. I can see no other way than for you to know the truth. Having learned that truth, you must decide what to do with it. However, I am not the person to tell you - that is for Madame Lauran.

'We have remained in contact over the years - I have spoken to her and she has agreed to meet you. You must understand that for her the memories are more painful than you can know. We are both old and our time is nearly done; we had hoped the horror would die with our generation but it seems that it is not to be. There are a few here who remember but I believe that only Madame Lauran and myself know the full story - but her demons are more alive than mine.'

She passed a slip of paper to Harry on which was written an address.

'I am giving you the opportunity to gain information that could do much damage to many people, perhaps even to yourselves. Please think very carefully how you use this knowledge.' She rose from her chair and shuffled to the door where she stood and waited with her gnarled hand on the handle. 'Once you leave here it is inadvisable to return. I doubt we will meet again so I will bid you adieu.'

'Thank you,' said Mary quietly as they walked past her into the chill evening. They had only spoken two words throughout the brief visit.

Chapter 20

They had returned the hire car to the airport the previous evening and taken a bus to the station. It was now 7.55 on a Sunday morning and the over-night sleeper from Toulouse trundled slowly through the outskirts of Paris towards Gare D'Austerlitz. Grey clouds had given way to low, early-morning sun which reflected back from the windows of track-side properties.

Mary was asleep on the top bunk of the six-berth couchette they had shared with a family of four from Toulouse. The two teenage girls on the middle bunks had tittered at Harry's laboured attempts to clamber onto the top deck. Mum and Dad below had sighed and tutted. Harry had slept little, too hot, too noisy, too much buzzing round in his head.

For no apparent reason, during the night, the train stopped for two hours in Limoges giving Harry the opportunity to stretch his legs until being unceremoniously herded back on board by an irate and incomprehensible night-porter. Harry judged the occasion unsuitable to try out his 'avalanche' phrase so complied with the 'unsociable, power-mad rail-person' (as he later described him to Mary) and re-boarded.

He had spent the remainder of the night leaning against a window watching a damp dawn creep in. He returned to the couchette, climbed the ladder and gently shook Mary awake. 'Come on, we're on the outskirts of Paris, come and see.'

The clickety-clack of the train on the track was slowing as the journey's spring wound down.

Mary had slept for over six hours. She leaned towards Harry and kissed him gently on the nose.

'What did I do to deserve that?' he asked.

'Just because,' she replied with a smile.

They had checked out of the Hotel du Bois the previous evening (no charge for today, they were told) and had driven straight to Toulouse. Harry had told Maurice that they wished to catch a train to Paris and it was he who suggested the over-night sleeper that left at 10.00pm. Harry had felt that Maurice was glad to see the back of them and, although they had been treated very well, felt he had been especially helpful with their departure. They had eaten dinner in a tiny back-street restaurant and chatted over coffee while waiting for their train. Harry thought he had glimpsed Robert from the café in Caylus but dismissed it.

They had tried to figure what was such a secret, something that involved four English lads forty years ago, all of whom were now dead, something that had begun before the boys visit to Felines and something that was important enough for innocent people to be hurt in the present. Sure, the boys' experiences were awful enough in themselves, but something greater was even now holding the spirit of a corner of France under its spell.

Harry changed his mind about Robert from the café in Caylus when he saw him watching through the railings as the train pulled out, a telephone to his ear.

The taxi driver showed not a scrap of interest as he watched Harry lift their cases into the high-lipped boot of his Mercedes. They climbed into the taxi that was to take them to the hotel booked for them by Maurice on the internet. In the Latin Quarter, Hotel de L'Ile (short break in Paris three-star variety) was situated on Rue des Quartier, three blocks south of the Seine. When he parked up, the driver flipped the boot lid without leaving his seat and Harry lumped the cases onto the pavement. 'Twelve euros,' said the driver through the open passenger window, 'plus three for the luggage.' Harry was flabbergasted and stared at the cabbie.

He handed over the money in a crumpled heap. 'Fifteen euros, including tip.' He fumed. The taxi drove off.

When it was out of sight, Harry told Mary to wait. He marched round the corner and re-appeared a few minutes later, picked up the bags and asked Mary to follow. They entered the two-star Hotel Lausanne, registered as Mr & Mrs David Jenkins and were shown to a twin room on the third floor.

'What was all that about?' asked Mary with a puzzled look.

'Just being cautious,' he replied. 'I'd rather no-one knew where we were, at least for the moment. Well, they'll know we're here, but not exactly where we're staying. I'm not sure, but I think we were followed and watched onto the train. It's probably nothing.'

Mary wasn't convinced.

Trying to change the subject he grumbled, 'Do you believe that bloody taxi driver charging for the luggage? He didn't exactly bend his back did he? - Damn cheek.'

Their hotel was a third of the way down a narrow street about 200 yards in length. Their room overlooked a boulangerie / café. Its large plate-glass windows allowed passers-by to watch the bakers at work and the lovely smell of freshly baked bread permeated the air, even in their room. Looking at the magnificent display in the adjoining shop Harry wondered how Parisians stayed so slim. He patted his own belly and grinned - he had lost nearly half a stone himself since he'd stopped boozing.

There was a market on the street below and a dozen or so stalls were selling home-made fare including pates, wines, fruit and meats. Each stall was covered by a red and white-striped canvas. It was just after nine in the morning and people were milling about. On another occasion this would be somewhere Mary would love, she adored the tradition and bustle of city life. Harry broke the spell.

'Madame Lauran lives about half a mile away on Rue Poplar, it's here on the map. It's nine-twenty now, a bit early, so let's leave it a couple of hours and get some breakfast.'

Mary was aware that they were sharing a room, albeit with twin beds - not that she was nervous, just aware. She knew Harry was a friend, a good friend. Two single people in a twin room, even in all innocence, changed the emphasis somewhat. He probably snores like a hog, she mused, re-directing her thoughts. She chuckled.

'What's up?' asked Harry with a little-boy frown.

'Just thinking,' she said. 'Look, why don't you go the café in the bakery over the road, I'll have a quick shower and join you in a while.'

Conscious that she probably needed some space, he slipped out of the room. She watched him walk across the road into the bakery. He'd taken his phrase book along so goodness knows what he would end up with. Probably ask for some brake fluid or something.

She smiled to herself.

Chapter 21

Harry did experience some difficulty. A thimbleful of strong, bitter coffee accompanied by a tooth-shattering bread roll with frozen butter was not his breakfast of choice and radical modification of the assortment was beyond his basic semaphore. Thus, half an hour later he was not only hungry but also concerned because there was no sign of Mary.

A further fifteen minutes and he was worried.

He returned to the hotel to find the room empty and his heart began to thud. This became a full-blown panic when he discovered signs of a struggle in the bathroom. The contents of Mary's wet pack were strewn over the floor and a there was a shattered glass in the basin. 'Mary!' he shouted. He ran out of the room, down the three flights of stairs taking two or three at a time and demanded of the receptionist if she had seen Mary leave. When she said no he ran to the hotel door and out into the street, looking right and left for any sign of her. He went back in and asked if there was a rear entrance.

'The kitchen door is the only other exit.' replied the girl.

'Show me,' he said, 'quickly.'

She hesitated for a moment then came out from behind her desk and led him through the breakfast room where an elderly couple looked up from their newspapers. She took him through the service door into the small kitchen where she pointed to a door at the rear that stood ajar, 'There,' she said. He ran and looked out into the deserted alley. He pointed to another door at right angles to the exit and said to the girl, 'Where does this lead?'

'That is the rear stair-case used in case of fire. It leads to the upper floors.'

He opened the door and shouted again, 'Mary.' Nothing.

'Jesus,' he screamed in frustration.

'Are there no kitchen staff, surely they saw something?'

'We have only two guests apart from you. The chef only lays out bread and cereals. When he has prepared the tea and coffee machine he leaves. At this time of year we have few people staying, he was gone by eight o'clock.'

'Are you sure you saw or heard nothing, nobody coming in or out?' he asked.

'Nothing, I'm sorry.' She paused. 'Look should I call the police?

'No, wait.' He stood for a moment thinking. 'I'll go and check the room again. If I need any help I'll give you a shout. Can I go up the fire stairs?

'Yes sure.' He hurried out of the kitchen.

The stairwell was gloomy and scruffy, concrete treads and flaking paint on the walls. A bare lightbulb on each landing was turned on by a timed push-switch at the top and bottom of each flight. The lights turned off automatically after about 30-seconds. Above each entry door to the stairwell was an emergency light that presumably only came on in the event of a fire. He lit each floor as he ascended but saw nothing by the time he reached third floor. When he got back to the room it was as he left it, empty.

He was breathing hard - not fit, he thought.

He looked around the room. Mary's handbag was on the dresser and next to it Harry's mobile; '1 new message'. He grabbed the phone and opened the text message.

"Call 07995 447653 from a public telephone. Speak to no-one."

Timed thirty-five minutes ago at 09.34 the caller's number was withheld.

'You bastards,' he said under his breath, 'If you hurt her I'll bloody well kill you.' He turned to see the wide-eyed receptionist at the door.

'Is everything alright; have you found your wife?' she asked.

'Uh, no,' replied Harry, 'She's left me a message though,' waving his phone at her; 'She's, er gone to have a look at the market. Thank you anyway. We'll be fine now. Sorry to have disturbed you.'

The girl looked doubtful but said, 'OK if you're sure, I'll get back downstairs.' She cast her eyes quickly round the room and left.

Bloody hell, he said to himself.

He put Mary's handbag in the top drawer of the dresser then grabbed his phone and some loose change and left the room, locking it behind him. He ran down the stairs again but slowed and forced a smile as he passed reception and made his way out into the street.

The street-market was busy now and he had to barge his way to the end of the road. He asked a man, whose poodle had just crapped on the footpath, where he could find a public telephone. The gesticulations that accompanied unrecognised words told him that it was down that way somewhere and on the left. He found it but had to wait for a short, stumpy woman with a fur coat and too much jewellery to finish shouting at someone. He moved round the glass case putting himself in the woman's eye but she turned her back on him and shouted some more. Finally, she slammed the receiver down and marched away muttering giving Harry a fearsome look as she waddled off. Silly old sod he thought uncharitably.

He dialled the number displayed on his mobile. It was answered after four rings. 'What have you done with her?' he yelled, 'don't even think of harming her.' There was a long pause which dragged on for such a time that Harry wondered if there was anybody there.

'You are not in any position to issue threats,' said someone finally, 'please keep absolutely quiet and listen.' The male voice spoke English but with the trace of an accent that Harry could not place. He spoke slowly and deliberately. 'This is the last time you will be able to contact me, this telephone will be destroyed following our conversation. Our next communication will only transpire if I contact you. I know who you are, I know where you are, I know where you have been and I know where you are going.'

'I will not stop you from visiting the old lady, neither will I prevent her from telling you what she must. But believe me, I could prevent both if I so desired.' Harry believed.

'I am depending on you to be very circumspect in how you react to what she tells you. By borrowing your friend I am issuing a warning against any rash behaviour on your part, either immediately or in the future. We have taken her just to show you we can. Please remember that. She has not been harmed, nor will she be if you are very careful. I assure you that if you act honourably, you will be reunited with her in due course. Go now. We will be watching.' And with that the call was ended.

Harry stood rooted to the spot with the receiver to his ear. He stared transfixed through the canopy as the continuous tone whirred in his ear. He only reacted when a walking stick tapped on the glass impatiently indicating that he should make way. He replaced the receiver and mumbled an apology.

He regained his bearings and began to walk slowly back towards the hotel thinking about what he had been told. Be careful with what, and how could he keep Mary out of danger. The man had sounded threatening but only in the sense of his slow deliberate delivery, menacing even - he somehow felt that Mary would be alright as long as he did nothing stupid. That was going to be the difficult bit, how would he know when his actions became a threat? From the way the man spoke it implied that, though he would not exactly welcome Harry speaking to Madame Lauran, there was a sort of cautious endorsement; as if by listening to her he would understand.

By the time he reached the hotel the only thing he knew for sure was that he must, in fact was desperate, to protect his friend. He had to go through with the meeting and the sooner the better.

With no sign of the receptionist he went up to the room. Trying to make things look as normal as possible, he re-packed Mary's washbag and put it on the shelf above the basin. He picked up the larger pieces of glass and wrapped them in toilet paper before putting them in the waste bin. Finally, he took Mary's handbag out of the drawer and put it in a plastic shopping bag to take with him; he didn't want a nosey chambermaid rooting in it, besides if she had gone shopping she would have taken it with her.

Then he had a radical re-think. He packed everything in their two small cases and took the lift down to reception where he checked out. As he was counting out the cash the girl had returned to reception and she asked, 'You found your wife I hope?'

'Yes, she's fine thank you. I'm meeting her at the station after lunch. Thanks for your help this morning, I was in a bit of a panic. We've not been married long and I'm a little over-protective sometimes. She's run into a friend and we'll be staying with her so we shall not be requiring the room after all.'

The receptionist apologised that she would have to charge fifty percent for the fee explaining that it would have to be cleaned and readied, despite the fact that they hadn't stayed the night. She made out a bill but Harry paid without question. He quickly left before he got himself in any more of a tangle.

He slung his sports bag over his shoulder and pulled Mary's case by the retractable handle. He clattered his way through the streets scanning the physiognomy of an unfamiliar city hoping to spot the eyes within that were watching him.

There are few more lonely places than a crowd. Everyone knows someone, everyone knows where they are going, everyone feels comfortable - except you. In these busy streets Harry felt very alone. He also felt vulnerable and rather frightened.

People drank coffee and smoked at café tables on the pavement. Some chatted, others observed, many were merely there just to be seen.

Harry was another fleeting spirit who would amble by, depart and leave no trace. Small manicured dogs, a trendy accessory of the fashion conscious, quick-stepped beside fur coats and pointy boots. Little dogs frequently doing what dogs do - Harry watched where he put his feet and made his way to meet the lady who would hopefully give him some answers.

Chapter 22

Madame Lauran lived in a quiet street of three-storey Georgian houses. The highly glossed, bright blue door of number seventeen was framed by a dormant climbing rose. He used the shiny brass doorknocker, stood back and waited.

The door was opened by a lady of equal age to Madame Chambrée. There the similarity ended as Madame Lauran looked every inch the classic Parisian Lady. She was without doubt refined, her light blue dress immaculate, black shoes highly polished and her grey hair beautifully coiffured. She stood straight as she appraised Harry with deep blue eyes. A pearl brooch above her left breast matched her earrings.

She looked briefly at Harry's luggage and introduced herself. 'I am Cecile Lauran, you are doubtless the young man of whom Madame Chambrée spoke, Monsieur Dunn. Please come in. You may leave your bags here in the hall.'

Four mahogany doors and a matching staircase led off the square hall. One door to the left and two ahead were closed. Madame Lauran walked through the one to the right, indicating that Harry follow. The polished wooden floor of the hall gave way to a rich burgundy carpet in the large lounge.

Dominated by a magnificent marble fireplace and hearth, the room was dotted with classic furniture tied together by a sumptuous cream suite. But it wasn't the beautifully proportioned room that drew Harry's eye, nor the classic landscape paintings hanging regally under individual picture-lights, no, it was Cecile Lauran herself.

There was something about her. Strength and dignity sure, but there was something else - had he seen her before?

They stood apart looking at one another; she appraising, he searching – neither appeared to reach a satisfactory conclusion.

'Please sit,' she said. 'You would like a cup of tea or coffee perhaps?'

'No thank you, I'm fine.' He replied. Although his breakfast had been the complete antithesis of a 'full English', he had no appetite.

'Where is my friend?' he asked rather aggressively. 'Do you know who has kidnapped her?'

'Please do not be too dramatic,' said Mme Lauran, 'she is fine. It was not my idea to hold her. People, frightened people, with a lot to lose have become very nervous but they do not wish to harm her. When you hear what I am about to tell you, you will understand their concern.'

She spoke with the authority and confidence borne of wealth and position. She had come a long way from apparent humble beginnings in rural France. As she spoke her piercing eyes speared Harry and pinned him to his armchair. Her authoritative manner left Harry in no doubt that she was to be neither rushed nor dominated.

She glanced out of the window for a few moments then began to speak.

'Before I begin I would be grateful if you would tell me what you know.' Her eyes were still bright but they flickered briefly. A demon came and went. 'I am taking a big risk by talking to you. I do not fear for myself but the reason why I have said nothing for more than forty years will become obvious. I believe you have become an unwitting victim of the deeds of people a lifetime ago. Perhaps I need the courage of a problem shared to help me.'

So Harry told her.

She said nothing when he had finished, just looked him in the eye with an unreadable expression.

She polished her glasses on a silk cloth but left them hanging from a gold chord round her neck. Then she rested her hands in her lap and raised her eyes to meet Harry's.

'They were known only as Les Dix, which as you may know translates as 'The Ten'. Ten people whose identities are largely hidden but whose actions are a scythe that still threatens to rip apart many people two generations on. Actions that indirectly may well have led to the death of your father and his three friends. To this day I can only be sure of two names – one of them my brother, Guillaume Leport, the other, Guy Bezier, who died fourteen months ago in a village near Pau in south-western France.

His death caused quite a stir in the newspapers, albeit briefly.

When he died he left his cottage to a trust which had been set up to assist people on release from prison – an officially endorsed organisation that helped prisoners re-integrate into the community. The cottage was ideal as its remoteness was away from prying eyes – and those out for revenge.

While they were clearing the house, a journal was found hidden within the base of a wardrobe. The text contained information about Guy Bezier's friendship with my brother and made brief reference, or perhaps inference is a better word, to their being part of Les Dix, hinting that the two of them were the sole surviving members. As my brother had died nearly forty years ago, the journal was obviously old, Bezier may well have forgotten about it. I doubt it, but it's possible.

A journalist scented a scandal and the story rumbled on for a while in the papers with speculative hints about satanic cults and the abuse of children but the reports faded without them realising how close they had come to the truth. They questioned people in Caylus, Felines and other nearby towns and villages, but learned little – the communities closed ranks. They questioned me too but I denied all knowledge of Bezier or the alleged activities of my brother. I had no choice.'

Madame Lauran paused. She stood and walked to the fireplace where she adjusted the position of a photograph on the marble mantelpiece. She looked briefly in the mirror, then turned and stood with her back to the unlit logs and pine cones in the unlit fire. Gazing, unfocussed, somewhere over Harry's left shoulder she continued.

'But the real story began fifteen years before my brother was killed.

We lived in a village about three hours' drive north of Felines called Tremiére. It had suffered as badly as any place during the occupation; many men had died fighting during the war and as the conflict drew to a close, the village was left devastated and rudderless. Many French people hated the Germans but there were some, those who thought the occupiers would prevail, who sympathised and sided with the enemy. Unbeknown to most people and behind the backs of their countrymen these traitors passed information to the Nazis, betraying families and friends. My brother and Guy Bezier were two such people.

Eight German officers came to our village on a regular basis either individually or in groups. They drank in our small bar, played cards and demanded food. A few of the women went with them, whether or not they were offered a choice is debatable, I suspect there was a degree of coercion. Although in my youth I was reasonably attractive, I was left alone - probably because of my brother. Outwardly they were reasonable people, but they were arrogant. We were in no doubt that they were in charge, we were the vanquished.

My brother, Bezier and the eight Germans were christened Les Dix sometime after the war, a macabre and reviled legend that haunts still.

There were forty-six villagers living there as the war neared its conclusion, a mix of the elderly, women and children. Allied forces were prevailing and time came for the occupiers to pull out.

One day a message was sent round the village stating that the Germans wished to thank us for what they described as our tolerance and forbearing. They wished, they said, to host a simple party for the villagers in a barn on the edge of the village, everyone was invited. An invitation was an order, so with a degree of uncertainty, but also relief that we would soon be free of our unwelcome guests, we prepared ourselves.

On the eve of the party, I was ready to leave the house when Guillaume came to me and ordered me not to go. I asked him why but he wouldn't say. He told me to prepare some food and warm clothing. We were to go together to the small wooden lodge in the nearby forest. The lodge was about two kilometres from the village and was used, particularly during the winter, to shelter local people who hunted in the woods.

I had suspected for some time that Guillaume was collaborating with the Germans. He would often come home with meat, wine and brandy, things not available to most people. I also knew that he spent much time with Bezier.

I regret to this day leaving my friends but my brother was insistent and together the two of us slipped out of the house and away into the forest.

When we got to the lodge he was obviously very nervous and became unusually assertive. He forced me to sit in an old wooden chair. To my astonishment he bound my hands and feet to the chair and left me. He apologised quickly and said he would return. I had tried to resist him but he was too strong and despite my increasingly desperate pleas he left.

The lodge was cold and, after he left, as silent as a mausoleum. I couldn't move as he'd secured me well - all I could do was wait. I was truly terrified.

I must have dozed because I was woken by the distant chatter of gunfire. Though not unusual, there was a war on after all, it was less common during the hours of darkness. I had no idea what time it was. Some time later there was more gunfire.

I will never forget the feeling of isolation I experienced that night. My bonds were tight and my limbs ached but it was the utter solitude and helplessness that frightened me most.

Guillaume returned, this time with Bezier, late in the night. Both men were quiet, especially my brother, who looked gaunt and ill.

My questions went unanswered. Guillaume lit a fire and both men sat and stared into the flames. They freed me from my bonds and as I frantically demanded what had gone on, Bezier ran to me and slapped my face with such force that he drew blood. He yelled for me to be quiet, the look in his eye that of a mad animal.

I left the lodge under the pretext of collecting firewood, then ran, my aching limbs screaming in protest. Guillaume followed but I outpaced him. He shouted after me begging me not to go. I ran all the way to the village.

As I drew near I saw the blackened wreckage of the barn and my heart leapt. It was completely destroyed, all that remained was a heap of ash and smouldering timbers. I could see no-one and nobody replied to my shouts.

But it was what I found in the sties, previously hidden from view behind the barn, that nearly felled me. In each of the seven pens were the bodies of my friends and neighbours; six or seven in each. They had been shot. Women and old men horribly mutilated, lying beneath or across one another, some at impossible angles, the children strewn on top, lying where they died in terror and agony. Blood-drenched torsos and annihilated faces, unrecognisable as the innocent, beautiful, gentle people of our village. It was an orgy of horror I have seen every waking moment for fifty-five years.

Nothing moved, there was not a breath of wind, yet I could hear the distant echoes of their screams - I still can.

How long I stood there I don't know but when I turned, Guillaume was there. His face was devoid of emotion, dead eyes stared into mine.

He told me that it was never meant to happen like that. He didn't know what they were planning. They'd had told him they were to select a few villagers to take with them, that was why he wanted me out of the way. I suppose he was trying to convince himself that there was a speck of decency left in him.

He spoke in a monotone and told me that they had taken the elderly and women to the stables and murdered them. Guillaume and Bezier had fled and hid in the edge of the forest when they realised what was happening. They watched in disbelief as the children were raped, four boys, three girls, the eldest eleven and the youngest little girl just two. They too were then shot.

The soldiers drank wine and brandy at the table in the barn. They laughed and sung as if nothing had happened, eating the food prepared by the villagers for their own party.

The two had waited till the Germans had drunk themselves into a stupor and were asleep either resting on their arms at the table or on the floor where they had slumped. They crept back into the barn and shot them where they slept, all eight of them, with their own weapons. They covered the bodies with straw and set fire to the barn, then retreated to the forest once again and waited. Finally, when the building collapsed in on itself, they returned to the lodge.

The two of them discussed what to do with the bodies of the villagers. They agreed that they were appalled by the executions but in reality they were frightened for themselves so I suspect that was all said for my benefit. Though both men were affected, neither showed real remorse, rather a fear of being implicated in the horror.

It was several days later that I learned what had subsequently transpired.

My brother and I returned to the lodge where Bezier had passed out through drinking Brandy and the following morning the three of us set off heading south. My brother assured me that he would do right by the villagers.

We arrived at an abandoned cottage in the early afternoon and I was told to wait till the two men returned, probably the following day. I never saw Bezier again. Guillaume told me when he returned alone at noon two days later that they had doubled back and gone to a neighbouring village to report the tragedy. He told me that several people from the village of La Forge had helped him bury the dead, decent burials in the graveyard of the small church in our village, Tremiére. They had found a local priest to conduct the funerals. Bezier had left my brother the previous evening to go and stay with a relative so Guillaume returned to the cottage alone.

My brother and I then made our way further south to the farm in Felines. We travelled in an old Citroen van he had stashed at the cottage.

He had bought the smallholding in Felines eight months previously. I asked him where the money came from and he said that he had managed to save a little, he also told me cryptically that war could be a profitable business. He couldn't have saved much as our existence was simple prior to and during the war, so in my heart I knew that he had somehow been paid for assisting the enemy. It must have been a profitable business. I knew he was a traitor and, by implication, so was I. Particularly as I had run from the village and would not be accounted for during the recovery of the bodies and subsequent burials.

But there were others. The original ten involved in and around Tremiére were the ones who became infamous because of the massacre but my brother knew of other traitors both from our district and further afield. I presume he learned of them through his contacts with the Germans – he held a great power over many people. Whether he blackmailed them I don't know but if he did it may well have been a lucrative source of income. What I suspect is that he used his knowledge to manipulate them, his trump card was the fact that he could expose one or more of them at any time. I am almost certain that a number of these traitors settled in Caylus and I believe it went further than this deception.

You know, from what you told me in your story, that my brother was also a sexual predator. Your friend's recollections are confirmation that he preyed on children; I assure you that his disgusting behaviour did not stop with his niece. I don't know whether he was in contact with Bezier but he created a network of revolting monsters that abused and raped children. Not only was he responsible, at least on the periphery, for the deaths of 43 innocent people, but his depravity continued in other guises throughout his life.

Over the years he integrated with the community, he used the support of the townspeople over whom he had influence and can you believe he even rose to be notaire, the approximate equivalent of your mayor. Quite astonishing hypocrisy. Throughout, his behaviour away from his official duties didn't alter.

Why did I not stop him you may ask? Well, he could have ruined me too. I have no idea what he would have concocted against me but I am ashamed to say that I was basically a coward. I let it go on for fifteen years.

His killer was never found. I am not sure how determined the authorities were to pursue the investigation, but everyone suspected that it was not Celine who was responsible. Even if she had been, I believe the town would have gathered round her and somehow protected her. No-one would have blamed her in any event - but I never believed it was her.

Thanks to you, I know who killed him. It took a complete stranger, someone who had not even witnessed anything first-hand, to show us what courage was. I am sorry your father's friend ended his life the way he did; he is one of the few people whose hand I would shake. Myself and others owe him a debt, one that will never be repaid.

Having heard your story, Monsieur Crabtree's actions are the factor that finally persuaded me to tell you what I know. Even before you arrived today I was not sure how much to reveal.

Celine came to live at the farm when she was only four years old. Her father, our other brother, who neither of us had seen for over twelve years, lived with his wife here in Paris. Both were killed days before the end of the war and my brother was finally traced to Felines. We were Celine's only living relatives and my brother agreed to take her in. I found out later why he was so keen.

We had lived there for about eight months until I moved to a small house in Caylus, paid for by Guillaume. He persuaded me that the farm was a better place to raise a child so she remained with him.

I would drive to the farm each morning and attend to their needs, make breakfast, do some washing and so on, then drive Celine to school. I would pick her up and take her home in the afternoon when I would prepare a meal for them and return home. She attended the local school but no-one was aware of the abuse to which she was being subjected at home. She was a shy child, rather introverted, but everyone thought it was the loss of her parents and leaving her home in Paris that was the cause.

Throughout these years the town's heart beat with a very different rhythm – it was sick and we were in denial. Suspicion grew like a cancer to the point where nothing was said. Many decent people were sucked into a world of silence, a world where fear ruled, fear for personal safety yes, but also fear of guilt by association, fear of being linked to deeds both past and present. It became a place where the actions of a few gradually throttled a way of life.

Periodically someone from outside would come and ask questions about the past, about Tremiére and 'Les Dix'. The whole town would snap closed, no outsider was welcome.

Probably, the only person who knew the extent of both his own and others' treachery was my brother. I'm sure some secrets died with him but he left a legacy of evil and mistrust.

After he died, Celine came to live with me but within a week I took her away. We just up and left one day. You see, she was pregnant. Nineteen years of age and carrying the devil's child.

I'm not even sure that she knew exactly what was happening. She left school at sixteen but after that rarely left my brother's farm.

The only person with whom I talked was my then neighbour, Madame Chambrée. We lived close to one another in Caylus and I had to tell someone, had to speak to someone about my fears. I would have imploded otherwise. She is the kind of friend of whom we all dream - understanding, loyal and most important of all, non-judgemental. I had no right to have had such a friend.

Before the war she was a nurse and had worked in England before returning to France to care for her father. He died just before the outbreak of war but she stayed on and worked as an assistant to the local doctor.

She knew of a private hospital called The Grove near Pewsey in Wiltshire where they would care for Celine. She wrote to the hospital, specifically to a gynaecologist she had befriended during her time there, and he agreed without question to help her.

We initially came here to Paris where we rented an apartment but within a week she was on her way to England. I went with her on the train to Calais and saw her onto the ferry. She would be met in Dover by an acquaintance of the doctor and accompanied to Wiltshire.

I never saw her again.

I did write both to Celine and the gynaecologist, a Mr Brierley – Celine never replied and the doctor's letter told me that she had left the clinic not long after her arrival. I was naturally worried about her, I even travelled there myself about six months later but was told again that she had left. She was, they told me, in good health, but had transferred to another location at her own request. They led me to believe that she didn't want to be found. I returned to Paris with only their word that she was safe. The gynaecologist was a pleasant, kindly man and I had to make do with his reassurance. Needless to say, I have often wondered what became of her. I pray that she found contentment somewhere.'

Madame Lauran was finally silent.

She lowered her eyes and stared at her hands folded on her lap and released a deep shuddering sigh. She had relived and recounted her extraordinary story. A single tear ran down her cheek – she stood and walked from the room. She walked upright and proud, continuing to defy the demons and guilt that would have crushed many. Harry listened to her steps cross the wooden floor in the hall, a door opened and closed and he was left with the ticking of a clock.

She returned ten minutes later with a tea tray. She had busied herself as a distraction – she had probably done the same in one form or another for many years. She invited Harry to help himself, then poured her own.

'The thing I cannot help you with is the link to recent events,' she said. 'Why, after such a long time, have we seen the beast raise its head once again?

I have thought about it since I agreed to speak to you but the only apparent occurrence of significance was the death of Bezier.

I hope you understand that I trust you to protect people who have suffered enough. You have in your possession knowledge that could cripple the already weakened spirit of people who have struggled with their demons for a lifetime. The children and grandchildren should not be blamed for the sins of their forebears. They are still fragile and they are frightened.' She paused and took a sip of tea. 'What do you intend to do?'

Harry drunk his own tea and was silent for a while before answering. He realised that the action he took from here had the potential to cause irreparable damage, but the overriding factor in his mind at this moment was Mary's safe return. He had seen first-hand the suspicion in Caylus and now he knew why. He would get nothing more from there, indeed he didn't want to return. At best, questions would be blanked, at worst he could end up in a hole in the ground in the forest. There were a couple of threads to follow, both rather feeble – one was Bezier, but perhaps the more likely was Celine. Chances of success after all this time though seemed slim.

'My main concern at this moment is Mary,' he said at last. 'She has worries of her own without being held captive. Whatever happens from here I can assure you that I want her safe.' He tried to sound aggressive but felt he was making a poor fist of it. 'If that means doing nothing further, then so be it.' He knew this wasn't strictly accurate and as he said it he metaphorically crossed his fingers. He didn't appear to have convinced his companion.

Her eyes remained fixed on him but she said nothing, so he continued, 'I do not want revenge but I would like answers. I would like to know why my parents died, for I believe it was no accident, likewise the recent death of my godfather. I will go back to England as I think the solution is there, I will not return to Caylus, you have my word on that. I will do everything in my power to protect the people there.'

They looked one another in the eye for many moments until eventually she said, 'I believe you, I must trust you. But always remember, there is much at stake for many people.'

She sat quietly while she thought. Harry finished his tea – his china cup had rattled gently on the saucer so he put it down and placed his clammy hands on his knees. He desperately tried to remain calm.

'Now you must leave,' she said suddenly, all business again. 'You passed a small brasserie on your way here called La Fleur Noir. Go straight there and wait, a taxi will collect you. This house we are in,' waving her hand, 'belongs to a friend; he is away. Please never come here again nor try to contact me by any other means. Remember all I have told you, use it wisely and use it very carefully. We shall not meet again.'

With that she left the room, clip-clopped across the hall and opened the front door where she stood and waited for Harry. He picked up the cases and as he passed he said, 'Thank you.'

She didn't meet his eye and made no reply as the door closed behind him.

He sat in La Fleur Noir and, though he didn't want one, ordered a coffee. A move he considered prudent after repeated glares from the miserable looking bartender. He reflected that he'd been in the city for barely seven hours yet it felt like a lifetime. His window table allowed him a view of the street and he was constantly on the look out for a taxi. He saw more dogs and plenty of expensive clothing but it was a further forty minutes before a large black Peugeot taxi came to a halt outside. He left ten euros on the table, grabbed the cases and rushed outside.

An elderly lady got out of the car which drove away again. He looked at the lady waiting for her to say something but she walked straight by him into the café. 'Damn', he muttered and sat down at one of the outside tables. A waiter approached and gesticulated. He was encouraging Harry use the café for its intended purpose, when another car pulled up, this one a cream coloured Mercedes and sitting in the back, Mary. Harry barged past the irate waiter and yanked open the rear door.

She looked pale but unhurt and as Harry climbed in she slid across the seat and hugged him tightly. She wept against his shoulder and mumbled, 'oh Harry.'

'Baggage,' said the driver gruffly and Harry disentangled himself and put the luggage in the boot.

The car set off at some speed down the narrow street and Harry asked the driver where they were going.

'I believe you are leaving. We are going to Orly,' he replied, then to clarify. 'The airport.'

Chapter 23

They sat together on a vinyl-covered bench-seat. Refurbishment hadn't reached this distant departure lounge where they waited for BA 004 to Heathrow.

Mary, legs curled up beneath her, leaned on Harry resting her head on his shoulder as they sat quietly. Harry wasn't keen on flying at the best of times but was especially twitchy after his episode on the outbound flight. 'Just a panic attack,' Mary had said. Understatement, he thought, more like an attack that he thought was his final performance in full view of a load of strangers who probably though he was drunk. His hands were clammy.

'What are you thinking about?'

'Nothing, just dozing,' replied Harry.

'Liar.'

She was right but he pretended to doze some more as a trickle of sweat ran down his back.

The taxi driver had handed them flight tickets and refused payment for the ride. Someone was keen to ensure they didn't linger.

Harry tried the mystery man's phone number and as promised the line was dead.

He thought about Madame Lauran. What a mixture. She'd spoken variously with tenderness, regret, fear, remorse and disgust but the one overriding impression throughout was impermeability. Her polished shell protected both herself and others. A single tear had squeezed through the husk, the only outward sign of any true emotion. Unless her humanity had genuinely withered and died over the years, it had been a hell of an act of self-discipline.

Harry inwardly chided himself for his cynicism but then, thinking of his parents and the burnt-out farmhouse, became angry.

He mulled over the reasons she had chosen to speak to him; 'To help him; because his family had suffered; to put an end to it.' He could add to that; 'To warn him off, to protect herself, to keep murder and child abuse buried, to protect a town.' Without doubt, the reputations of innocent people could be ruined - people a generation or two on who could not be held responsible for the actions of their forebears.

But was it possible there could be another reason altogether; were they protecting something in the present? Come to think of it he'd not seen a single child in the town. In fact, the only person under forty he'd seen was the hotel receptionist, Claudette, that was her name. Bloody unusual. Something stirred his sub-conscious but he couldn't button it. Mary wriggled and scratched her nose.

'Coffee?'

'Yes, and a large brandy and a cigarette,' she replied.

'You don't smoke do you?'

'Not yet.'

'I'll be back in a minute.'

It wasn't quite as easy as that though.

He queued and asked the spotty man behind the counter for coffee then had to back-track because it was self-service and he'd lost his place in the queue. He'd pushed one of a selection of coffee buttons and got scalding water all over his trousers - then the spotty man had tried to charge him for the coffee he'd slopped. Fortunately, the man's English didn't run to colloquialisms as Harry said, 'If you'd get off your backside and provide a service worthy of the name things like this wouldn't happen,' - fortunately this wasn't understood.

Harry and the man behind him in the queue exchanged scowls and both muttered expletives in their respective tongues so Harry returned to Mary in a tizz. 'Don't ask,' he said.

Mary spotted his dam patch and laughed. 'Shut up,' said Harry.

'I'll go and get the milk and sugar then should I?' she asked

'Good idea.'

The plane was half an hour late which from Harry's point of view was a mixed blessing. On the one hand it would prologue his life by thirty minutes should they plummet into the channel but conversely it required the expenditure of an extra thirty minutes worth of nervous energy. God he hated flying. France had got on his nerves too.

Chapter 24

They were on the M4. The windscreen wipers on their hired Citroen squeaked. A French car, they couldn't escape its clutches. With each pass of the blades the lines on the screen on the passenger side in front of Harry resembled splayed fingers as the wipers hopped across the glass. It was a maddening distraction through which forward vision was nearly impossible. But Harry's mind was elsewhere because he had just received a text message from Quinn; 'Boat trashed. Speak later.'

Harry went pale.

'What on earth's the matter Harry?' asked Mary.

'Something's happened to the boat.'

'What do you mean?'

'That was a text from Quinn. He says the boat has been trashed. He says we'll speak later. Look can you pull into the next service station, I want to ring him but not from the mobile.'

'Yes, it's about fifteen miles.'

They were quiet for a few minutes.

'This is going from bad to worse,' said Mary, 'it surely can't be connected with anything we've done in France, we've only just left. You gave them assurances that you'd be careful.'

'I suppose someone was looking for something,' said Harry.'

'The laptop?' she asked.

'That's as good a bet as any. But who this time?'

Harry had told Mary Madame Lauran's story during the flight. They'd had three seats between two of them and he'd been careful to keep his voice down. They'd agreed to hire a car, go and see if they could find anything out in Wiltshire, and get back up north as soon as possible.

Mary's abductors had not harmed her, just frightened the life out of her. Two of them had come into the room and told her that if she didn't come with them quietly, she would never see Harry again. While she'd dressed one of them, a man with a stocking over his head, had thrown Mary's' toiletries on the floor and smashed a glass in the basin. He'd wrapped the glass in a towel to keep the noise down. They had gone down the fire-stairs and she'd been bundled into a car waiting in the alley.

They took her to an apartment or hotel room about ten minutes drive away. She'd no idea where because she was made to lie on the back seat and they'd covered her with a rug. They'd locked her in a windowless bedroom and told her to keep quiet. A woman, who looked like a clown dressed in wig, large glasses and too much make-up, came in and told her that no-one was going to be hurt and actually apologised for their behaviour. Apart from the fact that she'd been kidnapped it was all pretty civilised.

A couple of hours later she was taken down to an underground garage. They had driven a short distance and she lay on the seat again till told to get out and wait, a taxi would pick her up. This arrived within thirty seconds and they had driven off to collect Harry.

The service station was like any other. The aesthetics and planning considerations seemed to encourage the weary traveller to leave again as soon as possible. Harry phoned Quinn and they duly left as soon as possible.

Quinn had softened his approach somewhat and seemed sympathetic towards Harry's boat. He had left it by Bridge 51 when he went to France in a fairly isolated spot, the towpath used only by boaters and occasional walkers. The break-in had occurred sometime during last night. The Shropshire Star had carried a story by a certain female reporter under the headline: 'Boat ransacked; assault link?' Although Quinn didn't go into detail the inference of the article was that Harry was questioned by police over an assault on a local business lady and although no charges were brought, there were questions to be answered. Not least of which, where was the boat's owner at the time of the damage?

Harry got his retaliation in first and phoned D.S. Groves from the car explaining that he had been to France for a short break and was making his way back to Shropshire. He would call at the police station the following day. 'Make sure you do,' was the curt response. He disconnected.

'Is there no pity?' asked Harry.

'Apparently not,' replied Mary who was still driving.

'I haven't had chance to fall in love with the boat, but I do feel real sadness for Will, even though he's gone.' He paused. 'What the hell do you do with a wreck in the middle of nowhere? That was my house. I hope the insurance pays up, otherwise I'm snookered. They probably haven't even got the letter telling yet them I'm the new owner, I only posted it as we came away. What a mess.'

'It might not be so bad; and anyway, you've got the flat, don't worry, you'll be OK.'

'You mean we'll be OK,' replied Harry. He looked across at Mary and patted her knee; she smiled.

The rain had given way to bright sunshine but by the look of the clouds another heavy shower was not far off. Driving was tricky as the sun reflected off the wet road, miniature-rainbows danced in the spray from vehicles ahead. The Logical Song by Supertramp played on the radio and Mary smiled, 'I saw them in a baseball park in Montreal in the late seventies. It was a fabulous show. My goodness it seems like a long time ago.'

'Yes, I remember them, they were good, never saw them live though.'

They chatted about the past, far enough back for it to be safe for them both and agreed that things were not as good these days – as did every generation.

'We sound like old duffers' he said

'Middle-aged maybe, but you're quite right, it's not the same. Things rarely are.'

He pointed. 'Look I think this is where we turn off.' He looked at the map. 'Yes, come off here and head for Marlborough.'

Twenty-five minutes later they dropped down into Pewsey where they asked directions to The Grove as they filled up with diesel. They took the road heading towards Honeystreet and passed through the village of Wilcot. Half a mile further on they passed a garage, a pub, a wood-mill and a large smelly farm called The Criftins before turning left onto a gravel road bordered on each side by a sturdy post and rail fence.

Cows grazed in the fields and four hundred yards further up the gentle slope a gold on blue sign, set on one of a pair of stone gateposts, announced: The Grove. Private Clinic. A cattle grid chattered and gravel gave way to tarmac. Lawned gardens now straddled the drive and someone had been busy with beautiful box yew hedging forming what looked like a maze. Ahead of them was an imposing double-fronted three-storey stone building. Ivy clung to its face; variegated leaves bordered white-framed sash windows. A large oak front door was sheltered by a portico that in times past would have welcomed the horse and carriage of the privileged. Not falling into that category, Harry and Mary were directed around a central fountain to the rear of the building and the visitors' carpark.

There were only two other cars and when the engine was turned off and they were out of the car, the thing that struck them both was the peace. In the far distance they could hear a tractor grumbling away but apart from birdsong and a clattering woodpecker everything was peaceful.

The rear of the building was more functional and they had parked facing a single storey extension that looked to be either private wards or an accommodation block. This more recent addition ran away at right angles from one end of the main building and in the angle formed by the new wing a modern conservatory-style entrance.

Automatic doors slid open noiselessly and they approached the reception desk across the deep blue-carpet of the foyer. In the waiting area an ash-coloured, glass-topped table was surrounded on three sides by two-seater sofas and some imported daffodils looked on from a glass vase. Inoffensive landscapes adorned magnolia walls and at each end of the foyer were sturdy wooden doors. Each had a rectangular glass panel at eye level. One door led away to the new wing and one towards the older part of the building.

'May I help you?' A lady had materialised from a further door to the rear of the reception desk. She wore a lilac blouse with dark blue skirt and a pair of wire-rimmed glasses hung from a cord round her neck. Her name was Margaret Walcott, as portrayed on a discreet gold name plate pinned to her blouse. Around forty, she was attractive with deep green eyes and short brown hair.

'Good afternoon,' said Harry in his 'Sunday-go-to-church' accent, 'we are looking for information on a young lady who was resident here in 1961.

'Really?' She replied, stony-faced.

'Yes, really. She came across from France and I believe she was looked after by a gynaecologist called Mr Brierley.'

The lady looked at Harry for some moments before asking; 'Are you a relative?'

'No,' replied Harry, 'she is the niece of a friend of mine. My, our friend,' he corrected looking at Mary, 'lives in the South of France and is sadly not well, she has asked me to try and trace her niece as a matter of urgency, if you understand my meaning.' A blank stare met Harry's raised eyebrows. He had the feeling he was making rather a mess of his introduction but soldiered on. 'We understand that she came here in the spring of 1961 but no-one has heard of her since. My friend realises the likelihood of tracing her niece are slim but the only avenue open to her is your clinic. Her name is, or was, Celine Leport.'

'I do sympathise, but I am sorry we are unable to give out information on any patient unless they themselves instruct us to do so. There are a few exceptional cases but I'm afraid in this instance it will not be possible.'

He was getting nowhere. 'What if I threatened to shoot you?' said Harry.

Margaret Walcott's eyes widened and she blanched. Then she returned Harry's huge grin. 'My goodness,' she said, 'I've heard some things in my time but that's a first.' Then with a mock frown on her face 'No, not even if you threatened to shoot me.' No mug is our Margaret thought Harry.

'We've had sob stories, attempted bribes and journalists promising all sorts, but I'm afraid the answer is always the same. We take confidentiality at The Grove extremely seriously. I hope you understand our position.'

'Yes, of course I do. But if there anything you could suggest that may help us find her we would be very grateful.'

'Look, people come here for all kinds of reasons but apart from the excellent care we offer, one of our main attributes is discretion. What I am trying to say is that some of our clients wish to be anonymous and it is not unknown for them to leave and not want to be found. Even if your 'friend's niece' she emphasised the words, 'could be traced through our records, which is not a certainty after such a long time, it is very likely she herself chose to leave no clue as to her whereabouts. I'm very sorry. You could try Somerset House but it would be like looking for a needle in a haystack and I wouldn't hold out much hope. She may have changed her name at any time or left the country. It is not that difficult to disappear.'

'We believe she was pregnant when she came here,' said Mary, 'it would be wonderful if our friend at least knew if she had another relative. Maybe more than one if she'd had a family of her own.'

Margaret shrugged in sympathy.

'I don't suppose that Mr Brierley is still around,' asked Harry.

'You are talking about forty years ago, that's a long time. Even if Mr Brierley were still here he would tell you exactly the same as me, as would any other member of staff.'

'Yes; shot in the dark,' he replied. 'Look, can I leave you my phone number in case you think of anything?'

'Certainly, but I don't think it likely.'

Harry wrote his mobile number on the proffered pad, they said their goodbyes and returned to the car.

'Shoot her?' laughed Mary.

'Chat-up line.' He replied as they climbed into the car.

'You realise we were on camera in there. They probably heard all you said, they could have you locked up.'

'I'm getting used to handling the old bill, no problem. After D.S. Groves anything else would be a doddle. Come on let's go and find somewhere for a coffee.'

They passed a lady clipping the box hedge on their way down the drive. The tiny camera on the gatepost swivelled and followed them until they had crossed the fields and turned back the way they had come.

An old man sat in his suite on the third floor and watched them go. There were three screens on the desk in front of him. The left hand one was tuned to the security camera positioned high on the gatepost, the one in the centre covered reception and the one on the right was interchangeable between another six cameras sited throughout the clinic. An identical set of screens was situated in the main office to the rear of the reception desk. A bored security guard had also watched the visitors leave, happy to do as little as possible and focus on his ham salad roll. He was however alert enough hear the exchange in reception and place a phone call.

The old man sat in a wheelchair, a rug covering him from the waist down. A black and white film played silently on the television in the corner of the room. The only other sound was the gentle hiss of the oxygen cylinder that fed the man through tiny tubes in each nostril. He was ninety-four years of age but remembered clearly the young French girl who had been in his care so briefly forty years ago.

He picked up the telephone - his hand with paper-thin, translucent skin, trembled slightly as he held the receiver to his ear. 'Margaret,' he said with cracked, breathy voice, 'would you kindly bring Celine Chambers file up to my room. Ask Simon to pop in too please.'

'Certainly Mr Brierley, at once.'

He leaned back in his chair; tried to relax to allow the oxygen to flood his body and quiet his thudding heart. Perhaps, he said to himself, it's time. He moved the joystick in the arm of his motorised wheelchair and guided himself to the window. The view of the rolling Wiltshire countryside was one of which he had never tired.

Much of his body protested his longevity but his mind and eyes had remained sharp. The thing he detested the most was his reliance on other people, but he had two aids in whom he trusted implicitly - literally with his life. Margaret Walcott was one, the other Simon Fairweather. More than a nurse, he had been a confidante but was now a friend, their association spanned more than thirty years. Presently fifty-four years old, Simon had come to work at The Grove straight from medical school and had never left. Roger Brierley had recognised something rare in the young man, a tenderness and compassion that cannot be taught, and had taken him under his wing. For the past six years though, since his master had required constant supervision, Simon had been his ever-present companion.

Margaret was Roger Brierley's eyes and ears during the day to day running of the clinic. The six-strong management team, led by Chief Operations Executive Susan Wolfe, ran the clinic without interference from their patriarch, but Margaret provided a verbal weekly report to the old man. She had a staggering memory for facts and figures so no written record of their meetings existed.

Every member of staff loved the old man and held him in the highest regard - in his current state he was aware that he couldn't afford to alienate them. He was also aware that his hold on his beloved clinic was maintained by a thread, His sole bargaining chip was his stewardship of the Trust that owned the property and business outright. The only way for the situation to change was if the old man voluntarily rescinded his control or he died.

Only he and Simon knew that he had left provision for the Trust to continue after his death through a complicated series of investment funds and a predetermined management structure, under the guardianship of Simon. Simon in turn would report twice yearly to what the old man jokingly described as 'the three wise men in their temple of gold'; three trusted partners in a substantial City accountancy firm that would continue to manage the Trust's accounts.

The management and staff trusted the old man, they always had. Staff had come and gone over the years, their common bond the affection and esteem in which they held Roger Brierley.

A gentle tap on the door preceded Simon and Margaret, the latter carrying a slim buff folder.

Chapter 25

Harry drove as Mary slept beside him. His mushy mind tried desperately to determine a link between the clinic and what went next. According to Madame Lauran, Celine had definitely been there but where did she go and with whom? Did she have the baby and if so did she raise it? Was the child adopted? She must have gone somewhere for medical attention whether she gave birth or had a termination. They would stand a better chance if the baby had been born for the simple reason that there would be two people to try and trace.

His choices he figured were the adoption agency, hospitals, both private and public, social services. There must be a record of births accessible through the internet. But what name would he look under. He wasn't even sure of the bloody surname for God's sake. He was getting a bit ratty. He needed some help. Mary slept on.

Just when he was getting desperate enough to pull into Frankley service station on the M5 he remembered something and with some relief drove past. Will's solicitor, Edward Parker, had mentioned something about a donation to a clinic in Wiltshire. Small donation he had said. Now why? Surely it was too much of a coincidence for it not to have been The Grove. How had Will known about the place? With Edward Parker's demise the only thing he could try was to phone his secretary, Irene Daniels. It was a long shot - if she would tell him anything - if she was still there.

Now they were sitting in a jam on the M6 and wished he'd stopped when he'd had a chance. Rush hour on the outskirts of Birmingham in the drizzle, desperate for a pee and a dull musty headache – it didn't get much better than this.

He turned on the radio and listened to a discussion about a cabinet minister who had 'allegedly' used an R.A.F. Hercules transport plane to take her from a late parliamentary session to her constituency in the North East of England. Crucial meeting the following morning etc. etc. – nonsense, thought Harry, lying, cheating bloody politicians. He was tired, angry and frustrated and turned the radio off. Blaming a cabinet minister for his troubles.

His mind wandered back over the previous few days. So much had happened in such a short time it was hardly surprising he was muddled.

'Why the frown,' asked Mary who'd finally woken up.

'I can't see an end to it. We've travelled halfway across Europe, met some unlikely people and learned some extremely unpleasant things - none of which really gets us anywhere.'

'Let's just calm down a bit,' she said rubbing sleep out of her eyes, 'we've been on the go for days, it's not surprising you can't think straight.'

'I wasn't much good at that at the best of times.'

'Where are we anyway?' asked Mary.

'About forty minutes from Shrewsbury, we're on the last leg.'

It was just after eight in the evening, the flat was warm and the Chinese they'd picked up on the way in was now a pile of rubbish - not much different to when it had arrived, thought Harry.

They sat at the kitchen table in silence and shared a bottle of Shiraz. Drinks number two and three of the new era he thought.

His mind drifted back to Madame Lauran. There was something, but he couldn't button it. Something she'd said, something about her, the house - it wouldn't come. He shook his head in annoyance and walked through into the lounge where he stood and stared in disbelief at the empty table - the lap-top was gone.

'Mary.' He shouted. 'Did you hide the computer?'

'No.'

'It's gone. The bloody computer's disappeared!'

She rushed in and stared at Harry and said quietly, 'someone's been here - my God.'

'Who the hell had broken in without any sign of having been there?' The cheap printer that Mary had bought sat on the table, umbilical unattached. 'Is anything else missing?' he asked.

She looked around. 'Not that I can see straight off. There wasn't much worth stealing; nothing I would miss anyway. I've lived without it for so long I couldn't even tell you half the stuff that's here.' She paused. 'I did print off a copy of Will's story if that's any good, but heaven only knows what else was on there; addresses and so on.'

'No, I never looked properly either. No point reporting it to the police, they didn't even know I'd pinched it in the first place. Bugger!' He muttered.

'It's the fact that someone's been here that gives me the creeps.'

'Yes, I know, but I don't see what we can do.' said Harry.

'Change the door lock for one thing, put something more secure on.'

'It's a bit late for that. It's obvious what they were after, I can't see whoever it was coming back again. There's not much we can do tonight in any event.'

They sat together on the sofa and drank the coffee Mary had made.

'How do you suppose Will knew about the Grove?' asked Harry.

'What do you mean?'

'He left them a donation in his will. His solicitor mentioned it. I'm going to call his secretary tomorrow; see if she's still there.' He paused. 'There's no reason for her to know though is there? Problem is I don't know anything else we can really try.'

After a moment Mary looked at Harry. 'You don't think that you're being railroaded out of Wales has anything to do with it do you?

Harry stared at the flame-effect gas fire. The mere mention of that chapter of his life made him shiver. 'I don't see how. I never really fitted in there and my relationship with my wife and in-laws had deteriorated to a point where we were all bloody miserable. I certainly wasn't much of an asset to the company and Susan and I might as well have lived at opposite ends of Europe the amount we had in common. In retrospect I'm glad it came to an end when it did.'

'Shunting you out the way they did was pretty drastic, especially consider-ing what we now know about what happened in France. And there was the fire at your parents' house which you now think may have been no accident.' She was quiet for a while before continuing 'Your Dad, Will and Parker were mates and they're all dead – more than coincidence surely.' She raised her eyebrows and looked questioningly at Harry. He remained silent until Mary continued. 'I really don't know. It's just more questions that need answering.'

'Derek Crabtree took his own life out of guilt and his inability to face his past, but that was years ago, I can't see a link to my dad's death or the others, can you?'

'Not directly no, but there is the French link.'

They were quiet for a while.

'Something has happened recently, but I can't see it. It really started with your parent's death didn't it? Can you think of anything around then?'

Harry just shook his head.

Should he approach his ex? The thought made him shiver.

What he did know was that Mold was the last place he wanted to go. Deep in his sub-conscious part of his recent past lay cocooned. His conscious mind quaked as it slowly brought the tangled knot of misery into focus. Like a leaky tap when trying to sleep, the crescendo of noise hammered home its message. He tried to steal himself to deal with it.

He was suddenly glad that they'd bought only one bottle of wine.

'I'll make some calls tomorrow. Quinn, Jan and Irene Daniels, then go and see the police. After that, if I'm let out, I'll go and have a look at the boat.' He smiled thinly. 'I feel as though I'm looking at all these new people in my life through a film of oil on a dirty window. They're all indistinct - one of them puts their face close enough to see then retreats again into the fug.'

'You're rambling.'

'They're taunting me.'

'They are probably just as confused as you are. Quinn was Will's friend so feels some moral responsibility, Irene Daniels was doing a job and poor old Jan was going about her everyday stuff when she was attacked. I'm sure they're all just as keen as you to put an end to it.'

Mary fell silent and leant over to snuggle next to Harry. He could smell her hair, fresh and clean - he'd forgotten the comfort of closeness.

Chapter 26

When he woke, he was lying on the sofa wrapped in a rug. The first glimmer of dawn shimmered behind the curtains, he was cold and Mary was gone.

A note on the kitchen work-top near the kettle told him 'Call you later. Don't be too hard on the police.' He could see her smiling. Why the early start he wondered?

He made coffee and went to shower. Although he didn't ferret around too much, he saw no sign of Mary's old clothes. He didn't like the thought of her trooping round on her own - didn't like being without her full stop.

He turned on his mobile phone to send a brief text to Quinn and saw an incoming message waiting for him; caller unknown, number withheld. 'Please call 07967 443762 at your convenience'. It was convenient so he called. An anonymous answer machine prompted him to leave his own message, which he did, saying that he would have his phone with him all day.

He then sent a brief text to Quinn; 'Can you meet me at the boat at 4.00pm'. The reply, a few minutes later, was unhelpful and brief. 'No'. Great, he said to himself.

He phoned directory enquiries from Mary's landline to get the number for Parker and Williams which he keyed into his mobile for later. It was too early to call Jan either at home or the hospital so he made himself another coffee and turned on the television. Yet more problems in the Middle East, Health secretary under fire as a result of the loss of thousands of nursing jobs, Arsenal Manager grumbling about an incompetent referee. Weather forecaster blathers her way through a pack of lies. Local newscaster with an adenoid problem offering uninteresting titbits to the wrong camera.

He turned it off again but the silence challenged him to try and think constructively.

He found some 'Bran Flakes' in the kitchen cupboard and recalled a conversation with his wife, back at a time that semi-civilised conversation was still possible. 'It's good for you.' She had said.

'It tastes like chopped up leaf mould.'

'Put some honey on it to make it taste better.'

'If I need to enhance its flavour, why don't I just eat the honey?'

'It's good for you.'

'It's vile.'

'You need roughage.'

'What for?'

'Digestion; keep your gut healthy.'

'It is healthy and supremely efficient,' he'd said indignantly.

So, he'd had a bacon sandwich to be bloody minded.

That was just before all his troubles started. He felt it unjustified to blame everything on bran flakes but it made him think back to a previous existence - his wedding, his new wife and his portly father-in-law, so proud of his daughter but barely tolerant of Harry.

John Wainwright gregarious, smiling at everyone, till his gaze settled on Harry when the smile left his eyes - wine-flushed cheeks set in a flabby grin like a politician in crisis facing the cameras.

'Pop' had bloomed for the wedding, become the centre of attention, a position earned by the cash he'd laid out for the spectacular. He'd made a passable speech at the wedding breakfast, 'man who sinks into woman's arms soon has arms in woman's sink', that sort of thing. Head still, eyes down towards Harry; the butt, his straight man.

Susan's mother, hat smothered by an assortment of garish flora, had sat steadfast in her pink two-piece, smiling fixedly, wondering why the summer fruit puddings had collapsed, inwardly raging at the incompetence of the caterers. Her Jimmy Choo's throttled her feet - crazy, they spent most of the day hidden under white tablecloths anyway. She'd not only lost a daughter but had gained an oaf. He was a nice enough bloke 'our Harry' but he was an employee for goodness sake, poor stock.

Harry never felt he had married above himself – never felt much at all really except early on perhaps when he had the tingling of what he thought was his first true love. His best man had been a chap on the same course at university, their common interests, Grand Prix Motor Racing and Led Zeppelin.

Mind you, he was third choice. The previous two had turned out to be gay and were on their own 'honeymoon' in Malta. Not that it bothered Harry either way really, he would probably never see any of them again. Jonathon was the chap's name and he and Harry had been forced to collaborate on his speech to find anything vaguely amusing or interesting to say. The smell of the pit lane or the drum solos of the late John Henry Bonham had limited appeal to the mass audience. Most of the guests probably thought that Formula One was a baby food.

They'd come up with a fabrication about the pair letting a herd of cows loose onto a golf-course in Norfolk. 'And it's lovely to see so many familiar faces again here tonight' – which had bombed.

Confidence now in tatters, he had wished the gride and broom many years together and forgotten the toast. 'If you're ever in Slough, look me up,' he'd said before making a hasty exit. Harry hitherto never had and henceforth never would.

He leaned on the kitchen worktop and looked through the window. Outside the day was overcast and gloomy. Just about sums it up, he thought.

The concrete and glass of Shrewsbury Police Station had not seen a renaissance since his previous visit as he walked up the steps to go and face his nemesis. Harry wondered how a monstrosity like this could ever be built in such a lovely market town. Shrewsbury has an Abbey, a castle and historic, timber-framed buildings – how could the town planners think that this awful lump would enhance the town? Not his problem, just a shame.

He was half-way through the revolving door when his phone chirped so he carried on round and took the call outside. 'Mr Dunn?'

'Yes.'

'This is Margaret Walcott from The Grove.'

Harry's heart raced. 'Good morning, was it you that left me a mystery message earlier on?'

'It was late last night actually.'

'Oh, I'm sorry. What can I do for you?'

'The girl was called Chambers. She did not register under the name you gave me but as Celine Chambers. I hope that helps.'

Dumbstruck, Harry replied, 'Yes, I'm sure, er, thank you. You don't, um, know where she went by any chance?'

'No, but I can tell you that the person with whom she fell in love was, I believe, one of the people who worked on the extension to the clinic at the time.' After a brief pause she said quickly, 'I must go now, goodbye.' And without allowing Harry another word, she rang off.

He stood rooted to the spot when a familiar voice, very close to his ear said, 'Mr Dunn, you're facing the wrong way. Not thinking of disappearing again I trust.'

She glared at him, all fifteen stone of her, narrow-eyed as he turned to face her. A good three inches taller than Harry, her physical attributes were only part of her overall superiority. 'Follow me.' She said.

Same room, same format, same friendly disposition.

'Yes, I've been to France on holiday......'

'Near Toulouse......'

'Three days......'

'With a friend of mine......'

'That's none of your business......'

'It was purely a break. I just needed to get away,' glaring at his opponent, 'purely recreational......'

'A different place each night. Small Gites, I can't even tell you the name of the nearest village......' (Lie one)

'Why is taking a short holiday suspicious for goodness sake? I'm back and here voluntarily under my own steam. I have done absolutely nothing wrong. I am here to help you if I can......'

'I was informed by a friend via a text message......'

'His name is Roger......' (Lie two)

'No, you cannot have his bloody address just so you can go and frighten the life out of him......'

'I think it was insured. I mean I posted the amendments on the way to the airport. I hope they got the letter in time......'

'In time for me to be adequately covered......'

'No, I am not having any financial difficulties......'

'How can my boat being trashed be perceived as convenient? It was my house for God's sake......'

There was a pause while D.S. Groves left the room allowing both of them to calm down. Harry sighed and leaned back on the metal-framed chair looking up at the grubby ceiling. How the hell do you get coffee stains and fag burns on an eight-foot high ceiling? When she returned after around five minutes it was with a cup of tea – for herself.

'No, I have not seen the man with grey hair......' (Lie three)

'Absolutely sure. I've been on holiday......'

'No, I haven't seen my boat. I'm going there when I've finished helping you. I don't suppose you have found whoever was responsible.....?

'Well perhaps if you stopped hassling me you may have more chance of finding them......'

'I'm not trying to be rude or irritate you, I'm here to try and help you. I'm the victim here. My home has been broken into and I don't know why or by whom. I am rather frightened and would appreciate a bit of understanding. Do you treat all victims like this.....?'

'I'm sorry you don't like me but that's not my fault......'

'If the boat is habitable I will stay there, otherwise I will stay with a friend......'

'No, because I haven't asked them yet, but you can always contact me via my telephone. I have absolutely no intention of running away......'

'No, it's not the mate with the dog. Our friendship came to an end when he rendered me homeless......'

He walked away from the station knowing he had lied and considered buying a pad and pen so he could make notes but decided against it. Three little porkies, he'd remember them.

He got on the bus and as it rattled and wobbled its way to Ellesmere he promised himself a little car. Now the money from Will had cleared he was suddenly flush.

He walked towards his boat with trepidation, slowing down as he approached, not wanting to get there. From the outside it looked as if nothing had happened. The curtains were drawn and the cover over the front well-deck was zipped tight. The first sign of a problem was a deep gouge out of the wooden door near the lock where someone had obviously forced it with a jemmy or crowbar.

The interior was a complete mess, he could see that even before he drew back the curtains on the canal side. Paper strewn on the floor, the door of the fire open, ash and small lumps of coal on the rug; a knife had been used to slice open the leather seat and footrest and the foam had been ripped out. The contents of the cupboards were all over the floor; CD's, glasses, spare batteries all thrown about in a frenzy. The kitchen cupboards were open and pots, pans and cutlery were scattered on the linoleum. He was staring at the mess when he felt the boat sway as someone came aboard. D.S. Groves crouched in the doorway expressionless.

'Anything missing?' She asked, descending into the cabin.

'What the hell are you doing here?' asked Harry angrily, 'why didn't you say you were coming, you could have given me a lift.'

'Don't want to make things too easy for you - and to check that you did what you said you were going to do - for a change.'

Harry shook his head and sighed. He reached up to the ceiling and flicked a light-switch but nothing happened.

'Never a dull moment eh?'

'Ha, bloody ha.'

She smirked.

'Well, what's missing?'

'How would I know? It's all my uncle's stuff, I didn't know what he had.' He turned away from her and on hands and knees made a show of putting things back in the cupboards.

'Don't bang your head on the way out, will you?' he said.

'Look here funny man,' said D.S. Groves to his back, 'I don't believe half of what you said this morning. Believe me, I will find out. Too much has happened around you for it all to be coincidence and I intend to get to the bottom of it and that will happen sooner rather than later. Now think carefully how miserable you would like me to make your life. You were quite right back at the station, I think you are a clever little bugger and I dislike everything about you. If I could come up with a reason to arrest you right now I would, but by the skin of your teeth you can stay here in this mess - off the record.'

'I WILL see you again - on the record.' She bent double and clambered out. Despite the onslaught, Harry's final view of her inelegant contortions and substantial posterior made him grin. Despite everything, he chuckled, the tension broken.

It took him an hour and a half to fill a dustbin-liner with ripped clothing, broken glass and china. He put a bath towel over the chair and another over the stool to hide the slashed leather. The cupboards were in some sort of order - his order now.

By lunchtime he was hungry but sadly out of beans. With a choice of pineapple chunks or a tin of button mushrooms he made do with a coffee, black. The telly wouldn't work because he'd moved the boat and the aerial was pointing at a stand of trees and there was no hot water. Apart from that, he thought to himself, everything's pretty good.

He thought about taking the boat back to the marina but thought again as he was facing the wrong direction. He'd have to turn it round sometime but had no idea how far the next turning point was. There was one a hundred yards behind him but there was no way he was going to go backwards without help.

He tried Mary's phone but it was switched off, the hospital told him that Jan had been discharged and the answer machine was on at the B & B where he left a message. He sent a text to Quinn saying, 'HELP!'

'Fat chance,' came the reply, 'Lock Tavern 2.30.' He was obviously close by and had seen Harry, at least he appeared to have some sense of humour. It was still only 1.30pm so he had plenty of time. He phoned Parker and Williams; 'Office temporarily closed'. Mm, thought Harry. He fell asleep and woke at

2.15, swore loudly and jumped on the bike. The towpath had dried out but despite that he found it hard work and arrived at the pub fifteen minutes late, wobbly-legged but dry.

Harry had lunched on a packet of dry-roasted and a bag of cheese and onion when Quinn arrived ten minutes later. It was difficult to conceal such a physical presence but dressed in brown brogues, green corduroys, Barbour jacket over a chunky-knit grey turtle-neck jumper he looked more country farmer than highly trained defender of the realm. Add to that a neat haircut, no moustache and a pair of wire-rimmed glasses under a tweed flat cap he was a different man. He carried a black hold-all and performed the same observational routine as on the previous occasion and only joined Harry after a suitable interlude.

'Well?' he asked.

'Fine thanks,' replied Harry.

'Don't get smart,' growled his companion, 'what have you learnt?'

Harry had anticipated this question but his brain turned to mush at the critical juncture. He knew, had seen with his own eyes, that this chap was not someone to try and hoodwink and had decided an exchange of information was the only way to keep him onside - and keep himself out of hospital.

'Look,' said Quinn, 'I'm trying to be patient and I've got better things to do than follow you about. Be straight or be on your own.'

Harry talked. He spoke about France - Felines, Caylus, Paris and he told him about The Grove. He summarised his talk with Madame Lauran and thought he had captured the horror of the story but judging by Quinn's reaction he might as well have been talking about Winnie the Pooh. He told him about his interview with the cops and the call from Margaret Walcott.

'Busy boy,' said Quinn, 'what next?'

'Insufficient planning then another lurch into the unknown probably - but to be honest we're rather stuck. The name Chambers is our first concrete lead - it's as if someone wanted us to probe, give us a titbit to get us going. It originated at The Grove so it seems to me that the clinic is pivotal.' He paused and asked 'What was Will's connection to the place? He left them something in his will didn't he?'

Quinn sat silently and stared at Harry, motionless, waiting.

'There is something else. I didn't tell you the name of Will's friend, the one who actually shot Leport. I'm sorry I kept it to myself, but I didn't know you from Adam and I wanted to hold at least one card even if it didn't seem to be of much significance. The guy was called Derek Crabtree. It turns out he'd been abused as a child and the episode in France had affected him deeply. Anyway he..'

'Committed suicide.' Said Quinn, 'I know.' Harry froze.

Quinn unzipped his holdall and brought out the laptop.

'You! Why?'

'Two reasons. One, to find out what you had not been telling me and two, self-preservation. There were things you hadn't told me. Not much I'll grant you but I'm glad you've put that right. There may also have been something on here that could compromise my safety - unlikely, but possible.'

'Jesus Christ!' said Harry loud enough for the two people at the bar to turn.

'Shut up,' said Quinn quietly, 'and listen.' So Harry did.

Chapter 27

When he got back to the boat he'd phoned Mary but she'd been reluctant to tell him where she had been after leaving the flat so early. He eventually prised out of her that she'd had a hospital appointment. Before that she'd sat by a radiator and had a quiet word with one of the two people she truly trusted.

Not realising that he was one of them, Harry had been miffed that she hadn't confided in him. He would have gone with her he'd said. He'd been so pre-occupied with his own feelings that when he'd finally got round to asking her how she'd got on, she wouldn't tell him, which had made him feel even worse.

His sleep had been broken by a series of terrible dreams.

When he'd woken, reality and horror were intertwined. He dripped with sweat and his chest ached. Fingers and toes tingled and he was back on the plane, trapped and terrified. When he'd tried to raise himself from the bed he was unable to move, a force held him flat on his back. He was aware of his surroundings but something in his sub-conscious had taken control, trapping him, forcing him to face his demons. Finally released from his nightmare he leapt from the bed and stood on shaking legs. In sweat-soaked T-shirt he leant on the cabin wall breathing deeply, trying to calm down.

An hour later he felt better. He walked up to the road and made his way into town in the Ford Focus he'd hired for a fortnight and went to see Mary. He parked in Tesco's car park and took a roundabout route walking to the flat - through Tesco, along the riverbank, down unknown roads, back through the superstore and finally to the flat. He felt like a sleuth and if he hadn't been weary and wary would probably have enjoyed himself.

He gave Mary a warm hug and asked how she was; 'OK', she replied. She looked tired though and he watched her as unobtrusively as possible. She sensed him looking out of the corner of his eye until she caught him and had told him to stop fussing.

They had a quiet couple of hours – he because he was worried about feeling guilty and she because she was worried.

She decided to tell him the truth in an effort to alleviate both sets of feelings; told him that she had had to have a liver scan. This was one of the places where the cancer may spread or re-appear and she had been having some discomfort. The results would be back in a week and if the news was bad the prognosis would probably be worse. Yes, she was worried.

Harry felt a surge of adrenalin, then cold fear, then helplessness. He berated himself because the first instinct was fear for himself, fear of losing a friend and the possibility of being alone again so soon. Then he realized his selfishness.

Later he thought more rationally, trying to imagine the terror that Mary must be feeling.

He realised that however much he pulled himself together and supported her; she would walk a lonely road.

He saw her in a new light, as someone vulnerable. He felt a desire to protect her from her fate, to treat her gently, wrap her up, make it all go away. Impossible he knew. Take it minute by minute, hour by hour; just be there. She was the same person as a few moments ago, but knowledge changed things, especially if it was something you didn't want to hear – subconsciously it changed the way he saw her. When you're suddenly faced with the possibility of losing someone, they become all the more important.

He wanted to help her but at the same time was desperate to ignore it. She had lived with the threat for a lifetime, a horror she locked away in a dark place and that fickle finger held the only key.

He made her a cup of tea. Well, that's what you do isn't it?

Smile, try and keep the sympathy out of it. In the end it would be her strength that would drag them both through. He had to help give her that strength.

He understood why she had broken down in the hotel room in France – could begin to understand the pressure, the conscious effort required to suppress the demons that danced before her eyes every waking moment.

He'd had two hours of it, she half a lifetime. And he was sure that there were things she had not told him.

Jesus!

Later he found out more as during that same afternoon they'd set out in the car. Harry's attempts at frivolity were met with pursed-lip smiles, so they were silent. He drove following Mary's directions and they arrived in Nantwich about an hour later. They parked fifty yards from Brine Leas High School on the opposite side of the road.

Mary wrapped a scarf around her head and put on a pair of horn-rimmed glasses retrieved from her handbag. She got out of the car, leant with her forearms on the roof and looked in the direction of the school. Harry got out and stood beside her. They stood quietly for a few minutes as other vehicles pulled in around them waiting for the children to emerge from school.

With the smallest nod of her head towards the gates, Mary said, 'the blonde girl there, blue top, black trousers, sports bag over her shoulder; that's my daughter.' Harry turned and stared at Mary, then back towards the school.

The girl, who Harry thought was probably eleven or twelve, stood chatting and smiling with her friends. One by one the group dispersed to be driven away by their guardians.

The girl climbed into a red VW Beetle and as the car drove towards them Mary turned away to lean with her back to the car. Harry watched the Beetle pass and saw the girl talking to the woman driver. From a brief glance the driver was young with dark, curly hair and the daughter's profile was instantly recognisable as a young Mary.

Harry turned to look at her as a tear ran down her cheek. She took off her glasses and scarf and stuffed them in her bag then climbed into the passenger seat.

'Your daughter?' said Harry quietly as he got in beside her.

'Lucy. She's twelve.'

Harry knew when to keep his mouth shut, so he did. He squeezed her hand gently and drove off.

'I had to let her go Harry. She was seven years old and I had to let her go. Oh dear God.' She put her hands to her face and wept.

Chapter 28

As they had entered the flat, Mary said, 'I'd like to be alone for a little while.' She gently squeezed his upper arm and smiled. Then she walked into the bedroom and closed the door behind her.

Harry walked into town. A steady drizzle soaked his anorak and drips of water fell from the rim of his hat onto his trainers. A few hardy shoppers traipsed up and down Pride Hill and the lights from the shops dissolved in the murk. As he trudged aimlessly it dawned on him that any problems he had were mere trivia.

The shabby girl with her Big Issues was working overtime and a market researcher was huddled in a telephone shop doorway smoking. People shopped out of necessity, no levity, it wasn't a day for enjoying it.

He tried to concentrate on his own predicament but couldn't focus. His mind always returned to Mary. He travelled with his emotions this time, allowed himself no succour. Don't hide them, don't let them become Crabtree's knotted fist. Let go, acknowledge the fear. He had even been on the verge of tears at one point, but as he arrived at the flat there was an underlying anger not only at Mary's nightmare but also how someone had manipulated and mashed his own life.

He could do something positive about both of them and as he unlocked the door to the flat he felt a new resolve. Mary's appointment was six days away and to be strong for her he needed to be in a fit state himself. He shivered, shook his head clear and walked into the flat.

Harry had sat and read the Shropshire Star. Under the headline 'Council to charge charity shops', the brief story that followed had outlined council bosses plans to charge charity shops for the removal of rubbish for the first time. They'll just have to put it back on the shelves Harry had thought. He was still smiling as Mary came into the room.

'Don't stop,' she said.

'What?'

'Smiling. Each one is worth a thousand pats on the head.' And smiled herself. 'What's tickled you anyway?'

He showed her the article and related his unspoken response.

'You are unkind.'

'It's the adverts that really tickle me, here listen to this. In the for sale section here: 'For sale: Girl Guides uniform to fit nine-year-old. £15. On the page opposite in the wanted section: Wanted: Girl Guides uniform to fit 10-year-old. Also Bull-worker. Must be cheap.' Now this chap really has got a problem. He chortled again.

Mary laughed and for a precious moment her worries disappeared.

Lesson here, thought Harry.

They shared a bottle of Wolf Blass yellow label Shiraz with their pizza. 'Love it,' purred Harry holding his glass to the light. Mary smiled at her friend.

The following morning Mary had gone to the public library to investigate the name Celine Chambers on the internet because Harry had stupidly left his laptop on the boat. The Office of National Statistics, Family Records Centre, UK BMD and various genealogy sites had all failed her. Dead end, she'd told Harry. Unfortunate turn of phrase, he'd replied.

She'd even tried the Deed Poll register but as only one in two hundred name changes are 'enrolled', thus made public, that proved a non-starter as well. If Celine had changed her surname prior to the birth of her child, if she actually did give birth, then any record of the child would be virtually untraceable anyway.

They discussed it and concluded that Margaret Walcott's supplementary information regarding the builder was perhaps the avenue to follow. But first they had an appointment.

They'd met in a Little Chef off the by-pass to the south of Shrewsbury. Quinn sat with his back to a corner, eyes on permanent patrol, Mary and

Harry faced him. He'd greeted Mary with a hug – Harry could hardly believe his eyes – not jealous, merely astonished at this show of affection. Surely not the same man who acted like a hard-ball and whose piercing stare could drill for diamonds. Harry had looked sideways at Mary who either hadn't seen him or had ignored him.

The Grove, he had told them, was and still is a very private clinic. Because of that, certain associates of mine had cause to be guests (as he termed it) on a rehabilitative basis. Although we do not use the clinic nowadays, it was used sparingly back then, as were one or two similar establishments. Someone injured on a deniable assignment required a place of total privacy and discretion to recuperate, secure from unwanted intrusion or awkward questions.

In the early sixties a high-ranking operative was 'in residence' when a junior officer was dispatched to deliver some important papers to him. The documents were too sensitive to trust to the postal service so were delivered in person – that junior was Will. He'd only been in the service days so it was quite a responsibility.

Because of the nature of their work, a list of all residents was forwarded to HQ whenever one of our operatives was there. Will would have had access to this list and it appears that Celine being there at the same time was merely a freakish coincidence. I can only presume that, because of what happened to the girl in Felines, Will showed his gratitude to the clinic by means of a legacy.

She was not there long and he was probably unaware that she had left shortly afterwards. Under no circumstances whatsoever would Will reveal the true nature of The Grove. Quinn told them he doubted that the place needs financial assistance because the 'guest list' has read like a who's who for decades and I'm sure that gratitude has been liberally dispensed.

The Grove is owned by an organisation called The Freedom Trust whose registered office is that of a firm of City accountants called Hardy, Squire and Partners. The Trust owns two further clinics, one near Rhayader, Mid Wales called Wye Lodge and a third in North Yorkshire called Sternthorpe Hall, seven miles from Scarborough.

The name of the company that built the extension was G.D. Howarth & Co. They were based in Devizes, Wiltshire, and were in turn owned by Western Estates Ltd whose H.Q. was in Bristol. Howarth's ceased trading in 1984 but Western Estates remains to this day and continues to thrive in Property Development, Land and Asset Management, Timber Imports and Archaeological / Environmental Evaluation.

He'd presumed that the Walcott lady had not spun them a yarn, so had made some enquiries.

He'd handed Harry two typed sheets of paper and asked him to read and digest them before passing them to Mary. There is, he had said, something you may find of interest.

They did.

Chapter 29

Harry leant on a dry-stone wall wrapped up against the chill. Clouds close enough to touch, rolled above him as he stared down on the farmhouse that had once been his home. A bobble hat was pulled down over his ears and gloved hands nestled deep in the pockets of his green quilted coat, collar upturned to keep the cold breeze off his neck. His reminiscences were plucked away by the frigid air and scattered over the bleak terrain.

It was the same house but barely recognisable from the rough and ready place he had once called home. The farmer who had bought the place from Harry had sold it within a few months at a substantial profit. The new owners, obviously people of means, had transformed the smallholding into something for which estate agent's flowery rhetoric was invented.

There was no sign of the burned out wreck that was Harry's lasting impression. New slate roof, sandblasted freshly-pointed stone walls, hand-crafted timber-frame windows and a gravel driveway that crossed the field from a white gate some three hundred yards distant ending in a semi-circle in front of the house big enough for a dozen cars. The pale gravel like an anaemic scar slashed into the landscape. One car sat there now; a red Range Rover, looking like it had been born there.

The whole property, around five acres, was surrounded by new post and rail fencing on the three lower boundaries, rising to the fourth, the wall upon which Harry now leant. A large pond had been dug surrounded by newly planted trees and shrubs that awaited the warm breath of spring. Pathways criss-crossed levelled fields surrounding the house; a landscape-gardener's dream, an illusion created by a computer programme with little sympathy for the past. The whole a tasteless splash of colour on an age-old sepia landscape.

Would there be more reward for the guardians of this clinical panorama than experienced by his parents throughout their daily grind? Yes, very probably, he concluded.

The only tinge of regret, if that is what Harry really felt, was purely financial. This could all have been his and worth a fortune. But would he have wanted the full package? Timber Merchants, in-laws, Susan, golf club, damp depressing town, memories best left alone - all the real cost of this house. He had moved on, or was in the process of doing so, and he had glimpsed a future. Mary's cancer gathered out to sea like a bank of storm clouds - he prayed for an offshore wind. But overall, no he wouldn't swap.

He knew he had to lay his ghosts to rest and his thoughts turned to their meeting with Quinn. Indeed, he was back in Wales as a result of that meeting and what the report contained.

Chapter 30

He saw Susan leave the golf club entrance and walk to her car. She looked thin and pale. She was on her own and was dressed in golfing garb - red slacks and dark blue Y-neck jumper over a white shirt. She walked unsteadily carrying her black handbag in one hand and a white baseball cap in the other. It took her two attempts to unlock the car door with the remote control and when she slid into the driving seat she leaned her head back and exhaled, puffing out her cheeks. Susan was a wreck.

Harry sat in the Ford across the road from the car-park entrance and watched her manoeuvre out of the gate. He started the engine and followed.

His mind drifted back to their time together.

Theirs had been a union of what? Not convenience, not necessity - maybe what they thought was love.

As he followed the silver BMW away from the town he thought about the house they shared, their few friends at the golf club - her friends now. Their increasingly inert marriage had been rumbling up a blind canyon even before the intervention of her father - a rift valley, he thought with a sardonic smile.

Their life may have looked fine to the townsfolk. They had enough money and status but they were large fish in a murky pond and had choked on the silt thrown up by her father's misery. Even if they could have found some common ground they'd never stood a chance.

What Harry couldn't figure out was why Pop Wainwright had suddenly turned against him with such ferocity. He was here to find some answers. His stomach churned at the prospect of tackling Susan but by the look of it she wasn't doing well herself.

She turned through the gateway of a detached brick-built house. Perhaps three-bedroomed and private, it stood alone back from the road and was surrounded by a six-foot beech hedge which someone had kept neatly trimmed. There were no other cars on the herring-bone brick driveway so he followed her in and parked close behind her.

She leapt from the car, turned and looked aghast 'What the hell do you think you're ....', and stopped. She stared and her rheumy eyes re-gained their focus. 'Harry! What in God's name are you doing here?'

'Hello Susan.'

'What do you want?'

'Just to talk.'

'You shouldn't be here. I'll call the police.' But it was said without conviction and her body appeared to surrender as she leant on the car and looked down at the drive. 'You aren't supposed to be here,' she said weakly. Her eyes were bloodshot but to a casual observer she could have been crying.

He was silent for a moment. 'I just want to talk to you Susan. I think you owe me that.'

'Owe,' she said, 'what's that meant to mean? It was you that left; you that ran away. You're weak Harry. You couldn't face up to your grubby crimes so you just up and left.' She was recovering some initiative 'Can you imagine how I felt? My husband was a pervert - I had to face our friends, listen to their fake sympathy, endure their knowing looks, it was awful. You bastard!' She turned and set off towards the front door but Harry ran up and grabbed her elbow.

'Let go of me this minute or I'll scream.'

He spun her round and looked her in the eye, 'No you won't; you'll listen.'

She shrugged herself free and walked into the house. He followed her down the hallway into the kitchen where she leant with her back to the worktop and folded her arms defiantly.

'You've got two minutes, then I'm calling my father.'

'Look, can we just talk like two sensible adults. How about a cup of coffee?'

'I don't need any bloody coffee, I'm listening.'

Harry sighed and looked beyond her through the window to the neatly trimmed rear lawn. A few white and yellow narcissi were dotted around the border but the roses and shrubs were skeletal. The small figurine fountain in the centre of the lawn looked dead, vanquished by the long winter.

'I didn't do it Susan. Whatever I am or was, whatever my faults, I would never hurt children. Someone set me up, planted that stuff on my computer and made sure it was found. God knows I'm not perfect, you of all people know that, but someone was out to ruin me and whoever it was made a pretty good job of it.' She made to interrupt but he held his hand up. 'Please let me finish; then if you want to throw me out you can.'

He paused gathering his thoughts. 'The images were found by someone brought in by your father to work on the office computer system. I didn't know the guy and find it hard to believe he was wholly responsible, though he must have played his part. I believe the person behind this was your father. Why, I'm not sure, but an awful lot has happened recently. I'm sure you agree that at the time we were going nowhere and I admit that, pathetically, I just gave up. I need to find answers and I think you can help me and hope you will.'

'I can't help you. Even if I could, why should I?'

'Because one thing you possess, however deeply buried, is integrity. I don't particularly blame you for anything that happened to us. It takes two to make such a fuck-up of a marriage and I am willing to take the lion's share of the blame. I'm not surprised you took up with someone else, I'm sure he was a better prospect than the boring old fart I'd become. What I want you to believe is that though I may have been dreary, I am not, nor ever have been, a pervert.'

Without objection from Susan he walked over and filled the kettle. 'Like one?' he asked.

'Coffee's in the cupboard over there,' she said pointing vaguely.

'How do you have it?'

'Strong, black, two sugars.'

From the tree he took two mugs; 'Home sweet home' embossed on the side. Mm. While the kettle boiled he leant on the worktop, arms straight and locked, with his back to Susan. Not wanting to push his luck, he had his coffee black too. He'd spotted one cup, saucer and side plate in the sink and judged that milk was probably not something she required, being on her own.

'How is your father?' he asked handing her the mug.

'What do you care?'

'I'm just trying to be civil.'

'If you must know, he's not very well. He's worried about mother. She was diagnosed with leukaemia last year and it's taken its toll on both of them. I sometimes think he's worse off than she is.'

'I'm sorry to hear that. It must be an awful time for you. I understand how difficult it can be.'

'What would you know about it?'

'More than you think.'

'Are you ill?'

'No, it's someone I know, a friend. I know it's hard. If you let it, it can take over.'

She was silent for a time. 'Where did you go?'

'I went to stay with an old school-friend in Shrewsbury. When he kicked me out I rented a squalid room in a doss-house.'

'Who's this friend of yours, the one who's ill?'

'Just someone I met. We had plenty in common - like no money, no prospects and one friend each.'

'You don't look like you're on the bread line.'

'I took a job in a supermarket,' he lied, 'I'm getting by but I do need to know why what happened did. I'm not after money or anything, just the truth. As far as I'm concerned I must go forward and I have to start by nailing the past.' He wasn't keen on lying but he was less keen on telling the truth.

She studied him; 'Look, say I could help you, what exactly is it you want?'

'I would like you to talk to your father. Ask him what happened and why. But I don't want him to know that it was me that was asking. Make out it came from you, as if you're trying to reconcile what went on last year, so you can move on,' with the emphasis on the 'you'.

'Don't want much do you? You're asking me to deceive my own father so you can get your life back on track. You've got to be joking. Besides, I've only got your word for it that you're not a pervert.'

He looked her in the eye. It was she who broke contact. She looked down at the floor, 'I'm sorry, that was uncalled for.'

'Forget it. Look Susan, I know that what we had wasn't perfect but if you won't do it for me alone don't you feel you owe it to yourself to find out the truth. Perhaps it will help you move on too, allow you to hold your head up with your friends. The only person who will convince you is your dad. Maybe he thought I wasn't good enough for you and devised a way to see me off. He had to discredit me to such an extent that I would disappear and he made a pretty good job of it. Please help me.'

She turned to look out of the window and said finally 'I'll think about it. Now I'd like you to leave.'

He'd left his mobile number and said that she could call at any time, day or night. Had he done enough to win her support he wondered?

He was sure of two things; firstly, that he was right not to tell her everything, especially because of what Quinn's notes had revealed and secondly, that the moment he had seen her bloodshot eyes he had come to a dreadful realisation.

Mary was waiting for him in the lounge. They'd agree to meet at the Castle Hotel in St Peters Square, Ruthin some 10 miles from Mold.

'How did it go?' asked Mary with a note of concern.

'Just like we'd never been apart - not much communication, no mutual trust, one of us pissed and the conversation lasted about five minutes.

She grinned. 'Will she help us though?'

'I don't know honestly. As we agreed beforehand I didn't tell her much, but I played on the self-help angle. In other words, she could help herself as well as me by learning the truth.'

'And?'

'Not sure. We'll have to wait and see.' He leaned back on the sofa they were sharing and studied the art deco chandelier.

'There's something else isn't there?' asked Mary. 'What is it? Do you still feel something for her?'

Harry looked quickly at Mary and took her hand. 'Absolutely not,' he said and smiled. 'We never really had anything in the first place and what there was has been demolished. I was thinking about how I can learn from previous mistakes, like not being overpowered by a bully father-in-law.'

'No danger of that here,' said Mary and gripped his hand.

They'd agreed with Quinn beforehand that using Susan was probably the best way to go forward. The key was getting her to speak to her father. They had to have someone on the inside. Even if they got no direct answers through her they may 'shake something loose', as Quinn put it. This was why they also thought that keeping both Quinn and Mary out of the way for the time being would be safer. In effect Harry was being hung out and any feedback or repercussion would land on him. Bait.

Quinn had said he would 'keep an eye on him'.

It was forty-eight hours to Mary's appointment and neither had spoken a word of it since their discussion in the flat two days previously. God it was hard. A news bulletin or a glimpse of a newspaper reminded Harry of the disease that caused such misery; 'new wonder drugs', 'treatment post-code lottery', even the bloody horoscopes – constant reminders.

Every indication brought a surge of adrenaline. Don't worry about what you can't change, they say - but it's not that easy.

Why the hell is everyone so cheerful, don't they realise that my best friend might be dying.

Suddenly an image appeared – goodness knows where it came from but he thought of his dead mother's spectacles - a heartbreaking reminder of something so personal on which she had been totally reliant, now redundant. He swallowed.

Chapter 31

His palms were sweaty as he clung to the tiller. Beautiful countryside drifted by unnoticed. He was taking Box Car Willy back to Leebank. He'd plucked up courage and set off for a turning point a mile or so from where the boat had been abandoned for what seemed like weeks.

As he approached he gauged the turn and turned into the open space on his left but won no awards for style as he crashed the bow into the bank then reversed off at some pace. To prevent the ill-tempered monster reversing into the steel piling on the opposite bank he was forced to engage forward gear and rev hard, which flooded the towpath. A man on a nearby bridge looked down knowingly.

At least someone's enjoying it, thought Harry.

Seven-point turn (approximately) and he was heading home. He preferred the blind panic experienced during his failure to control sixteen tons of steel to the dull, to the desperate panic of Mary's wait.

'Good job there mon,' said the man on the bridge in a soft Shropshire accent. A hairy dog's head appeared and gave a solitary bark endorsing his master's appraisal.

'Glad there were no cameras about,' shouted Harry.

'Oh, I've seen far worse.'

Harry slipped under the bridge and out of sight, alone once again with his thoughts. The brief encounter with the stranger brought a flicker of a smile then Mary butted in and the smile died.

He phoned Ron and told him he'd managed to turn round on a wide stretch. Ron had told him it was a turning circle know as a winding hole. He wove an uncertain course as he dialled - even at four miles per hour it didn't take much to get off line. Ron said he fancied some fresh air so would walk out to meet him and give him a hand with the lift bridges. See you an hour or so, he'd said.

Ron had the bridge up and stood to attention as Harry clunked and scraped his way through the narrow opening. 'I've got some spare paint,' laughed Ron, 'keep going I'll walk down and get the next bridge.'

Negotiated with equal ineptitude this bridge was the last before the marina so Ron hopped on the back deck to join Harry.

'Thanks for that Ron. What kind of a welcome can I expect from Tom?'

'Actually, he's going through a good patch. You'll be OK I think, you've done him a favour. That reporter came asking questions but Tom convinced her that there was no major scoop and turned it round and got her to do a feature on the Marina. He's sold three boats in the last few days off the back of it. He's alright as long as he's in pocket and in charge.'

'I'll still keep out of his way for a while.'

'How have things been going anyway? Have you sorted it?'

'No, not really. I've had an interesting few days to say the least but it's got mighty complicated - I'll tell you about it sometime. We've stirred some things up so there's a chance that the doo-dah will hit the fan any time.'

'We?'

'Yes, me and a couple of friends, well, one friend and one puppeteer - I'm trying to keep them out of the way, especially the friend. As I say I'll give you the full story when I know how it finishes. I'll have you round for something to eat with Ralph, or we can go out for a pint.'

'I like a pint.'

'Good choice.'

Harry steered the boat onto the marina and after scraping more paint off on the jetty, tied up.

'Oh, by the way,' he said, 'I've got a red light on.'

'Where?'

'On the back of the toilet.'

'It's full, needs emptying.'

'What do you mean it needs emptying?'

'It's a cassette. You take it round and sluice it out in the building over there.' Waving airily towards the shop.

'Bloody hell,' said Harry, 'didn't bargain for that. I don't like the idea of carrying my own..... well you know.'

'You get used to it. All part of boating. Come on I'll show you what to do.'

With a sour look on his face Harry had performed his duties.

He'd half expected the Shropshire Star reporter to leap out from behind a wall and photograph him transporting his dangerous goods. He could see the headline, 'Assault suspect lugs logs to loos'. God, the ignominy.

The sun shone and there was a hint of spring in the air as he walked the short distance to the B & B. Before he had the chance to knock, the door was opened by a replica of Jan - younger and very pretty with mousy hair, cut short. He introduced himself and got a disinterested reception.

She wore an 'Eden Project' sweatshirt. 'Have you been there?' asked Harry pointing self-consciously at the young lady's chest.

'Mail order,' was the curt reply as she turned and walked away from him down the hall.

Jan sat in an armchair near the Aga and smiled warmly as he followed the girl into the kitchen.

'Harry, how lovely to see you.'

'It's good to see you too, you look great.'

'Liar.' She said.

'You do really. How are you feeling?'

'A bit wobbly but not too bad. You've met Cara, my daughter.'

'Yes, briefly. She's your spitting image.'

'With a bit of creative visualisation perhaps. She's staying for a few days till I get my strength back.'

Something touched the back of Harry's leg. 'Christ!' he shouted jumping forward clutching his thigh. He turned to see Dave, front legs apart staring in silent challenge. Both ladies laughed as the dog moved slowly towards Harry who was in reverse and heading for the wall.

'Dave,' said Jan, 'behave yourself, you know Harry. Leave him alone.'

There was a brief stand-off before Harry moved forward making appropriate noises and stroked the dog's head. He was rewarded with a brief wag before the dog settled at Jan's feet.

'I hope you're not going to cause any more trouble,' said Cara with some authority looking at Harry.

She was around twenty years of age and though young, had a determined air about her.

'Leave him love, it wasn't his fault. He probably saved my life, if it hadn't been for Harry goodness only knows what might have happened. Come here Harry, give me a hug.'

He bent forward and got a kiss and a thank you with his hug. Dave growled.

'I'm glad you got the dog back,' he said backing off and sitting in one of the chairs near the table, 'strained as our relationship is I hate to think of him in some pen.'

'Her.'

'Sorry, her.'

The dog looked at Harry from below her eyelids - he was uncertain if their friendship would develop but he was sure that it would be the dog that made the decision.

'How have you been getting on? Asked Jan.

Harry told her much the same as he had told Ron; that he was making progress and that he would try and explain everything soon. He was desperate to tell her about Mary but held back. He really felt as if he needed to share his fears, needed to be told that everything would be alright. Even though he was in turmoil he knew she had enough to cope with so remained silent.

'Where did you learn the medical stuff anyway?' asked Jan.

'I did a First Responders course with the Welch Ambulance Service in Ruthin. About the only positive thing I got from that bloody country. I never got the chance to put it into practice though before I left.'

'What's a First Responder?' asked Cara

'In rural areas,' explained Harry, 'ambulances can struggle to reach emergency cases within their allotted response time, about eight minutes from memory, so they've trained lay-people like me to take the calls and deal with things till the paramedics arrive.' He looked over at Jan, 'I was sitting next to you on the bed trying to wake you when you packed up. I'm bloody glad I took that course now.'

'Me too.' They smiled at each other.

'I'll make the tea then should I?' said Cara with an indignant note in her voice and stomped off. She made more noise than necessary trying to break the spell of an intimate situation to which she hadn't been invited. Jan smiled knowingly at Harry.

'Cara's been fantastic, I can't tell you how glad I am that she's here. I've got some guests booked in at the end of next week so I've got a target.'

'Blimey, that sounds a bit soon. Can't you put them off?'

'They're regulars and I can't afford to start turning people away. If they go somewhere else they might not come back.'

'I'll be glad to help if I can.'

'We'll be fine thank you,' said Cara pointedly as she poured the tea. 'We'll be glad of some cheerful company by then.'

Harry held up a digestive biscuit and looked at Dave who stared back unmoving, chin on the floor. Harry raised his eyebrows to Jan who nodded.

'Here Dave, want some biscuit?'

The dog didn't move a muscle so Harry leaned forward holding out the titbit. Still she didn't move. He got down on his knees and held half the biscuit towards the dog who opened her mouth but left her bottom jaw on the floor. 'Come on you lazy devil,' he said. He actually placed the biscuit in the dog's mouth and the jaws snapped shut. A couple of half-hearted chews and a noisy swallow later it was all over. The dog hadn't taken her eyes off Harry. Two wags and her eyes closed.

Jan invited Harry to stay for dinner but he declined saying he had some things to do so said his goodbyes and left. 'Don't get up Dave, I'll see myself out.' One wag.

As he walked down the road on his way to the marina his phone alerted him to a text message. 'Meet me at the bluff tomorrow at noon. Susan.' His heart pounded.

He'd forgotten about the bluff. It had been their secret, a place they used to meet years ago - Harry's idea of a witty. Their bluff was not a promontory or a headland, it was a graveyard. A place they could go in peace. Clandestine meetings in a sea of lost souls and fumbling about to an audience of ghouls. It hadn't got much better either.

They hadn't really needed to keep their relationship secret, the only people who really gave a damn were he and Susan. Except Susan's parents that is who would have preferred Harry to occupy the graveyard on a more permanent basis.

Whatever his feelings, as Quinn had suspected, they had indeed 'shaken something loose'. They were off.

He called Mary at the flat and told her about the arrangement and that he would see her tomorrow afternoon. She'd asked to come with him. 'No,' he said, 'I don't want to frighten her off.'

'Thanks a lot.'

'You know what I mean.'

'Don't exclude me Harry please, I'm not a cripple.'

'I know that and I'm not suggesting this for the sake of it. There's no point in exposing you. If you know what I mean,' he added quickly, 'I just think it makes sense in this case. I'm going to stay on the boat tonight. I'll see you tomorrow.'

'OK then. Bye, take care.'

'I will.'

He wanted to be with her, but selfishly he was glad to have some distance. He found it so difficult being with her having to share her distress. A night alone on the boat would re-charge his emotional batteries. He'd need them full because in less than forty-eight hours she was back at the hospital. He'd be there then.

He phoned her again.

'I just wanted to say that.....' he dried up, 'to say that I'm, er, very fond of you.'

Long silence.

'I'm very fond of you too Harry.'

'Yes, well, goodbye then.'

'Good night Harry.'

Chapter 32

Ruthin Church was originally a chapel-of-ease under the Mother Church of Llanrhydd. It is dedicated to St. Peter and was built and endowed in 1310. The church is famed for the beautiful Oak Roof of its north aisle......

.....He had arrived early and was browsing through a brochure trying to appear enlightened. None of it was of interest now, nor had it been when he'd tried to persuade Susan to have a fumble.

He was aware though that the fine, ancient building had stood up to a battering from the modern world better than his marriage.

The voice came from behind him and it certainly wasn't his ex-wife. 'Don't turn round. Stand still and say nothing. That way you might not get hurt.' It was however menacing enough for Harry to comply and he wasn't keen on the use of the word 'might'.

'You have been poking your nose into something that is causing certain people a great deal of distress. With some reluctance I am here to issue a final warning. I was of the opinion that we should take more decisive action but, fortunately for you, I was persuaded not to harm you - at this stage. Believe me it would give me the greatest pleasure to bring your little escapade to a sudden and messy conclusion. A dear friend of mine has lost an arm and half his face because of your meddling. He probably won't survive but if he does there is only a slim chance that he will walk again. I can categorically assure you that you will neither walk, talk, see, hear nor anything else ever again if it is deemed necessary for my services to be called upon in the future. Do I make myself absolutely clear?'

Harry swallowed. 'Absolutely.'

He'd been taken by surprise - it wasn't the first time he'd been caught with his pants down here but despite what was obviously a real threat he was angry.

'She had nothing to be frightened of from me. Why didn't she come herself?' he asked.

Silence. He went on the offensive.

'Look, my parents are dead, my uncle's dead, my reputation is trashed and I have one of Bernie's cronies threatening to kill me. What the hell do you expect me to do, stand on a hill-top and whistle yankee-doodle-dandy to the four winds? If you wanted to frighten me then well done, you've managed it, but I don't believe Susan sent you here to harm me.'

The blow when it came was delivered with such force that he saw a blinding flash for an instant, then darkness.

He thought he was dead.

A man in a dog collar was speaking to him, asking if he was alright. Behind the vicar stood an Indian man wearing a turban. 'A I in heaven?' he mumbled.

'No, but you are in God's house,' said the vicar.

'I'm sorry, I didn't realise that I'd spoken out loud.' His head throbbed.

'That's OK. You look to have had a nasty fall. Are you alright?' He helped Harry from his back to a slouch. 'Here, have a drink of water.'

'Holy water....?'

'No, mineral, from the local supermarket.' The vicar smiled.

Harry sat up, wished he hadn't and felt nauseous. 'Thanks,' he said taking a sip.

They'd obviously brought him into the church out of the cold. He looked round at the man in the turban who smiled and explained; 'I am a guest of Reverend Williams; I am merely visiting. I can assure you that you are not in heaven and I am not St Peter. My name is Varwender.'

Harry gently felt the big lump above his right ear and smiled, 'I'm pleased to meet you Mr Varwender.'

'Come, let me help you on to a chair,' said Reverend Williams, 'easy does it.'

'Thank you.' He drank some more water. 'I'm sorry to be a nuisance.'

'Nonsense anyone can have an accident. You're not the first person to trip down that step. As long as you are OK, that's all that matters.'

'I'll be fine thanks.'

'Will you come to the house and have a cup of tea?'

'No, really, I've been enough trouble. I'll be on my way. I came to look at the roof - should have been looking where I was putting my feet. Magnificent isn't it?' Lying bugger, he thought, and in church too. He mumbled a sincere thank you and walked out rather unsteadily. He left the good Samaritans concerned about his wobbly gait but relieved that their services would not be needed on a more professional level.

He looked at his watch – 1.30pm. He must have been unconscious for about an hour. He fingered his bump, 'Bloody hell' he muttered.

He phoned Mary and told her he had one more visit to make. No, he had not met Susan but he was about to put that right. He briefly explained his encounter with the thug, leaving out the bang on the head and his trip to heaven.

'Where does she live?'

'On the Ruthin road out of Mold, about a mile from town. Why.'

'Quinn was asking what you were up to. I think you need him to keep an eye on you. I'll tell him where you're going.'

'You two have a regular exchange of views don't you?' Silence. 'Fair enough I suppose, but tell him to keep out of sight, Susan won't say anything if he's lurking around. It's a detached two-storey place on the right surrounded by a beech hedge. If she's there, there'll be a silver BMW in the drive. If I'm there it's a red Focus. I'll come and see you as soon as I can.'

'Be careful Harry. Please.'

'Sure. Bye.'

She was there alright; asleep at the kitchen table with a glass of orange juice by her elbow - and a bottle of gin on the worktop near the toaster. He'd tried the doorbell and had gone round the back when there was no reply. He was now looking in through the kitchen window. He rapped on the glass but Susan didn't stir.

He returned to the front; the door was unlocked so he shouted her name went in. In the kitchen, she hadn't moved so he shook her by the shoulder. She stirred and mumbled then lifted her head a couple of inches before it slumped back down onto her forearms.

'Susan. SUSAN! For Christ's sake wake up!' he shouted.

Something registered so he shook her and shouted again. She lifted her head and struggled upright. Bloodshot eyes stared uncomprehendingly at Harry.

Gradually some focus returned and the blank expression turned to surprise, then fear, then hate.

'What the hell do you want?'

'Your undivided attention, come on sober up. Get with it.' He filled the kettle and brought a large glass of water to the table. 'Here, drink this.'

'Sod off,' she said reaching for the glass of orange. Harry snatched it away and poured it down the sink. The remnants of the bottle of gin followed.

'Now, drink this, I'm making coffee. Can you understand me?'

'I don't drink water. Mix me a proper drink. You can manage that I suppose?'

Good sign, the unpleasantness was returning, she was coming round.

'You're going to tell me what's going on,' he said. 'You sent that thug to warn me off. Why? What have you been up to? Or are you protecting your fat father?'

'Get lost.'

'Susan, listen to me. Can you hear me? Can you?'

She raised her head, looked up at the ceiling then closed her eyes. 'Yes! Yes, I can bloody well hear you!'

'Well then, listen.' He leant on the table, their faces eighteen inches apart. Her eyes were moist and yellow - like a pair of rotten, half-cooked eggs. He baulked at her sickly-sweet breath but stayed put. 'The police are on my back and I suspect that you don't want them on yours. I'm certain your old man doesn't want them on his. Unless you want me to cause you some real trouble, start talking.'

The kettle clicked and Harry turned to make the coffee. The chair clattered behind him as Susan staggered for the door. She was barely able to stand so he grabbed her and sat her back down with a bump. Her arms were thin, skin on bone, muscle dissolved in white grain and juniper. Lank hair fell over her face as she sat on the wooden seat, arms hanging limply by her side. What a mess.

Surely that wasn't a pang of pity he felt?

He brewed the coffee - black, strong, two sugars, and her nose twitched at the aroma. 'Come on, drink this.'

She looked at him through lifeless eyes then smiled a sick smile. She grabbed the cup and took a noisy slurp. 'Wouldn't you just love to know?'

There was malice, the mean look of someone who holds the ace, but there was desperation too.

Harry sat quietly and stared into his coffee.

'What's gone wrong Harry? What have I done to deserve this?' She waved her hand.

Ninety-five percent of the population would love a detached place in the country. However, they would be coming up to meet it, Susan was on the way down.

The tick of the clock on the wall behind Susan like hammer blows in the silence. 2.15pm - twenty-four hours and Mary would learn her fate. Fear once again gripped him but he forced it away and tried to concentrate.

'The fates have conspired against us Susan.' He didn't mean it but played her melancholy game. 'We've both been beaten and bullied by something out of reach. We still have the chance to win Susan. Both of us have the chance to regain our pride, get our lives back on track. I'll help you but you have to help me too.'

She said nothing but stared out of the window.

'My father's not fat. Not anymore.' She looked up, stared beyond Harry, somewhere far away.

He said gently, 'The Church, the bluff, I'd forgotten about it. In a strange way I was looking forward to seeing you there again.' Bullshit. 'Did you know it has a magnificent ceiling? I didn't, we never got inside did we?'

She brought her eyes to his; 'I knew. I've been back.' Harry was aghast.

'I went back because it took me back to a time when everything was alright. After you left I went back. Sometimes I sat inside but usually I sat in the graveyard.' She paused, then as if speaking to an audience, raised her arms to embrace the throng, and said clearly; 'Daffyd Williams, born 28th September 1844, died 4th November 1878 aged 34 years. With God.' She held his gaze till he looked down into his empty mug. Her arms dropped to the table with a thump.

'Daffyd became my friend. He was the only person who couldn't hurt me. He listened. I told him my secrets but he never judged me. I told him about us and he smiled. I told him my fears and he held my hand.' She got up, steadier now, and left the kitchen. 'Don't worry, I'm not running.'

He heard a flush and she returned wiping her face on a hand-towel. She threw it on the table and said, 'God, I hate him. I love him, but I hate him more.'

He knew she was close; he didn't move a muscle.

'Get me some more coffee.' Harry looked up. 'Please.'

Harry crossed the kitchen and had his back to her as she said quietly; 'He bought your farm you know. He bought your parents' farm. Before you left he made the farmer an offer that would 'see him through' and bought the bloody farm. They moved in a month ago - a new beginning he said. He put me in this godforsaken box and whisked my mother off to paradise. He said they'd earned it, they deserve it - bastard. He's spent a bloody fortune on it. It should have been mine, ours.' Harry turned and their eyes locked. She looked away. 'She's ill but I can't find it within me to feel sorry for her. It's because she's ill I found out.'

He crossed the room and placed the mugs gently on the table, gently so as not to break the spell.

'You know don't you?' she said, searching his face. Harry furrowed his brow; tried to look quizzical. 'Course you do, that's why you're here.'

He was motionless, waiting her out. She sighed and angrily wiped a tear from her cheek.

'She started to get sick about two and a half years ago. Up to then she was pretty fit for her age. She had a succession of infections she couldn't shake off and was eventually diagnosed with Leukaemia. She required a bone marrow transplant and as the best 'donors of choice', as they put it, come from close family, both my father and I were tested. It turned out that neither of us was suitable. She'd had a course of chemotherapy and while waiting for a suitable donor, father took her away to France for a holiday. When they came back, I could see that there was something terribly wrong. They wouldn't tell me but he had changed. He said it was the strain from mother's illness but there was something else.' She sipped her coffee and was quiet.

'What do you think it was?' he asked.

She looked out of the window again. 'I don't know about France but about a month ago I was helping them sort stuff out for their move. He'd removed the contents of his safe and put them in a box when he got called into work for some emergency or other. I was trying to be helpful, trying to show some enthusiasm. I was taking the box to my car, thinking that he wouldn't want important stuff left lying around, when I saw a haematology report from the private hospital in Rhayader. That was where mother was treated and we were tested.' She looked back at Harry who held her gaze. 'You know what it said. He's not my father is he?' She knew of course but had to hear it from someone else, needed someone to say it out loud to make it real.

'No, I don't think he is.'

She shook her head slowly. 'He didn't think to tell me. What a bastard. How could he not tell his own daught........how...?' She grabbed the towel from the table and covered her face.

He walked round the table and squeezed her shoulder, then went to the window and stared out over the garden.

Finally, she let the towel fall to the table but she hadn't finished speaking. 'There was also a newspaper cutting, in French, about some guy who died. I don't know what that was about, I suppose he must have picked it up while they were over there a couple of years ago. The only other thing was a single sheet of paper. It had five names on it. Two names were crossed out - one of them was your father. Your name was at the bottom, circled in the same red ink, with a big question mark against it.' Harry tried not to betray his dread. He knew the other names; they'd have a line through them now.

'I didn't mean for you to get hurt. I sent him to warn you – there was no point me talking to you, you wouldn't have listened to me.' She gave him a thin smile. 'You didn't listen anyway did you?'

'I did listen but chose not to hear. I've had enough Susan. I have to get on with my life. Thank you for trying though, I appreciate that. He did belt me round the ear mind so I would still question your choice of friends.'

'What are you going to do?'

'I'm going to see your fa....I'm going to the farm.'

'What will you do?'

'It depends on what he says.'

As he walked out of the kitchen he turned and said, 'stay out of the bottle Susan. It'll kill you.'

'Is that all?' She muttered under her breath.

Chapter 33

Concerned about the possibility of a reception committee at the farm he phoned Mary to ask of Quinn's whereabouts. She quoted his sketchy reply verbatim, "He's a big boy, he'll be OK."

Not the ideal response, thought Harry. Of course he was worried, scared even, and Quinn as back up would give him the courage he needed to face this. No way he could just stop now though – he had to see this through with or without help.

He told Mary that his ex-wife had taken their slot in the gutter but she had confirmed what Harry already knew, that John Wainwright was not her real father. He told her that he would explain everything later and that right now he was on the way to try and lay it all to rest once and for all.

'Will you call by?' she asked.

'Hopefully later this evening. I'll crash out on the couch if that's OK. I'll give you a ring when it's over.' He paused. 'And by the way, I'm coming with you tomorrow.'

'We'll see.' She replied. 'Be careful.' And she was gone.

He suddenly felt isolated.

If he'd dreaded the thought of tackling Susan, facing the man who had all but ruined him was something else altogether. Mary's forthcoming appointment frightened him but it also steeled him.

He drove three miles and turned right onto a rough track that ran uphill by the side of an open-sided hay barn. Two hundred yards later he cleared a copse and approached the new gate set in its post and rail fence. He'd seen it from the above, it didn't look much from up there. From his lowly position in the car he was faced with a virtual rampart.

He knew that fear was laying siege to his mind, feelings of insecurity and embarrassment ran riot. He thought back to the times he had walked this road as a child, a pitted dirt track that led him home where he was safe. Ignorance and innocence protected him from the responsibilities and worries of the grown-up world. If he'd foreseen the complexities of adulthood he'd have stopped where he was.

He climbed out of the car and opened the gate. Every move could be watched from the house above and he shrivelled in anticipation of a verbal volley - or a gunshot. Neither came and he clattered over the cattle grid and closed the gate behind him.

The wind had died and the clouds had lifted. Weak sunshine hinted at what the reclaimed farm may offer in times to come.

He recalled his father chugging over the field on the old Massey Ferguson with threadbare cap and cigarette hanging from the corner of his mouth. Wrinkled eyes peered from his weather-battered face as he squinted against the sun. The clatter of the ancient grass cutter echoed round the age-old moors. Each spring the rudimentary machinery was coaxed back to life ready to stagger through another season. No ambition then, just survival.

The Range Rover was gone and there was no sign of life but as he approached, he saw the front door ajar. He climbed three stone-flag steps and called out, 'Mr Wainwright'.

'In here.' A female voice, distant from deep within.

Cautiously he entered and noticed the smell of fresh decoration, then toast. 'Come in Harry,' the voice louder now, terse. It came from an open doorway to his left so he crossed the hall. The house was silent, his footfall whispering on the thick burgundy carpet as he entered what was obviously the lounge. Bare white walls, white ceiling, cream carpet, crimson three-piece suite – clinical and functional but somehow extravagant. Anything the interior could offer however was eclipsed by the views of the landscape through two large picture windows, one looking down the hill to the front, the other up the hillside to the west. The light fittings were brass, one triple in the ceiling, four wall-lights and several picture lights awaiting the paintings and framed photographs stacked on the floor to the left of the stone fireplace.

The dominant smell now was that of the sick – indefinable, yet distinct, the odour of creeping death. The source was a crumpled figure, buried in a crimson armchair.

He stared for a moment. 'Hello Celine.'

No surprise, no acknowledgement. 'Sit down Harry.'

The slim girl his uncle had seen more than forty years ago was slim again; now destroyed by disease. Harry knew her to be around sixty but her rotting blood had aged her another twenty.

Harry baulked but her eyes showed no sign of caring, nor did they seek sympathy – though sunk within a jaundiced, leathery face, they were fierce. A fire burned within. It may have been hatred or determination; it was certainly not submission. No surrender to him, to life, to anything.

'I've sent him away.' Her voice was cracked but strong. 'I knew you'd come. All my life I have expected someone to come.' A pause and a thin mirthless smile, 'you're just in time. Sit.' He remained upright, she seemed not to care. 'I wouldn't let him face you. He would be no match for you now however pathetic you are. He's broken – a worthless adversary. You would gain nothing; you would win a toothless victory.'

He was silent. He knew how they had worked in the past as a couple, had seen it first-hand. Gain the higher ground then attack, embarrass, pummel – wound the victim, make them bleed, watch them wither.

He was no longer afraid. He spoke quietly and with reason, without force but with strength.

'I will find him if I have to. Before I leave I will know the truth. Did he kill my father?'

'That worthless oaf who scratched and whimpered his life away in a pigsty? He was nothing.'

He fought his anger at this seething hatred but kept his voice level, 'He was my father. He was perhaps not a success judged by your warped standards, but he was a decent, honest man. A man with a conscience who loved me and who loved my mother. He chose to live the way he did. He hated insincerity; he hated the fake authority of wealth, believing that respect was earned. He lived his life with a burden - a burden that, to many, seemed too insignificant to dominate a lifetime. Outwardly his conscience manifested itself as weakness but in his morality he had strength.'

'Morals don't pay the rent.' She sneered; teeth too large for her shrunken face.

'When the rent comes due we'll find out how much they're worth... won't we?' Her sneer fell away and he persisted, 'you didn't answer my question.'

'We managed; we were in control. After all that had happened we had survived. Your idiot father, that stupid brainless fool, ruined it all.'

Now Harry was lost.

'Even after Bezier, John never fully understood - it was only when your father opened his mouth.'

'I don't understand. What did he do?'

She was silent. Her breathing laboured, she was building her strength.

'He gave John the missing piece, led him to the thing that finally drove him over the edge. They got drunk, my John and your worthless father, here in this house, when it was a shack,' another malicious smile, but this time it didn't linger and she lowered her eyes. 'He inadvertently gave him the link between me and Susan's real father. Your father was too dim to be aware of it - just told a tale about his trip to France and their witnessing a rape.'

'My father never knew that you were the girl he saw that day.'

'Probably not, but John thought he did. Or more importantly thought he might have done. He couldn't cope with the thought that someone else knew. He wouldn't allow them to tell, couldn't bear for anyone else to find out.'

'How did he come to know of Leport at all?'

She looked out of the window, staring unblinking into the past.

'That was my fault, my moment of weakness, my first real mistake.' The fire had left her voice now and for the first time she sounded like a dying woman. 'We were in our hotel in Pau, France, when I came across the report about Bezier's death. When I read the words 'Les Dix' I cried out. I couldn't stop myself - it was like that singular moment of grief when a loved one dies and the mind lets go. I told him then about Leport, had to. Much of it I kept back, but I told him about my rape, not that he wasn't Susan's father, but enough apparently to set John on a course.'

A voice from behind Harry startled him. 'I found the truth about the devil-child that I had raised as my own'.

He turned. John Wainwright stood in the doorway, arms hanging by his side - in his right hand was a gun. 'How the hell to do cope with that?' He was shouting now. 'How do you carry on when you discover that the woman with whom you've spent a lifetime bore the child of a bloody monster?'

'What are you doing here you fool?' snarled the old woman.

'It was my idea.' Wainwright turned towards the figure behind him raising the gun. Quinn grabbed the old man's wrist and the gun discharged low into the timber door frame. 'Drop it. NOW!' The old man struggled for a moment and the gun fell to the floor. Quinn back-heeled the gun into the hallway and with his free hand smashed his fist into Wainwright's jaw. He crumpled but Quinn held firm. The old man twisted and fell to the floor. He was half sitting, half-lying on one hip till Quinn released his wrist and he slumped the rest of the way and lay on his side in an approximation of the recovery position. With one arm trapped beneath him, his free hand flapped gently as if waving and blood seeped from his mouth onto the carpet. Quinn roughly shoved the old man's upper shoulder with his foot rolling him onto his back. He let go a pitiful moan.

'I found him lurking about in the trees at the bottom of the road,' said Quinn, 'thought you might like a word with him.'

'Get up!' Quinn grabbed two huge fist-fulls of lapel and shirt-front and lifted him clear of the floor. He took two paces and threw his burden onto the sofa like a rag doll. Wainwright moaned again and covered his face with his hands.

Harry looked at the old woman. She remained impassive, eyes now a mix-ture of fire and hatred. For whom he couldn't be certain. 'Congratulations,' she said scornfully staring at Quinn, 'quite a conquest. Am I next?'

'No, I don't think so. Nature's doing just fine don't you think?'

The ghost of a smile fell from her face, 'who the hell are you?'

'A friend of a friend who's here to see fair play. I think the playing field's level again now, don't you?'

Harry walked behind the sofa and manhandled the old man into a sitting position. 'Now,' he said, 'start talking.'

John Wainwright looked towards his wife who stared back at him blankly as if saying, 'your mess, you sort it.'

He touched his lip with a finger, moved his hand where he could see it and stared at the smear of blood. He leaned forward and rested his elbows on his knees and said, 'I loved her from the first moment I set eyes on her.' He shook his head slowly. 'A lifetime ago. I held her hand as we walked through the garden at the clinic and never wanted to let go.'

Harry leant on the back of the sofa looking at the back of the old man's head and Quinn leant against the door jam, arms crossed. He'd retrieved the weapon from the hallway, pocketed the bullets and slipped the gun into his waistband.

'I was working for my father's timber yard in Wilcox - we supplied timber for the extension at The Grove. I was young but being groomed for better things so was instructed to follow the project manager and learn all I could. We'd only been started a week or so when Helen, or the woman who I was to know as Helen, arrived in a car driven by one of the staff. Within a couple of days we spoke for the first time and began our regular walks. She soon spoke of wanting to get away, to start afresh. She told me she wanted to be with me.

I was used at first, I can see that now, but I like to think that in time we grew to be real friends - perhaps even fell in love. We were lovers from the beginning - that bloody maze, do you remember?' He smiled quickly and looked over at his wife. She showed no sign of having heard him and concentrated on her gnarled hands resting in her lap. 'Anyway, I fell for her wiles and vowed to get her away.'

'Why did she have to leave?' demanded Harry.

'Because she needed to be one step removed from any direct contact with France. If she moved on she believed that no-one would find her. You can't exactly blame her for that, can you?' He looked back over his shoulder at Harry who merely raised his eyebrows. He turned back and started picking at his fingernails. 'Of course, at that point I had no idea she was pregnant.'

'So how did you spirit her away?'

'I'm getting there, be patient.'

'Don't you dare tell me to be patient,' Harry exploded, 'after what you have done to me I should break every bone in your body and leave you to rot.'

The old man sighed and whispered, 'I'm sorry.' He shook his head slowly and continued. 'As I said, my father owned the local timber yard but he was also a director of Western Estates who in turn had a place on the board of The Freedom Trust who owned The Grove.' Quinn and Harry exchanged imperceptible nods. John's father, Michael had been mentioned in Quinn's 'Little Chef' report. 'Roger Brierley ran the Grove and had recently been appointed to the Trust's board. It was he who organised Helen's transfer to their sister clinic outside Rhayader in Mid Wales. The only people who knew of her true origins at that time were Roger Brierley and Helen herself.' He ran his tongue over his bloody lip and swallowed. He looked up at Quinn and asked him if he would mind bringing him a glass of water.

'Yes'. Replied Quinn who remained motionless and when Wainwright held his eye, 'I do.'

The old man shrugged.

'She left soon after. One day she was there, the next gone. I visited her regularly at Wye Lodge and when I learned she was pregnant was told by my father in no uncertain terms that I must do what was right by her. Like an idiot I believed it was my child - I was blind but genuinely besotted. When Susan was born, I was told the baby was premature, a month early, and up until about two years ago, I truly believed she was our child.'

'I had continued to progress at work and my father set us up with a house in Mold. Under his guidance we opened the timber yard and when he died it came to me. Everything was fine until you fell for Susan.' He looked over his shoulder once again. 'God knows what she saw in a scrawny little bugger like you, but I was forced to accept it.' There was a hint of defiance creeping back. 'I gave you a job, clothed and fed you, but we both thought that you and your family were losers.' Harry gripped the back of the sofa willing himself not to crack the old man on the back of his head. When he remained silent the fire left Wainwright and he shrunk forward again.

'Then Helen got ill. Part of her treatment was a bone marrow transplant so she, Susan and myself took blood tes...' but Harry interrupted. 'I know all about that and your trip to France. What about my parents?'

This time Wainwright turned on the sofa and stared at Harry with genuine astonishment.

'How did you know....' then it dawned, 'Susan told you didn't she? You've seen Susan. You callous...' But he ran out of steam and went quiet.

'My father, what happened to my mother and father?'

'I had to stop him. I couldn't let him tell anyone, couldn't afford for anyone else to know. I'd have been ruined. We'd have had to leave, sell up and start again. I couldn't let that happen. I found out by chance that your father knew about Helen. I wasn't absolutely certain he knew but I wasn't going to take that chance. I found out when I went to scc him after Helen was diagnosed. I needed an ear, needed to let off steam. When you get to my time of life in my position you don't have friends, you have business associates. It shows how desperate I was that I went to see your father.'

'Yes, and you got drunk. What did you do to him?'

Wainwright looked at Helen once again but she hadn't moved. Her head had sunk a little lower on her chest but she wasn't going to help.

'Look,' he said, 'what about Susan. You have the power to break her, to cripple her. She had nothing to do with anything. What will you do?'

'I'll treat her with a damn sight more compassion than you have. Now I'll ask you again, did you kill my father?'

'Can you assure me that you will leave Susan alone?'

Now!' he shouted. 'Did you start the fire that killed my parents?'

'Please, look I was under enormous pressure, my life was falling apart.'

'TELL ME!'

'YES. Yes, for God's sake, yes. I did it. I set fire to the house. God forgive me but I trapped them in the bedroom and set fire to the house. I put a wedge under their bedroom door and rid myself of a problem.'

'A PROBLEM? A BLOODY PROBLEM? Is that what you consider decent human beings? Just another sodding problem? They were my parents, my flesh and blood for Christ's sake.' He slapped the old man on the side of the head who tumbled sideways. 'What gave you the right to kill two innocent, decent people?'

The old man had clambered upright so Harry slapped the other side of his head. Wainwright tumbled off the sofa onto the floor. Harry ran round and kicked him hard in the ribs. He curled up to protect himself. 'You bastard, you goddam miserable bastard!' Another kick slammed into the old man's elbow bringing a cry of pain.

'OK Harry. OK. Leave him now.'

Harry turned and looked at Quinn who said, 'OK, that's enough.'

'No, it's bloody not.' He aimed another kick but Quinn's arms circled his chest and pulled him away. 'Come on mate, enough.'

'God damn him!' he said as he struggled in Quinn's arms. His breaths came in staccato bursts and his head swam. Gradually he calmed. 'OK. OK, I'm OK.'

The old man lay facing the sofa curled in a foetal position, his breathing laboured a result of the kick in the ribs.

'Get up,' said Quinn and grabbed Wainwright by his jacket collar. He yelled in agony and clutched his chest as he was dumped back on the sofa.

'For pity's sake,' he moaned.

'You haven't finished yet. What about the others?'

Wainwright looked up through rheumy eyes, desperate now and genuinely fearful. 'What others? I don't know what you're talking about.'

Quinn and Harry exchanged glances.

'You know bloody well,' said Quinn, grabbing Wainwright's lapels again. His face was nine inches from the old man's, 'you have one chance,' he took the gun from his waistband and pushed it hard into Wainwright's neck below his right ear. He didn't know the gun was empty - his eyes were wide with terror.

'Please. I know nothing about anybody else, you have to believe me.' He was plainly petrified.

Harry joined in, 'I suppose you know nothing about a computer full of porn and a certain son-in-law ending up in the shit?'

He whimpered. 'Please,' he said pushing Quinn's arm away feebly. Quinn backed off. 'Yes, I did that. I had to get you away. I'm sorry, but I swear on my life I never hurt anyone else.'

'You can swear on your life all you like but it's worth jack-shit, said Quinn, 'I don't believe y.....' but he pulled up short as a phlegmy rattle came from the arm-chair across the room. As the three men turned in unison to look, a ghost of a smile died on the old woman's lips and her head slumped forward onto her chest. Then she was still. There was a moment's silence.

'NO! Oh God no!' Yelled Wainwright as he struggled off the sofa and stumbled over to his wife. He knelt before her. 'Helen! Helen, no, no, come back, for God's sake, not now.' He grabbed her shoulders and shook her. The dead woman rocked and swayed and her head flopped from side to side like a rag doll. 'Noooooo!' He buried his face in her lap and his body, overcome with grief, shimmered and shook.

The two men stood and watched. Neither betrayed emotion, neither spoke.

Many minutes later the old man raised his head and knelt before his wife. He placed his hands on her cheeks and lifting her haggard face, kissed her gently on the forehead. 'I'm sorry my love. I'm truly sorry.' he whimpered – a pitiful pathetic noise.

Quinn, still holding the gun, retrieved one bullet from his pocket and placed it in the chamber. There was a metallic click and John Wainwright turned and stared impassively. Quinn looked the old man in the eye for a full minute then placed the gun on the carpet in the centre of the room and said quietly. 'It's too good for you.' Then he motioned to Harry and the two men left the room.

As they climbed into Harry's car they heard a single shot. The muffled crack rumbled across the valley then died in the evening air.

They drove through the gate at the bottom of the long drive and approached a dark blue Land Rover at the edge of the copse. Quinn inclined his head to the man who stood leaning on the bonnet smoking a cigarette. The man returned the gesture.

'Friend of yours?' asked Harry.

'Insurance.'

They pulled up beside the 4x4 and Quinn got out of the car. He exchanged a brief word with the man who passed an envelope to Quinn.

Through the window Harry said, 'I'm going to have a word with Susan before I head back. I feel I should tell her what's happened.'

'I don't think that will be necessary,' he said, passing the envelope to Harry. He opened the letter and read.

Chapter 34

Dear Harry

Goodbye.

No, that's hardly enough is it?

Let me start again. I'm sorry about your mum and dad - truly. They were alright and didn't deserve such a miserable demise. I can see where 'Pop' was coming from when he broiled them but perhaps what he did was a bit drastic. He had 'position' though you see and could hardly afford the adverse publicity that they could unleash.

I know, I know, it was not even certain that they knew anything. They had to know more than they let on because, let's face it, they were a bit dim weren't they? Uncommunicative, isolated. Nice in their simple way but not exactly Mastermind material. But Pop had a reputation to protect - and Mum of course, and me.

In all truth Pop collapsed a bit after the 'incident' and rather ran out of steam.

He got a bit confused, what with Mum catching the pox - and later, with all that non-parent issue, well, he just about folded. But it seems that the females of the clan were made of sterner stuff. We figured out, in a way perhaps that only real survivors can. We realized there were another couple of naughty beavers waiting to gnaw away at our family tree. (Poetic eh?).

Just to regress for a moment, I can confirm that I was shagging Paul (Mercedes, flat, pots-o-cash etc. etc.) but even he proved a bit of a disappointment. The Merc was a company car and then he lost his job, he sold the flat and went bust. That was the turning point really. I realised, with a bit of a parental nudge from mum, that the only person you can really rely on is yourself. If you want a job doing properly......etc. etc.

Pop was a bit tangled up with kids anyway. I thought his way of shunting you out was pretty appropriate. He had no problem getting hold of a few 'naughty photos' anyway - silly, dirty man! Didn't you feel that the geek that helped him was the archetypal 'fiddler'? I did. God knows, if that was the kind of muppet he was associating with it's not surprising he got himself in a mess.

Anyhow you'll be wanting to know what happened to the others.

I'm telling you, by the way, because I will disappear (or have already done so when you read this). I know how to do it and the world is a big place. I have made a few influential friends in the hide-and-seek department along the way. A couple of flights, a change of hair, a change of clothes, plenty of cash, change of eye colour, change of name etc. etc. OR a selection / combination of that lot!! They've even taught me how to disappear from them – silly billies!

I know, I know there'll be fingerprints, hair and bits and bobs lying around but one thing they won't be able to trace me from is my blood sample. I had that switched – before they tried to match me with Dad – not that it would have mattered. She doesn't know. You can tell her if you want. That would be a good, her knowing I'd gone behind her back – magic! Unless you've killed her of course or 'Pop' has, or that goon of yours, or contrary Mary, or little Lucy-loo.

Harry went cold.

That's shaken you up a bit hasn't it?

Don't worry, keep calm, no harm will become to the chosen few. You see, I actually like you - or did. No, I think I still do. You've told me you want to start again and we both have a little something on each other don't we? I've got a bit more on you perhaps, but we both have enough...! Know what I'm getting at?

Course you do.

Anyway, I seem to be 'off topic' as they say on the internet forums.

Where were we? Oh yes. Good old Uncle Will and the gawky brief.

Yes, it was me who engaged the services of a certain 'private dick', he of indeterminate credentials. Your dear papa spilled the beans to Pop during their 'pre-barbecue soiree'. God knows how Pop had remembered, he came home in a right state but I held his hand and shared his troubles.

I wrote what I can only describe as a brilliant letter to Mr Parker threatening to expose him over the death of a man many years ago in La belle France. I added a few embellishments here and there including vague hints about 'long memories' in that part of the world and long arms from that part of the world. I suggested he meet with an intermediary and put the matter to rest once and for all for a little financial consideration.

Now here's the clever bit! The meeting was to take place on neutral ground - a bandstand in a local park to be precise. He was feeble but desperate and turned up. What he didn't know was that we had 'borrowed' a young girl, given her a bit of a sleeping draught and propped her up behind the bandstand. Her clothes had been re-arranged a bit and she had been parted from her panties.

Good Samaritan Mr Parker, though suspicious, couldn't ignore the pitiful cries for help that in the words of Blue Peter 'I had prepared earlier' and recorded onto a handy tape recorder. As he bent over the child to investigate he was snapped by a conveniently placed amateur photographer.

I have to say the results were superb. Shot one, solicitor gawping at the child, hand on her shoulder. Shot two, solicitor's look of astonishment towards the camera.

The child I must tell you played her part like a pro - even if she was asleep. 'An associate' (business-like or what?) guided her into the police station and scarpered. She's alright.

Anyhow the photos were sent to the brief and had the effect that I could not have dreamt of. Poor bugger! Thought it would have been enough to keep him quiet, never thought he'd shoot himself. Silly old tosser.

'Uncle Will' was a different proposition. No way would he succumb to petty threats so we had to resort to the physical - sneaky but physical. We followed him to the Lakes and 'managed' to overhear his route. What's that mean? Well, 'solos' inform the Mountain Rescue bods when they are going on a decent hike.

A chance meeting on a high ridge with a friendly trekker coming from the other direction resulted in a tragic accident when one of them went tumbling down a nasty hill. One of them went walking back up the ridge again and one of them ended up in a heap in a valley.

Enjoy your boat by the way. I'm told it has lovely leather chairs - or did.

You can go after the private dick with pleasure, though I'm not sure what good he'll be to anyone. I understand he's in a bit of a state – your mate's doing probably. And his 'associate', well, I'm led to believe you never saw him did you? Mr ear basher I'll call him. For now that is. When I write my memoirs, I'll think of something more imaginative.

Well, that's it for this country. Oh! Except for a little private clinic in Wiltshire whose owner lives in the attic doing the basics of life through a variety of different sized tubes. He won't be a problem though, to start with he's nearly dead but while he struggles on he knows that a particular secretive woman's secret daughter has some rather interesting historical secrets concerning his younger days in a country across the channel.

Too many secrets wouldn't you say Harry my love?

AND: What about my theatrics? Pretty good eh? Played the piss head to a tee I felt. Did it fool you? Be honest now! Peel an onion, give the eyes a rub, splash some gin about. I've learned a lot over the years.

I wrote most of this before you came to see me. Just tweaked things here and there. Just after the bit where I shook you up I added that I still like you. And I do. Even though you came with your own agenda and all that bit about the church was a load of old crap, I really thought that when you walked out you wished me well.

Give my love to the girls.

I'll always remember the graveyard we left behind.

Your Susan.

Chapter 35

Harry sat in the Focus and waited. Mary was inside the house of God having a quiet word the owner, sitting by her radiator.

At least he imagined her by her radiator - perhaps she no longer needed the warmth. Perhaps his friendship was providing all the warmth she needed. Huh! He didn't think so, not after last night.

He had clammed up. Susan's letter had felled him. He'd never experienced such a mixture of hatred and evil, veiled threats and cold-heartedness. Never before had he felt so exposed, sliced open, second guessed and out-thought.

Mary had asked him more than once to tell her what had happened but he'd bumbled and fluffed his lines. Scraps came out but a complete sentence was beyond him. Chronological it wasn't, nor comprehensive - nor was it fair on his friend.

He fished the letter out of his pocket and read it again.

Susan had known about his parents. How in God's name could she keep that to herself? If she'd shown any remorse at the time he'd never spotted it. He'd realised their relationship was distant, to say the least, but surely he would have picked something up. Or was it another example of her acting. Perhaps their whole marriage had been a play in which he was an unwitting bit part.

He'd avenged his parents' death to a degree, or more accurately with Wainwright's death it had been avenged, but it was a hollow victory knowing that one of his allies, the person to whom he had been closest of all, was part of the plot and was away clean. Hiding, haunting.

Susan had chosen to side with her father and that bloody witch. His wife was unaware that 'Pop' was not her father at the time but nevertheless the betrayal leached through him like a cancer.

Christ, don't use that word, don't even think it. His eyes turned to the church.

His mind tumbled over and over.

All that had happened over the past few weeks had focussed on that gunshot in the farm.

That should have been it however awful and shocking, but the end all the same.

But it wasn't - Susan had won, she'd outwitted everyone and the only people that knew were the two of them; 'Till death us do part' they'd vowed.

Who could he share it with? How could he tell Mary he'd put her, and more crucially Lucy, in real danger? Well, he hadn't exactly, Susan had, but he was implicated and ultimately responsible. She would never forgive him.

He couldn't go to the police because that would put the 'girls', as Susan had termed them, in immediate danger. Same if he told Quinn. One whiff that she was being hunted or stalked would be all the excuse she would need. What was obvious was that Susan had friends, or accomplices - and bloody dangerous ones at that.

He imagined himself trying to explain everything to the D.S. Groves and shuddered. A dead man who was responsible for the death of his parents possibly still lying on his lounge carpet at the feet of his dead wife. Pop's co-conspirator, who was also responsible for two further deaths, he couldn't name because that would put the life of someone he had kept secret from the police in danger.

A bloke he'd never seen had clonked him over the head in a church doorway in Wales and his 'associate' was on life-support injured falling off a motorcycle sabotaged by someone else whose identity had been conveniently withheld. Marvellous.

Would you mind starting again Mr Dunn, this time for the benefit of the tape which we may send to the BBC Children's unit for airing on Tiggy Winky's Adventures in LaLa Land. But if you would be so kind, could you begin at the beginning this time and not in the middle of a pile of crap.

Bloody Hell!

Mary was right to be mad at him. He'd shared everything with her till that point, but he'd mysteriously clammed up after he'd crossed the finish line.

One thing was for certain, Mary had enough to worry about and if truth be known he was glad to have had something to worry about to keep him occupied.

He'd bought a packet of Benson & Hedges too this morning. He hadn't smoked for about five years, but the pressure of Mary's appointment and everything else was too much - he got out of the car and lit up. Clogging himself up was barely a consideration compared to the calming effect of the chemical concoction. He coughed but carried on with his ciggy till he saw Mary exit the church. Like a guilty schoolboy he dropped it on the floor and walked about pretending to stretch his legs.

'Not one of your strong points subterfuge, is it?'

'No,' he grinned sheepishly, 'I'm a terrible liar. I'm better off saying nothing at all. That way I can't be accused of telling porkies.'

'Saying nothing may be classed as subterfuge.'

'Even if there's a good reason for it?'

'Even then.'

'Well in that case I'm guilty.'

He paused then turned to her. 'I do want to say something to you. Come over here a minute.' He led her to a small garden by the side of the church where early daffodils were barely winning their battle. 'Here, sit down.'

He sat next to her on the mossy timber bench; a plaque read; 'Peter and Marjorie Jefferies. In loving memory.

He turned to her and looked her in the eye.

'You're making me nervous,' she said.

'I'm sorry, I don't mean to. Look, er, you know a little while ago I said I was fond of you. Well, I meant it.' He swallowed. 'I can only imagine what you have been going through these past few days. I really mean it when I say I wish I could take your place.'

'It's going to be alright Harry. It's going to be OK. I know you're rooting for me.

He reached into his pocket and handed her a small suede box. 'Here, just so you won't forget, take this in with you.'

She lifted the lid. Inside was a delicate gold ring inset with a small cluster of rubies. 'What's this?'

'It's a ring.'

'I can see it's a ring. What's it for; why?'

He smiled and looked down; embarrassed. 'It signifies friendship - a very special friendship. It's to wish you luck and to wish you well. And to tell you that .....well, just to say that....'

'You love me.'

'Yes.' He mumbled.

'I know you do Harry. I know you do.'

They fell against one another and held on tight. Mary wept and Harry pretended not to.

'Thank you. Thank you Harry.'

His hands were clammy. The steering slithered through his grip as he wiped each hand alternatively on his thighs. God he was nervous. Fear surged through him - it made him shake and he felt sick.

They were a mile from the hospital and they had said barely a word to each other since leaving St. Chad's.

Each was lost in their own thoughts. Harry hoped that Mary's were more positive than his.

He was a natural pessimist, that way you were far less likely to be disappointed. The downside was that he rarely felt the optimistic buzz of someone whose glass was half full.

Mary looked out of the windscreen, looked forward.

'Can I come for a ride on the boat with you?' She asked.

How can you possibly think of that at a time like this, he thought. 'Yes, course you can.' He said.

'We'll take a trip.'

Less than half a mile to go, he thought. 'That would be great.' He said.

'Will you let me drive?

Will you shut up and let me worry in peace, he thought. 'Probably not,' he said. He laughed. They both laughed. Harry felt like weeping.

'Good,' she said, 'I didn't fancy it anyway.'

They parked up - two quid - bloody cheek. Harry paid; it was the least he could do.

They sat still for a moment.

'Will you wait for me?'

Not trusting himself to speak he smiled and nodded. She climbed out of the car.

He watched her walk towards the out-patients entrance. He realised it was the first time he'd seen her in a skirt. It was calf length, dark blue and pleated. Below she wore flesh-coloured tights and mid-heeled black shoes that clicked on the footpath like a quick-ticking clock. A short olive-green woollen jacket kept out the chilly breeze and her hair hung down over her up-turned collar. She didn't look back. He swelled with pride that she was his friend.

He wondered if the chap in the church had recognised her in her finery. He hoped so.

As she walked past the smokers gathered outside the main door and disappeared from view he leaned forward and looked skywards through the windscreen. 'Help her please.'

He sat, fingering his upper lip, imagining her ordeal, living it with her, sharing her burden....

.....read the board: 'Mr Specialist. Clinic 4', down the stairs. Follow the signs into reception. Frightened patients hold hands with loved ones, pretend to read ancient Sunday supplements, nervous smiles all round, the incessant ringing of the phone.

Windowless and hot; is this hell's waiting room?

His imagination was running riot. What if? What then?

He got out and walked round the car park – decided against another ciggy. Passed the mobile flower seller and decided not to buy any. In a daze he found himself in front of the five-storey in-patient ward block. He looked up at the rows of windows – he could see various pieces of equipment, vases of flowers. One old lady on the second floor stood and stared down at him. He waved, she didn't, so he looked away. Some blinds were drawn – what awful things were they blocking out? Many people would get well, some wouldn't. Some wouldn't. He turned and walked away, returned to the car and sat in silence, palms sweating. A knock on the window dragged him out of his daydream.

'Mary?'

'Who else, of course it's me.' She stared wide-eyed. 'I can't believe you've been asleep?'

'I wasn't, no. No, I was er....I.....What did they say. Are you OK?

She smiled. 'I'm alright Harry.'

'That means you're OK, right?'

'Yes. Yes, he thinks I'm going to be OK.'

He jumped from the car and hugged her, almost squashed the life out of her. Looking up, he said under his breath 'Thank you.'

Harry leaned back and held her by the shoulders at arm's length. 'What do you mean thinks?'

'He reckons I've got polyps or cysts, but he doesn't think it's anything serious. Right now I'll take that.'

With a mock frown he said, 'Don't ever frighten me like that again, do you hear me?'

'You mean waking you up?'

'No, I do NOT mean waking me up. I wasn't asleep anyway, I was... concentrating. I mean don't even think about getting poorly again.'

'I'll try,' and she hugged him again. They stood for many minutes breathing deeply. 'Come on, let's get out of here. I don't get dressed up very often and I'm not used to it, all I want to do is to get this damn skirt off.'

'I beg your pardon?'

They looked at one another for a moment then laughed out loud, people stared but Harry didn't give a hoot. He took her hand to help her into the car - she was wearing her ring.

Chapter 36

Eight days later, Friday lunchtime, they walked into a café and approached the counter.

'Two teas and two bacon sandwiches please.' Said Mary

'Five minutes, I'm busy.'

'Could you make an exception, they're for Mr Branston.'

'I don't care who they hell they are for you'll have to wai......' He looked up. 'Bloody Hell! I don't believe it - Ale Mary. What in the name of the virgin happened to you? Thought you'd gone for good.' He looked beyond Mary and saw Harry sitting at a table trying to keep clean. 'And if it's not his Lordship. Come on your yacht Mr Branston?' He laughed.

'Hello Sid. Not lost your touch.'

'Not lost my touch with the butties either. I'll bring 'em over. Go and sit down Mary love. Where's your shopping bag anyway?'

'Oh, I binned it. It just fell apart.'

Mary grinned at Harry. Harry grimaced at his mug of teak brown tea. He wrapped a paper napkin around each hand and started the adventure that was one of Sid's bacon specials. To be honest he rather enjoyed it, there was something of great comfort having fat dribbling down your chin. He could have done without the surrounding rustling of the red-tops and bouts of hacking but it came as a package, he'd endured it before.

Sid's café had been their haven and they'd come to say goodbye. Having said that, as Harry chomped through his sandwich, he was already formulating a plan to make a sneaky return someday - probably incognito.

'What are you grinning at?' asked Mary.

'Oh, nothing.'

She held her cup to her lips with both hands and narrowed her eyes.

'You, er, not eating that?' he said, indicating her butty.

'I'm not hungry thanks.'

So Harry wrapped himself up and set off again.

'I'd like to introduce you to a Friend of Mine. Detective Sergeant Groves, meet Mary...uh...' Harry ran out of steam and looked at Mary, bewildered - he didn't even know her surname

'Harman,' said Mary.'

Hello Mary Harman,' said the detective.

'Hi.'

She smiled at Harry who looked dumbfounded.

How could he not know her surname for God's sake? He'd never asked, that's why. How could he have been so......well... uninterested? Unthoughtful? Whatever it was he felt a right charlie.

'So, you're the reason he disappeared off to France are you?'

He'd phoned the policewoman earlier that morning and asked her politely if there had been any developments with regard to the break-in on his boat. He'd again told her that he didn't think anything had been stolen as far as he could see but said that the insurance company may be in touch about recompense for his ripped seats - unlikely, but possible.

He'd also wanted to see if there had been movement on Edward Parker or his uncle Will's death. He couldn't ask her of course, that would have set her juices flowing, but if there had been anything untoward, he reckoned that she would have mentioned it. As it was she said nothing but told him to pop in if he was passing, there was just something that he may be able to help with.

Bugger, he thought. 'Oh? What's that then?'

'Just something I'd like to show you. Are you in town?'

'Yes, as it happens, I am.'

'After lunch would be convenient.'

'Fine' he said with more enthusiasm that he felt.

So here they were by the reception desk in Shrewsbury Police Station.

'We went on holiday together, yes.'

'Known Mr Dunn long?' she asked with raised eyebrows.

'Oh, a while, yes. We're good friends.'

'Are you? And what do you do?'

'I'm semi-retired actually.'

'Good for you. What about the non-retired semi?'

'I'm writing a book on the socio-economic divide in Victorian England.'

'Oh.'

Harry intruded and asked, 'Was there something you wanted me to look at Detective Sergeant Groves?'

She glared at them each in turn. 'This way. Come along if you wish.' Looking at Mary.

'Socio what?' whispered Harry as they walked down a gloomy corridor. Mary grinned.

'Have a seat,' said DS Groves as they entered an office. They'd climbed a floor and the window looked down over the station entrance.

The office was stark. Peeling paint clung to bare walls in haphazard patches and ancient, scuffed linoleum covered the floor. Two four-drawer filing cabinets stood guard against the far wall and sitting on the left-hand one a poorly succulent was dying a slow death. Against the opposite wall was a desk in front of which was a well-worn swivel chair into which DS Groves sunk with a loud creak. She looked Harry in the eye, challenged him to say something. He raised his eyebrows and looked down pretending to study his fingernails. He pursed his lips, desperate to suppress a smirk. He was in a good mood. Whatever the police threw at him now couldn't break that spell.

The desk held a telephone, half a dozen buff folders and a photograph of an air-force officer wearing a green flying suit. There was something familiar about the pilot. 'Husband?' asked Harry.

'No,' she replied.

The two visitors sat in chairs that may well have come from a defunct school. Harry sat next to the desk and Mary across the room between one of the filing cabinets and the window. From a drawer below the desk the D.S. Groves removed another folder, this one red. She opened the flap and passed a single sheet of paper to Harry.

It was a photocopy of a short newspaper article under the headline: Private Hospital Tragedy. As he read the brief article Harry hoped he had masked his surprise.

Following the recent death of his long-time friend Roger Brierley, Simon Fairweather tragically took his own life on Monday evening.

Mr Brierley, proprietor of The Grove Private Hospital, Wiltshire had suffered increasing ill-health in recent years and Mr Fairweather had been his constant companion and confidante for many years.

Spokesperson, Margaret Walcott, said; 'The relationship between the two men was like father and son and Simon was totally devastated by the death of his friend. Although Mr Brierley's death was not unexpected, it appears that Simon just gave up. It's all so hard to take in.'

Exact details have not been released but a police spokesman said that although an investigation is under way, no-one else is being sought in connection with the deaths.

Chief Operation Executive, Susan Wolfe said; 'This has been a dreadful time for everyone at The Grove and I respectfully request that we are left in peace to try and come to terms with this awful tragedy.'

Harry passed the paper back and hoped his hand wasn't shaking.

'Well?' she asked.

'Well, what?'

'Why are you sweating? Know anything about this?' waving the sheet of paper towards Harry who glanced across at Mary. She was looking out of the window.

He paused. 'We called there, The Grove, on our way back from our trip to France. My uncle Will had left the clinic something in his will. I was just trying to learn something about the man. It turns out that a friend of his was treated there years ago, a colleague from the forces, so I can only presume that he left them something as a thank you. That's all.'

'No, we never met Mr Brierley or Mr Fairweather......'

'We only spoke to the receptionist.......'

'Yes, I think it was Walcott.......'

'She didn't say anything specific because of patient confidentiality but when I explained about my uncle, told us that a number of members of the armed forces had been clients and it is not unusual for the clinic to receive payment in the form of a legacy......'

'No, I have not been back since........'

'Apart from Mary, the only other person who can verify this is Mrs Walcott... ....'

'I just presumed it was Mrs, but I've really no idea.......'

'I have been spending time sorting my boat out and..' Harry could feel himself curling up in an embarrassed, muddled heap. Mary was the one who broke the tension and asked to speak to DS Groves in private, 'if you wouldn't mind Harry?' He didn't. Without grace she asked Harry to wait outside. With a quizzical glance at Mary he bolted.

'I appealed to her better nature, woman to woman stuff, you know,' said Mary as they walked back to the car.

'No, I don't know,' said Harry.

'It was patently obvious to me that she was fishing. It was also evident that you were in danger of digging yourself a tunnel straight into the clink. I told her that I have been having a tough time and that you had spent every waking hour being my rock. It's not something Harry would wish to admit to you in person, I told her, but without you I wouldn't have got through the last couple of weeks etc. etc.'.'

'What did she say?'

'She said you were still a moron.'

'Charming. I hope you put her straight! Did you?'

'Of course...,' she replied, vaguely waving a hand.

'You didn't did you?'

Mary laughed. 'I told her you were a very nice moron.'

'Great! Where did she get the cutting from anyway?'

'The personal effects of a motorcyclist who died three days ago in hospital. It was in an unmarked envelope with £500 cash with a note that said, 'full and final.'

Harry felt that if he'd heard the last of D.S. Groves he would be a very fortunate man indeed.

Chapter 37

They were on the boat. Travelling east down the Llangollen Canal at the start of an open-ended cruise. 'We're going wherever we end up,' Harry had said.

For early April, the weather was warm and the countryside was showing signs of life. Yellow fields of rape defined the kaleidoscopic quilt that warmed this beautiful part of England. Spring was around the corner; birds flitted in and out of green-tinged hedgerows and a few brave lambs had made an early entrance.

They stood on the rear deck and sipped coffee as they chugged along. Mary tilted her head back and closed her eyes, taking in the fresh smell of spring and savouring their companionship.

They had talked.

Harry had talked because he knew that they should have no secrets - anything left to fester would surely poison their fledgling relationship. A relationship Harry felt they both so desperately needed to prevail. He told her all about his meeting with Susan, the miserable scenes in the farmhouse and he showed her Susan's letter. He told her of his sense of betrayal and feelings of emptiness and inadequacy.

She had not judged him, she had listened. She had taken his hand in response to the silent pleading in his eyes. A plea to be understood, a plea to be forgiven.

She had held him when he had begun to sweat and tremble as the confusion in his mind had surfaced.

She had held him tighter when he wept.

Later, Harry felt feeble and humbled as Mary had told him about her daughter, and he'd told her so. She'd replied that however difficult a situation becomes we handle it in our own way, the old cliché about there always being someone else worse off was of little importance when something takes over, particularly when problems stem from something beyond your control.

They'd both ended up looking at their own reflections from the bottom of empty glasses. The only way to hide and remain hidden was to fill them up again, drown out accusing eyes.

Throughout his 'wet period' (as he'd termed it) Harry had drowned reason altogether - at least Mary had sat by her radiator mumbling to an unseen saviour - though she now realised it had been more solace than solution.

She'd told him that she'd let Lucy go. When she got the cancer, she was told that her prognosis was dire.

She'd left her husband by then and was raising the girl on her own. Better to let the seven-year-old child live with her father now than see her mother wither. She was with someone else and they would support her. It was the best she could do.

Not surprisingly the girl felt rejected and didn't understand her mother's agony - perhaps never would. Would the girl's father allow his bitterness towards his ex-wife prevent him telling the truth - that her mother had made the ultimate sacrifice?

Mary had told him that her trauma and misery had negated her fear of dying. Even throughout her chemo when she had awoken to find her pillow covered in hair, rejected by the body she had come to despise, her first waking thoughts were for her daughter.

She had covered her head with a wig and her body with rags and fled.

They'd slept together that night for the first time.

Intimacy confined only to holding each other tight. Beneath her night-dress Harry could feel the irregular shape of Mary's breast. Violated, hacked away by the surgeon - but please God a lifesaver.

It was part of her - part of the wonderful, vulnerable being who was his friend. He would never let go.

Harry loved being beside her but his smiles were punctuated by the occasional furrowed brow as he thought back to the maelstrom of that tumultuous period a couple of months ago, in particular the letter he had received two days previously, delivered anonymously, by hand, to the marina.

Dear Harry

I'm loving it.

Things have worked out perfectly and I'm free.

I hope you feel the same elation with your poorly friend.

Poor Mr Brierley.

Mind you he was ancient; it can't have been much fun strapped to a chair crapping into a sack. His mate Fairweather must have been a bit of a wimp though mustn't he? I mean, shoving a needle full of nasties into himself just because his wrinkly old pal ran out of puff.

At least I presume he stabbed himself - the police seem to think so!

Perhaps it was the soppy little note he left.

Quite creative is our Margaret!!

She and I have made quite some progress by the way.

She's gay you know.

It took me a while to pluck up courage - the first kiss was the nerviest moment but after that things just slipped into place, if you know what I mean! Now I've taken the plunge, I have to say I really gain a lot of satisfaction out of it, and intend to keep my hand in. (Dear dear!).

Mr Brierly and his mate were just about the last threads to my past. Just about. But I don't foresee a problem from anyone else. Do you Harry?

I know they're dead by the way - miserable, cheating, lying bastards.

I can see him kneeling in front of her. What do you think of this?

Ode to a man who never was

With trembling hand

hold the murderous gun.

Gun-metal-grey, cold, deadly.

Forgotten, the crazy tortured path on which we tread

It is now.

Focus a desperate, spineless hatred

towards that lethal singularity.

Target locked.

Squeeze the trigger.

Eyes wide.

Breath held.

Fire.

An ephemeral eruption of sound and light

fractured stillness.

Every sense for an instant overwhelmed.

Mission accomplished.

Death.

Free to soar!

Love to the girls.

Bye bye Harry.

Your Susan.

He'd burnt it, at least the physical evidence.

The memory would haunt him as long as he let it. Miserable, hateful woman.

He shook his head to rid himself of the poison.

Look forward, Harry.

He did, then looked sideways at Mary and smiled.

Chapter 38

They moored near the lock tavern and he was nervous all over again. They ordered a drink from the bar and went into the snug. It was not long after opening time and they appeared to be the first customers. There was the musty smell of a pub that hasn't got going for the day but at least the wood fire in the grate was winning.

Then they were greeted by a growl.

Dave looked up from under the table, chin resting on the floor between her front paws, eyes unblinking, staring straight at Harry.

'Hello girl,' he said. No reaction.

Jan came from behind the table and hugged Harry. 'It's good to see you.'

Menacing growl.

'You too. You look terrific.'

'Liar.'

They laughed.

Also there, sitting on the brown vinyl seats, was Cara perched a suitable distance from Harry's new mates from the marina, Ralph and Ron.

Harry placed his arm round Mary's waist and indicating from right to left said, 'Mary, I'd like you to meet Jan, Cara, Ralph and Ron. Jan is the person to whom I've been the source of endless pain and Cara is her daughter staying with her Mum till she's back to health. These two guys welcomed me to the water and have been a huge help. And this is Dave.' Small grumble, one wag.

'Tha's lost a bit of weight.' Said Ralph

Ron looked at his mate with a mock frown, 'You can't say that! You've only just met the woman!' Then with a serious expression, looked at Mary, 'I apologise for my friend my love, they don't let him out very often.'

'I was talking to Harry,' said Ralph indignantly, 'not you Mary my dear. You are perfectly proportioned if I may be so bold.'

'It's the glass eye love – 'old rover' we call it. Can't tell what he's leering at.'

'Glass eye my arse! Oops sorry ladies.' He thumped Ron on the arm, 'now look what you've made me say!'

The dog wagged its tail.

Harry put a stop to it by asking if anyone would like a drink.

'Before that, there's a little something we clubbed together for you.' Said Jan and placed a bottle of Champagne and an envelope on the table. 'We know you've had a difficult time but here's to you, and welcome back.'

Harry felt a lump in his throat but before he could pick up the card, Ron grabbed it from the table. He retrieved the ever-present pencil from behind his ear and scribbled something in the card before putting it back in its envelope and replacing it on the table. He sat back and looked sheepish.

Harry, who was stuck for words, opened the card. It was signed by the four of them and read; 'Good to see you back Harry' and in pencil 'and Mary'.

'Thank you,' said Harry, putting his am round Mary's waist and drawing her close, 'that's very kind of you all, and a lovely surprise.'

Jan retrieved six wine glasses from the shelf under the table. 'Go on then, pop it open. I've had a word with the landlady and she's fine with it.'

They toasted each other.

'Mm.' Said Ralph.

'Blimey.' Said Ron.

Both the old boaters washed it down with a slurp of ale and seemed all the better for it.

Cara remained seated and looked tense and distant as another stranger was introduced into her mother's life.

They sat round the table and chatted.

Harry was nervous.

Dave went for a walk and a sniff around the small room and when she returned settled on Harry's feet. He was unsure whether this was an act of friendship or a means of preventing him going anywhere near Jan.

Mary and Jan chatted about the B & B, about how it was a lifesaver, having people around now she was on her own. Suddenly Mary stopped short. She held her breath and went deathly pale.

She stared out of the window looking up the slope to the towpath. Silhouetted against the blue sky was a man holding the hand of a young girl. The man bent down and said something before walking out of sight.

Mary turned to Harry. 'What......?'

He nodded his head. 'Go on then,' he said.

Mary had tears in her eyes as she stumbled from the room.

The girl had turned to watch the man go. A few moments later Mary walked into the picture. She stood a short distance from the girl staring, then moved closer and knelt down. Neither moved as they looked at one another. Mary held her arms out and for an agonising moment the girl remained motionless. The girl took a pace forward and knelt in front of her mother. The child's arms remained straight by her side as Mary hugged her daughter burying her head in the child's shoulder.

Quinn, dressed as the country gent, came into the room a few moments later, 'Nice idea,' he said, looking at Harry.

'Thanks. How did you persuade her?'

'I'll tell you sometime. Anyway, it was high time a very special lady was re-united with her daughter.'

More than six hundred miles away in a small town in a quiet corner of France, she sat with her cup of black coffee, two sugars. She sat at a table in the window and smiled to herself. She smiled because the fat man who'd come in, sat across the room and ordered a coffee, hadn't recognised her. She'd passed the test - he didn't know her, nobody knew her.

She detested the man but as a source of cash he was worth his weight in gold - and what a weight! He certainly paid top dollar for the orphan children she supplied.

She would nurture her client, her lover would help her do it, and they would both benefit.

Susan left the café and walked away to a new beginning and whispered, 'Au revoir Robert, au revoir tout le monde'.

About Jo May

I have two web sites

jomay.uk

A bit about me and my books

abargeatlarge.co.uk

You'll find an eclectic mix including:

Photographic records of Jo's boating adventures
A collection of stories, poems and articles
My avoidable health issues (Fat man gets into difficulty)
Links to all five books (to date)

There are contact forms within the websites
It would be great to hear from you

Bye for now, Jo

Printed in Great Britain
by Amazon

43018953R00126